S0-BCP-809

HARLEQUIN SUPERROMANCE
Celebrates its 20th Anniversary

*Two decades of bringing you the very best
in romance reading.*

*To recognize this important milestone,
we've invited six very
special authors—whose names you're sure to recognize—
to tell us how they feel about Superromance.
Each title this month has a letter
from one of these authors.*

Sandra Field, whose foreword you'll read in this
book, was one of the first authors approached to
write for Superromance. Her compelling and
dramatic stories, filled with very real and very
interesting characters, were perfectly suited
to the series—then and now.

Homecoming is **Laura Abbot's** seventh Superromance.
This former English teacher from the Midwest
creates wonderfully appealing,
true-to-life characters and puts them in
complete and familiar worlds—
both hallmarks of Harlequin Superromance.

Dear Reader,

What a powerful, compelling concept "home" is! For some, alas, it is a painful word, reflecting disappointment, failed expectations, even loneliness. For others, the mere word itself evokes rich memories, nostalgic emotions and a sense of belonging.

Homecoming was a project that moved me in many ways, not only because it was my privilege to work with some truly wonderful authors, but because through Tom Baines and Lynn Kendall I could explore to my heart's content some of the many connotations of "home."

One of the most important "homes" in this book, however, is Meacham House, a program for disadvantaged young people, "homeless" by virtue of the fact that they lack stable families, guidance and a place where they know they are accepted and loved. If your community has turned a blind eye to these rootless adolescents, I hope the fictional Meacham House will inspire you to take steps to make such a "home" a reality for them.

Finally, a generous thank-you to our wonderful new Hoosier friends who made my husband and me feel so "at home" as we toured Indiana while researching this book. You are special!

Happy homecomings!

Laura Abbot

P.S. I'd love to hear from you.
Please write me at P.O. Box 2105, Eureka Springs, AR 72632 or at LauraAbbot@msn.com. I also invite you to check out these Web sites: www.nettrends.com/lauraabbot and www.superauthors.com.

FOREWORD BY SANDRA FIELD

Homecoming
Laura Abbot

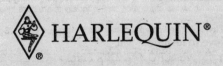

HARLEQUIN®

TORONTO • NEW YORK • LONDON
AMSTERDAM • PARIS • SYDNEY • HAMBURG
STOCKHOLM • ATHENS • TOKYO • MILAN • MADRID
PRAGUE • WARSAW • BUDAPEST • AUCKLAND

To my fellow Riverbend authors whose talent
and generosity of spirit have won my heartfelt
appreciation and respect.

And to the special young people and dedicated adults
of Lane House who furnished part of the inspiration
for this book.

ISBN 0-373-70937-4

HOMECOMING

Copyright © 2000 by Laura A. Schoffner.

Visit us at www.eHarlequin.com

Printed in U.S.A.

FOREWORD BY SANDRA FIELD

In the late seventies, I'd mapped out a clear course of action: move to Nova Scotia's Annapolis Valley with my two children and embark on a master's degree in psychology at Acadia University. I'd been writing for both Harlequin Romance and Harlequin Presents for a few years; this would furnish me with an income. Simple! And then George Glay, a Toronto-based editor with Harlequin, got in touch with me, asking if I would consider writing for a new series called Superromance, and I had to rethink my plans. I knew very little about the book industry, but I suspected it wasn't every day of the week that editors approached writers; the reverse, in my experience, was far more often true.

In those days, Superromances were 95,000 words in length, as opposed to the 50-55,000 words of the shorter series. A subplot was essential. So I invented another writing persona called Jocelyn Haley and went to work, and I never did do the master's in psychology. We did, however, move to the valley, where we rented an old farmhouse outside Wolfville. Flanked by barns and orchards, the house overlooked 3000 acres of farmland reclaimed from the Fundy tides by early French settlers called Acadians. Flat and fertile farmland, with a wide expanse of sky. Hawks, eagles, gulls and the waving grasses of summer.

For me, writing Superromances had something of the quality of that place. There was a spaciousness that enabled me to contemplate the joys and vicissitudes of love. There was room for my characters to develop, for the intricacies of personality and motivation to lead the hero and heroine in whichever direction they wished to go, and minor characters appeared as unexpectedly as the small, short-eared owls that would materialize at dusk over the ditches and dirt roads behind the house. There was ample time to play.

And isn't that, in the end, what writing is all about? About abundance. About enjoying the process. And, of course, about passing on the pleasures of that process to you, the reader of Superromances.

CAST OF CHARACTERS

Tom Baines: Prize-winning journalist, estranged father and River Rat

Lynn Kendall: Minister and newcomer to Riverbend

Ruth and Rachel Steele: Tom's twin maiden aunts, operators of Steele's Books

Kate McMann: Manager of Steele's Books and Lynn's best friend

Pete Baines: Tom's fifteen-year-old son

Libby Baines: Tom's thirteen-year-old daughter

Abraham Steele: Town patriarch and bank president, recently deceased

Prentice Jewett: Influential property owner and town curmudgeon

Charlie Callahan: Contractor, temporary guardian and River Rat

Beth Pennington: Physician's assistant, athletic trainer and Charlie's ex-wife

Aaron Mazerik: Former bad boy, current basketball coach and counselor at Riverbend High

Lily Bennett Holden: Golden girl, widow, artist and River Rat

PROLOGUE

Dublin, Ireland
Spring 1999

IT WAS AN ORDINARY MORNING, another routine assignment. Dense clouds hung oppressively over the city, and for the fourth straight day rain fell. Drenched pedestrians hurried to their destinations, heads lowered, black umbrellas offering scant protection. Automobiles, buses and lorries careered through the crowded streets, honking, vying for position and heedlessly splashing those on the sidewalks unlucky enough to be near the gutter.

Tom Baines leaned wearily against the seat of the press syndicate's staff car. The driver was skillful and, despite the heavy traffic, would get him and his photographer, Gordy Maxwell, to the assignment on time. With luck, the event would go off according to schedule, and he could return to the hotel, close the drapes and nurse the hellacious hangover thudding like thunderbolts against his skull.

"You want the standard stuff?" Beside him, Gordy fidgeted with the leather strap of his camera case.

Opening his eyes to a slit, Tom replied in a low growl, "Yeah, the diplomatic greeting at curbside, the politicians' handshake—you know the drill."

"That doesn't make the front page." Gordy, who

had a gift for stating the obvious, had been with Tom for eight years and, like Tom, chafed at routine assignments. The Scot's prize-winning photographs and Tom's incisive news dispatches and columns had established them as one of the premier partnerships in print journalism. Their success was the result of initiative, courage, even recklessness, and a bit of luck. By contrast, today's assignment was a no-brainer.

"You got that right, pal." Ever since the uneasy peace agreement between the warring factions in Northern Ireland, this posting had offered few big stories. "We'll do a quick in and out and be back at the hotel in time for lunch."

The driver swerved, and the movement increased the pain in Tom's head. He never should have had that final double scotch at the pub last night.

"Here we are, gents." The driver maneuvered the car near the spot where the press pool was setting up under an awning. Tom glanced at his watch. Five minutes to show time. According to protocol, the United Nations ambassador would be greeted curbside by the mayor. Despite the rain, onlookers had gathered, including a group of children wearing uniform blue jackets sporting their school insignia. Bloody Irish were accustomed to this nasty weather. Or else, as Gordy would put it, they were just plain daft.

Tom pulled a ball cap low over his forehead, buttoned his thigh-length raincoat and immediately stepped into a puddle. *Damn.* Gordy scurried alongside, his red hair already soaked.

Just as Gordy and Tom reached the shelter of the press tent, the rain slackened to a drizzle. The assembled journalists studied the motorcade's progress on a TV monitor. While Gordy pulled his camera out of its case and began adjusting lenses and settings, Tom watched as the police escort, several blocks away, led the limousine, UN flags on the hood fluttering in the breeze. The picture then panned to the functionaries huddled in the entrance to the government office building, including the mayor.

Members of the press pool surged nearer the site where the limousine would dispatch its eminent passenger. As usual, Tom and Gordy avoided the others clustering like a multilimbed journalistic beast on a feeding frenzy and, instead, walked partway down the sidewalk, past the reserved parking place. In the distance the limo appeared. The schoolchildren on the opposite curb pressed forward, even as their teacher admonished them to stay well back.

Perfunctorily Tom pulled out his small leather-bound notebook and pen and began jotting a few notes. Suddenly Gordy grabbed him by the elbow, his voice low and urgent.

"See that?" He jerked Tom's arm slightly and nodded to the left. Coming up the street, traveling in the opposite direction from the limousine, was a lone motorcyclist in a bedraggled green wool sweater and a newsboy's cap, with a large pack slung over his shoulders. The other members of the press, their backs turned, eyes trained on the mayor, failed to notice. However, two or three of the schoolboys, perhaps entranced with the motorcycle, stepped into the street. The hum of the limousine engine sounded in Tom's ears. One moment the scene was benign. The next he heard Gordy yell, "My God, the children!" and, beside him was a vacant spot where his friend had stood.

With dawning horror, Tom took in a series of nearly simultaneous images. Unaware of the two lads approaching him, the cyclist had paused, his machine idling beside the school group. Slowly, surreptitiously, he reached into his backpack. The limousine purred the last few yards before coming to a stop. Down the red-carpeted steps came the mayor and his entourage, welcoming smiles sprouting on their media-conscious faces. And Gordy was running toward the cyclist, whose mouth had contorted in a malevolent sneer.

"Gor-dy!" Tom's scream sounded in his ears alone, because at that moment, the cyclist retrieved something from his backpack and hurled it with unerring accuracy at the very spot where the envoy was emerging from the limousine, his right hand extended toward the beaming mayor. The earsplitting explosion knocked the two men to the ground and rocked the limousine, which then itself exploded, sending shards of flying metal and pieces of bodies into the air.

Tom ran forward through the dense, noxious-smelling smoke, headed toward the spot where he'd last seen Gordy. A piece of flying metal glanced off his shoulder, his shoes crunched against slivers of glass, and wails of fear and pain pierced his eardrums. His lungs, seared with the fumes of gasoline and high explosives, struggled for oxygen.

Gordy! God! Let him be all right!

Oblivious to the rain, now intensifying again and sizzling on the burning metal, Tom groped through the debris, his hand coming to rest on a motorcycle fender. Ignoring the heat searing his palm, he struggled on, his eyes burning and streaming.

A gust of wind swept down the street, and the smoke dissipated momentarily. Directly in front of him lay a mangled camera, the lens shattered, and there, just beyond was Gordy, his body flung, ragdoll-like, facedown, head bent grotesquely to one side, red hair matted with the darker red of blood spewing from a gaping wound.

Tom knelt beside his friend, and a howl erupted from his laboring lungs, through his parched throat and into the smoke-filled air, just as, far in the distance came the insistent sound of klaxons.

Gently Tom rolled Gordy over, the lifeless arms dangling across Tom's thighs. He intended to carry his friend away from this unspeakable place, to lay him to rest where soft rain would cleanse the familiar but now blood-soaked body, where the scent of lilacs would wash away the stench of evil, where nothing could ever hurt him again.

But as he gathered Gordy's body in his arms, he saw crumpled under it a much smaller figure, a boy whose thin legs were covered with the thick knee socks worn by Irish schoolchildren. That was what Gordy had been doing—racing to save this child from the terrorist's fury. Then Tom noticed something miraculous—the boy's bony chest was rising and falling, rising and falling.

Swiping a hand down over Gordy's eyes, Tom moved his friend's body to one side, pausing to rest his hand briefly on Gordy's shoulder in farewell.

Then Tom scooped the unconscious child into his arms, struggled to his feet and bore the young victim through the pelting rain and human confusion to one of the ambulances choking the street, now strewn with debris...and the dead.

CHAPTER ONE

Riverbend, Indiana
August 2000

NO WAY. Life couldn't be this serene, this simple, this innocent. Tom stood on the shady front porch of Uncle Abe's farmhouse surveying the scene before him. Neat fields of corn—broad green shoots reaching toward the azure sky, tassels spreading a gold blanket to the horizon—freshly painted barns and in the distance the meandering river glinting in the morning sun. A pastoral picture, even accompanied by a chorus of songbirds. So here he was, back home in Indiana. For whatever good that might do him.

He patted his shirt pocket, searching for a cigarette, before muttering a low curse. He'd given the damn things up. Old habits died hard.

But cigarettes weren't the answer any more than booze and women were. In the past year, God knows he'd tried to lose himself in both. To forget. Nothing had worked. The restlessness, the discontent persisted. Last winter, after abruptly abandoning his life as a foreign correspondent, the drifting had been welcome. At first. For a while.

Rocking back on his heels, he stuck his hands in the pockets of his rumpled khaki shorts. And now this. He looked around—at the large stone barbecue pit in the side yard, at the weathered chairs lining the porch and at the house itself, site of the raucous, male-only rites of long-ago hunting seasons—all of it now Uncle Abe's legacy to him.

Uncle Abe. Abraham Steele, Riverbend patriarch and benefactor. Admired, respected, sometimes loved and sometimes feared. Standing here after so many years was unsettling. Echoes of the shouts and laughter of his cousin Jacob and the rest of his group of friends, who had called themselves the River Rats because of their penchant for hanging out by the river, seemed borne on the breeze now feathering his face. He sighed. A long time ago. Another lifetime.

And now Jacob had up and disappeared, Uncle Abe was dead, and as for himself...well, who the hell knew?

He'd returned only once since his kids, Pete, fifteen, and Libby, thirteen, were born. And that was years ago. He'd wanted to show them off to their great-uncle. Show them the one place as a boy where he'd felt welcome. Now with his marriage long over and his son and daughter disenchanted with him, no place felt like home. But then, what did he expect?

Maybe it had been ungracious of him, but he'd written to his aunts, twin sisters Ruth and Rachel Steele, to request they give him some time by himself when he first arrived. He figured he might as well try solitude. Nothing else had worked. Besides, after only a few days in Indiana, he knew he wasn't quite ready for Riverbend.

As his gaze lifted to the tops of the century-old trees that sheltered the home, he had the disturbing sense that, for better or worse, this was the end of the line for him.

ON THE CARTERS' flower-bedecked screened-in porch,
Lynn Kendall laid down her pen, set aside the journal
in which she'd been writing and rocked quietly, hands
folded in her lap. The faint squeak of the wicker chair,
the rhythmic thump of the rockers on the wooden
floorboards and the cheery song of a nearby wren
filled her with contentment. At the edge of the lawn,
the Sycamore River meandered in its timeless fashion.

She wiggled her toes in her comfy slippers. When
was the last time she'd indulged herself like this?
Here she was, at eight-thirty in the morning, still in
her robe, and she didn't feel remotely guilty. Why
should she? This was her vacation. Four glorious
weeks!

She'd spent the first few days in Illinois visiting her
mother and married sister. Rockford had been a good
place to grow up in, and the house still evoked fond
memories of coming of age under the watchful eyes
of both her widowed mother and Nana, her grandmother. Nana. A smile hovered on her lips. What a
lady! How thankful she was for her influence. One of
Nana's favorite admonishments had been, "Take care
of yourself first, sweetie, because you have to be all
right before you can take care of anybody else."

Words Lynn was taking to heart here in this delightful sanctuary near Riverbend, which her friends
Seth and Mary Carter had generously made available
while they toured Australia. Without their kindness,
she could never have afforded such a complete and
restful getaway.

Granted, she was only a few miles from all her
responsibilities, but no one except her good friend
Kate McMann, who occasionally brought her supplies, and her secretary knew exactly where she was

vacationing. Rest, relaxation, study, meditation, exercise, fresh air, no alarm clock. What more could a woman ask?

As if challenging her complacency, Benedict, her enormous black tomcat, jumped into her lap and began kneading her chest. "You think I could use more, fella? Like what?"

Benedict drew back, cocked his head as if assessing her sanity, then, with a swish of his tail, settled in her lap, emitting a single ragged purr. "Maybe you're right. Maybe there *is* something else." Lynn ran her fingers absently along the cat's soft coat. If she couldn't fool one savvy feline, how could she hope to fool herself? She tried to be satisfied with her life. She'd known the path she'd chosen wouldn't be easy, and it hadn't been. But it had offered rewards beyond any she could've imagined. Even after only a year and a half in Riverbend, she had come to understand some of the pleasant implications of the expression "God works in mysterious ways."

She stopped rocking and watched a canoe, propelled by two teenagers, glide down the river. Yes, a difficult path, but one that would be even more fulfilling if it could be shared. Shared with a mate, one who would come to know and love *all* of her, not just the part she showed to the world. And one who could accept who she needed to be, who she'd been *called* to be.

She leaned over, burying her nose in Benedict's fur. Then she straightened. "Mysterious ways? I could sure use some now, Sir, if it's not too much trouble."

LATER THAT DAY, Lynn dragged her bicycle from the garage. She needed regular rides to get herself into condition for the charity biking event in which she was to participate in the fall. She was probably nuts to go out on such a hot, steamy afternoon, but the nearby country roads were ideal for cycling.

At the far end of her route, she stopped, her attention arrested by an untended country cemetery at the top of a rise. She wheeled her bike up the hill, noticing that from here she could see the river in the distance. Then she propped her bicycle against the stone wall, entered through the rusty gate and hunkered before the first of several stones. "Ebenezer Vale, Faithful Husband, Father, and Friend, 1809-1878." Awed by the dates, she brushed back the weeds from an adjacent marker. "Letitia Vale, Rose of Heaven, 1815-1871." Curious, she pondered their lives. What had it been like more than a hundred years ago, alongside the river? Had Ebenezer Vale been a farmer? A canal man? Perhaps a blacksmith?

As Lynn stood up to leave, she tripped over a small flat stone, almost completely covered with weeds. Kneeling, she plucked away the vegetation until she could make out the simple but heartbreaking epitaph. "Baby died."

A sudden breeze raised bumps along her arms, and tears obscured the etched letters. Gently she laid her palm on the stone and spoke quietly. "Rest in peace, little one." In that moment she felt a pervading calm before being pulled back into the present by the chirp of grasshoppers and the hum of a distant tractor.

Sighing, she rubbed her hands down her spandex cycling tights, then slowly rose to her feet, vowing to return and explore the cemetery. Maybe she'd bring garden tools and attempt to restore some order to this sacred place.

Feeling renewed, she returned to the road, hopped on her bicycle and started off, mentally contemplating what plants she might place in the graveyard next spring to honor those long-dead. She was coasting happily along a level stretch when suddenly her bike jerked, barely giving her time to brake with one foot. She saved herself from being sent sprawling, but one of the pedals scraped her shin, leaving a long painful abrasion.

Standing on the roadside staring at the broken chain, she chastised herself for riding this far from home alone. She knew better. Frustrated, she studied her surroundings. Across the road she spied a dirt driveway that disappeared into a tunnel of eight-foot-high corn stalks. In the distance she made out the top of a steep-hipped roof. Surely it would be safer to take her chances with a resident of the area than with a passing motorist.

Hooking her helmet over the handlebars and rolling the bicycle along, she started up the driveway. The breeze had died and the air was stifling. She knew her face was a mottled crimson and her hair damp with perspiration. And the abrasion on her leg was starting to bleed. Surely some kindly maternal type lived in the house, which she could now make out completely as the cornfield gave way to a clearing. It was a white two-story with a stone chimney and a deep full-length porch. Even though there was no sign of life, the front door stood open.

Lynn laid the bike on the ground, pushed back the limp strands of hair hanging in her face and climbed the porch steps.

"Who's there?" The voice was neither kindly nor maternal. Instead, it was gruff, unwelcoming—and distinctly male. A tall, broad-shouldered man with a short black crewcut graying at the temples, a two-or three-day growth of beard and a scowl on his face stepped out onto the porch. From the looks of him, he'd slept in his khaki shorts, and his wild Hawaiian shirt could have been previously owned by the proprietor of a dockside tattoo parlor. Her eyes drifted down hairy legs to the well-worn, water-spotted sandals on his feet. Whoever he was, he was no one's idea of a Norman Rockwell Hoosier. He eyed her. "You lost in the forest, Goldilocks?"

Biting back a grin and at the same time wondering what on earth possessed her, she decided two could play this game. "Granny, your eyes are failing. Don't you know Little Red Riding Hood when you see her?"

"Little Red Riding Hood, huh?" He stood, legs apart, arms folded over his chest. "Well, whoever, we don't want any."

"Any what?" She continued up the steps until she stood level with him, though several feet away.

"Of what you're selling."

"I'm not selling anything. I'm—"

"Furthermore, I'm a committed member of the Church of Perpetual Hedonism." He reached behind him and hooked his fingers through the screen-door handle. "Now, if you'll excuse me—"

Lynn took two steps forward. The arm with which she'd reached out to detain him fell uselessly to her side. "Wait. Please." The very least the man could do was let her use his phone. She could call Kate. "I've had some difficulty. See?" She pointed to her bike. "The chain broke, and I'm, well, stranded."

The man emitted an enormous sigh. "So you're...what? Looking for a Good Samaritan?"

Aptly put. "As a matter of fact, yes. And would that be...you?" She hoped she hadn't laid on too much sarcasm. Just enough to shame him into agreeing to help.

His brown eyes raked her body from top to toe. "You're bleeding."

She glanced at her shin. A trickle of blood was running down it to pool in the top of her sock. "So it seems."

He opened the door and stood aside to allow her to pass. "Come in. I'll get you something to put on the leg."

She stood her ground. "How do I know you're harmless?"

For the first time in their cautious exchange, she thought he might smile. "You don't." He shrugged. "For all you know, I could be the Big Bad Wolf." His eyes had a definite teasing glint.

"That's always a possibility." She studied him warily. He was not unattractive if you went for that Bruce Willis look. In fairness, cleaned up, he might even be...presentable.

"The question is, can you repair a bicycle?"

"We'll see. But not until after we look at that leg." He placed a hand behind her back and propelled her forward. "C'mon. We're letting flies in."

She stepped tentatively over the threshold. "You're sure I'm not disturbing your nap?"

"As a matter of fact, you are."

As her eyes adjusted to the dim light of the large high-ceilinged room, she noted that, indeed, a bed pillow with a dent in it lay on the large brown leather sofa. Mounted game birds and sepia-toned ancestors stared down at her from the cream-yellow walls. The massive mahogany furniture was definitely dated. But interesting. Even the most cursory inspection suggested that no one had run a vacuum or dust rag around the place lately. "Perhaps your wife could help me, and we can let you get back to your siesta."

"Fortunately that's one problem I don't have."

"What? A wife or getting back to your nap?"

"A wife."

Why was she not surprised? He hadn't moved from the doorway and, in fact, was continuing to give her a somewhat embarrassing once-over. "The alcohol? The bandages?" she prompted.

"Oh, sure. Sit down." He gestured at an over-stuffed armchair. "I'll be right back."

Perching on the edge of the chair, she tucked her hair behind her ears and looked around. A fireplace and ornately carved oak mantel dominated one wall. From the entry hall a set of stairs rose to the second story. Behind her, she could see an ample modernized kitchen. Her Good Samaritan had disappeared upstairs where, she supposed, the bedrooms and bath were located. Should she even be here? This man was a total stranger.

While she briefly considered fleeing—where? how?—he returned, his arms laden with washcloth, bandages, cotton balls and alcohol. He knelt beside her and set the supplies on the floor. "Here. Let me look." Before she could protest, he'd grabbed her leg and was swabbing the wound with the damp wash-cloth. Something about the cool cloth felt very pleasant but, she realized to her chagrin, not nearly as pleasant as the feel of his warm hand cupping the back of her calf. Her focus narrowed to the infinitesimal shifting of pressure of his fingers against her skin.

"Ouch!" She jerked away. "You might tell a girl when you're getting ready to apply alcohol to an open wound."

Expertly he stripped the backing off the bandage. "And a girl might pay attention, instead of closing her eyes and smiling that sappy grin."

She stared at him, lost for a comeback. Had she really behaved so transparently? And worse yet, so uncharacteristically? She nodded at the neat binding of the wound. "You've done this before."

He paused, then responded dryly, "I have."

He was still holding her leg, now with both hands. Wasn't he finished? She moved to stand up. "Thank you, Mr....er..."

He put his hands on her shoulders and pushed her back into the seat. "Sit still. I'll get you something cool to drink."

She exhaled. "I'd like that." And she realized she would. She was parched, tired and unaccountably curious about this man.

He returned shortly with two glasses of ice water. He pulled up a stool, sat in front of her and raised his glass. "Here's to little girls wandering in the woods."

She smiled, then gulped down a third of the liquid. "Since you're definitely not Granny, perhaps you could tell me who you really are."

He stuck out a hand. "Tom Baines."

She clasped his hand, then uttered a tiny cry of recognition. "*You're* Tom Baines?" She knew from her friend Kate that one of Riverbend's claims to fame was the Pulitzer prize-winning journalist's connection to the Steele family.

A soft smile crossed his lips. "I'm that former newspaperman in the flesh."

"Former?" When she questioned him, she noticed the smile fade, replaced by a look she could only define as guarded.

"It's not much of a life for an older guy. It's a young man's game."

"You don't look so old to me." In fact, he looked pretty darn virile.

"Thirty-six. That's over the hump."

"No way is thirty-six over the hump." What she'd intended as a riposte came out, instead, as a serious challenge. He stilled for a moment and she could see his jaw working.

He rose to his feet. "Believe it." He carried his empty glass to the kitchen, then stood by the door. "Ready to deal with your bike?"

Had she offended him? "Sure. I mean, thanks." She stumbled down the porch steps after him. "Really, I could call a friend."

"Not necessary." He hunkered down to look at the bike.

Did he always talk like this? As if he was barking orders? Maybe it was a journalistic occupational hazard—expending your store of words on paper, not in conversation.

After studying the chain-and-sprocket mechanism, he turned to her. "I have an extra chain, but it won't fit your bike. Sorry."

"Are you a cyclist?"

He picked up the bike and started around the house. "Not hardly. But I've found it's a cheap, efficient mode of transportation in places like Bangkok."

She trailed after him, wondering how many exotic

locales he had temporarily called home and what in the world he was doing at this isolated house. Surely if you retired from a career as a foreign correspondent, you wouldn't be satisfied in rural Indiana.

In the large detached garage were a sleek Chrysler convertible and an old red pickup truck. He hoisted the bicycle into the truck bed and laid it on its side. "Get in. I'll take you home."

Another barked order. She had to bite her tongue to prevent a sharp retort. After all, he *was* helping her. And he wasn't exactly a stranger, if reading his columns for years counted as acquaintance. She directed him to the Carters' house.

When they arrived, he lifted the bike out of the truck and propped it against the carport wall. In the gathering twilight he seemed to look at her appraisingly once more, then he ran his hands up and down her arms. She knew she should move, but she might as well have been carved in stone, for all the will she possessed. Next he did a curious thing. He stepped closer, gently brushed his knuckles across her cheek, then said, "Don't be too sure you didn't meet the wolf."

Abruptly he turned, strode to his truck and drove off, leaving Lynn leaning weakly against the wall, wondering why his words had set her heart racing. Wondering if God didn't have a particularly mischievous sense of humor. "Mysterious ways, indeed," she murmured.

AFTER A SUPPER of cold leftover pizza, a peanut-butter-and-banana sandwich and a wizened apple, Tom found himself back where he'd started the day—on the front porch, brooding. He'd kill for a cigarette.

He tilted his chair back on its rear legs, his feet propped on the railing, his fingers laced behind his head. Why did that woman have to come along to disturb his much-prized isolation? More baffling, why had he even let her in the door? Stupid question. He wasn't, yet, so much of a jerk as to turn away a damsel in distress. Besides, she'd looked awfully appealing.

Another enigma. Appealing? With that flushed face, those limp hanks of strawberry-blond hair, that determined set to her jaw and a leg dripping blood? About as appealing as… Words failed him, which was practically a first.

Because although the truth was she looked like the "before" model in a beauty makeover, something about her had nevertheless twisted his gut. Maybe the wide smiling mouth or the flirtatious twinkle in those soft gray eyes. Or the sprinkling of pale freckles across her nose and on her high forehead. Or perhaps it was something more elemental—like the way those tights clung to her nicely rounded bottom or the feel of her shapely calf in his hand or the pert breasts concealed by—

He was suddenly reminded of an article he'd read somewhere that suggested a man could tell within the first five minutes of being with a woman whether or not he wanted to go to bed with her. He hadn't believed it. Then.

He allowed the front legs of the chair to come down with a thump, then stood up. He'd diverted himself with women in France, Sweden and the Orient. But he'd never been so immediately or viscerally aroused on first sight by even the most glamorous or seductive of them as he'd been by... He slapped the railing. Hell! He didn't even know her name.

Under other circumstances, such an oversight would make him the laughingstock of the newsroom. Tom Baines, author of the internationally syndicated column "Hot Spots" and ace reporter who'd covered uprisings, pestilences, revolutions and disasters from Africa to Japan hadn't had the wits to ask the one vital question. Her name, for crying out loud!

He sat back down, but after a few seconds he uttered a triumphant "Hah!"

Because he *did* know all he needed to. He knew exactly where she lived.

CHAPTER TWO

LYNN RUBBED THE SLEEP out of her eyes, wiped her face gently with a damp washcloth, then brushed her teeth. Unbelievable. She couldn't remember the last time she'd slept until eight. Sighing with pleasure, she smeared lotion on her cheeks and forehead, soothing the sunburn her fair skin had suffered yesterday.

She examined her face in the mirror. She never wore much makeup, only enough to bring out her pale eyes and moisten her lips. On vacation, though, she was doing without, even if she did look a bit washed-out.

"Washed-out" was nothing, though, compared to how she must've looked to Tom Baines. Hot and sweaty, hair hanging in her face, thoroughly unfeminine. She grimaced at her reflection. What did she care? He had been rude and downright boorish.

And handsome as all get-out! Overnight she'd had to reassess her opinions of the Bruce Willis bad-boy look. And what had that final gesture been about? She'd expected irritation from him. Justifiable. She'd definitely inconvenienced him. Heaven forbid, she'd interrupted his nap! And yet... She remembered with vivid clarity the way his hands had skimmed her arms, the sweetness of that whisper of his knuckles across her sunburned cheek. There had been an unexpected, even incongruous gentleness in his leave-taking. Along with the decidedly suggestive growl in his parting comment.

She'd never imagined such a fleeting touch and so few words could cause the kind of seismic reaction she'd experienced as she'd watched him climb into the truck and drive away.

Enough. She gathered her hair into a ponytail, pulled her pink cotton batiste robe over her shorty pajamas and padded barefoot into the kitchen, heading straight for the coffee canister.

Benedict brushed across her bare legs, rubbing against the bandage, still neatly in place, despite the shower she'd had last night. "You sly kitty. You know how to wangle your breakfast, don't you?" She flipped on the coffeemaker, then, trailing the meowing cat, entered the utility room where she poured food into his dish. "Are you satisfied now, big man?" Contented chomping was her answer until suddenly the cat froze, ears forward in listening mode.

Then Lynn heard something, too—the sound of a car door slamming close by. Maybe even in the driveway. Before she could get to a window to investigate, there was an insistent pounding on the door. She couldn't imagine who'd be here at eight-fifteen in the morning.

She smoothed her robe, retied the sash, tiptoed to the kitchen window and peered out. The knocking resumed. There, parked big as life in front of the carport, was a battered red pickup. A familiar battered red pickup. Her mouth went dry. Tom? One thing was for sure. His manners hadn't improved overnight. The crack of dawn was no time for social calls. What could he possibly want?

Benedict was already in the front hallway in his guard-cat pose. She opened the door and stared at Tom. He wore a different pair of rumpled shorts—navy blue this time—and a white T-shirt. His hair was still damp from what she assumed had been a morning shower and he was clean-shaven.

"Ms. Carter?"

"No."

He looked puzzled. "That's the name on the mailbox."

"Yes."

"But that's not your name?"

"No." She, who'd spent her life helping others, couldn't resist the impulse to string him along. He brought out in her an impish, playful side that wouldn't be denied.

"Well, let me start over." He turned away, looking heavenward, as if seeking guidance, then faced her again. "Ms. R. R. Hood, I presume?"

She bit the corner of her lip to keep from laughing. "No."

He cocked an eyebrow. "You're not going to make this easy for me, are you?"

She shook her head.

"I must be rusty. Usually my interviewing technique is more productive."

"Interviewing technique? Pardon me if I'm misinformed, but doesn't interviewing usually involve, um, asking questions, rather than presuming?" She hugged herself. She shouldn't be enjoying this so much.

"Touché." He took a step forward, forcing her to retreat into the hall. As he advanced, she caught a whiff of some fresh-smelling soap, and it was enough to almost buckle her knees. Dear heaven, he was attractive! "So exactly what *is* your name?"

By now he had cupped her chin in his hand and was probing her eyes with his. Her mouth was mere inches from his. She mustered her voice. "Lynn Kendall," she said a bit too loudly.

"Lynn Kendall?" he repeated slowly, as if savoring the name on his tongue. His hand strayed to her shoulder. She was determined not to give ground, but the fierce fluttering of her heart alarmed her. Benedict tried to help by insinuating himself between their legs. Tom's gaze locked on her face. Finally he said, "Could a man get a cup of coffee here this morning, Ms. Kendall, especially since he's come to pick up a bicycle to be fixed?"

"He has? You are?" Lynn stumbled, then gathered her wits. "Coffee? Sure." Relieved to have an excuse to move, Lynn edged toward the kitchen, but somehow couldn't summon the will to stop looking at him. Then she nearly tripped over Benedict, loyally sticking to her side. Before she could regain her balance, Tom had grabbed her by the elbow, his arm snaking around her waist.

"You okay?"

Okay? Did "flustered" qualify? "Fine, thanks." She stepped out of his grasp, calling over her shoulder, "Black or polluted?"

"I like mine neat." He followed her into the kitchen, then sat on a stool and folded his arms on the countertop. *Neat,* she thought. He probably arranged his life like that, as well. No frills, no complications. She poured two mugs of coffee, shoved one across the counter toward him, then stood inhaling the rich aroma, grateful for the barrier the counter provided.

"So, Lynn Kendall, why isn't your name on the mailbox?"

"I don't live here."

"Oh?"

"I'm on vacation. The Carters were kind enough to let me use their place. I needed some peace and solitude."

"Is that a pointed remark?" He eyed her over the rim of his coffee mug.

She considered her answer. "It would be ungracious of me to provoke my Good Samaritan. I'm grateful to you for helping me yesterday."

"What about today?" He took a sip of coffee. "Have truck, will travel. To the bicycle-repair shop."

She wavered. With his pickup, it would be much simpler for him than for her to haul the bike. Then she made a reluctant admission. Accepting his offer would ensure that she would have one more encounter with him. Shameless, that was what she was. She ran her finger around the rim of her mug, then lifted her eyes. "Thank you. That would be most helpful. Maybe with my endorsement, you could start your own business. The Traveling Samaritan."

"I'm not always so generous." His mouth quirked and his eyes teased. "Only certain people qualify."

"Like hot, bedraggled roadside victims who stumble into your lair?"

He set his mug down and began rounding the

counter. ''No, like certain females with mischievous streaks who aren't afraid of big bad wolves.'' He'd reached her and put his hands on her waist, pinning her to the spot. He lowered his voice. ''You're not afraid, are you?''

Afraid? Terrified, maybe. ''Of course not.''

''Good,'' he whispered, and then his mouth closed over hers in a gentle, yet searing kiss. For support, she gripped the counter at her back. This couldn't be happening. But in spite of herself, she liked it.

He pulled away first and in his face was mirrored her own surprise. And something else. A fleeting seriousness, as if he'd overstepped a self-imposed boundary. He appeared to search for a means to defuse his impetuosity and finally said in an even voice, ''Lynn Kendall? That's a nice, solid name.'' With that, he started toward the door, but then turned and added, ''I'll let you know when the bike will be ready. In the meantime, don't befriend any other strangers.''

And he left. Just like that.

Lynn blinked. What on earth had possessed the man? Or more to the point, what on earth had possessed her? He had walked into the house, taken her by storm and walked out, a man obviously accustomed to getting his own way. And the worst of it was, she'd liked it. She liked *him*.

But this was vacation. This wasn't her world, her real life. She couldn't be sure how she'd feel if it was. She only knew she wouldn't be able to live with herself if he ever came to believe she was toying with him.

Yet in his dark eyes, beyond the surface humor, she read wariness. Down that path, she suspected, lay trouble for him. And if she became involved, perhaps trouble for her, too.

For that had not been an idle kiss.

She scooped up Benedict and wandered toward the screened-in porch, speaking in a quiet voice. "Surely, Sir, *this* isn't what You had in mind, is it?"

RUTH STEELE bustled around the kitchen, clearing the dishes, rinsing them and loading them into the dishwasher, all while maintaining a running monologue. "I don't know what's the matter with that nephew of ours. I know he asked us to give him some time when he got back, but I thought he'd have called by now. Something's peculiar. He's not himself. Aloof. Distant. Like Heathcliff."

Rachel Steele arched her eyebrows as her sister scrubbed the chrome of the sink faucets. "Easy, dear. You're going to take the finish off." She sat at the kitchen table quietly going through the newspaper, scissors in her hand, while her twin rambled on. Snipping out a column, she said, "Here's a good recipe for creamed spinach."

"Are you listening to me at all?" Ruth folded a tea towel over the drying rack and faced her sister. "Or don't you care about the boy?"

Her lips pursed, Rachel set down the scissors and looked up. "What a ridiculous question! Of course I care about Tom, but in case you haven't noticed, he's hardly a boy. And if he needs time and space, the least we can do is give it to him."

"I suppose. But we're going to have to tell him about Aaron soon. Before he hears it somewhere else."

Rachel considered Ruth's statement. She agreed with her and was, in some ways, just as disturbed by recent events. Ever since their brother Abraham's death and his son Jacob's mysterious failure to return home for the memorial service, things had been out of kilter. "Tom was mighty fond of his uncle. The news of Abraham's death must have hit him hard." She pressed a hand to her chest, massaging a dull ache. "And now we have to burden him with more when we tell him Abraham had an illegitimate son living here in Riverbend all these years. And that it's Aaron Mazerik. A new cousin from out of the blue."

Ruth sighed. "He won't like Abraham's harboring such a secret clear to the grave."

Both sisters had been thrown by the revelation about Aaron. But Rachel knew that Ruth had a difficult time realizing that Tom was a fully grown functioning individual who had been satisfactorily running his own life for years without her direct intervention. Although neither of the sisters was particularly bothered by the fact that they had never married, it was second nature to take family members under their wings. And sometimes even outsiders like Kate McMann—whom they'd hired to manage their bookstore—and her adorable twin daughters.

When Rachel fell silent, Ruth crossed the room and stood over her, frowning. "What can Tom possibly be doing out there at Abe's old farmhouse by himself?"

"After the frantic schedule he's kept during all those years abroad, maybe solitude is just what he needs."

Ruth scoffed. "Solitude? That's not what he needs."

"Oh?" Rachel waited. She always knew when her twin had a pronouncement to make.

"No. He needs a good woman. Not a stay-at-home like his first wife and certainly not one of those empty-headed jet-setters." She untied her apron and carefully folded it before facing her sister again. "No, ma'am. I'm talking about a truly good woman who will settle that boy down, bring out the best in him."

"Man," Rachel automatically corrected. That was, however, her only criticism of her sister's remarks. A good woman was exactly what their battle-scarred, rootless nephew needed, especially now.

WHEN TOM TOOK Lynn's bicycle to the repair shop, he briefly considered dropping in on his aunts at their bookstore just off the Courthouse Square. But he decided against it. As soon as he set those wheels in motion, he'd be inviting family involvement in his life, and he wasn't ready yet for their solicitude, their questions. Especially when he could provide no answers. Nor was he ready to get sucked into Riverbend's stifling social scene.

As he drove home, he pondered, as he often did, the direction his life had taken since the bombing. After Gordy's death, he'd handled his assignments perfunctorily, merely going through the motions until one day he had up and quit, rationalizing that a complete break would give him the chance to deal with his emotions. But in these past few months no amount of traveling—to Waikiki, San Francisco, Vancouver, New York City—no well-intentioned interventions of friends and colleagues, had insulated him from his darkest thoughts. On top of everything else he was now suffering from writer's block. In fact, his aimless searching had seemed increasingly meaningless. He couldn't even identify what he was seeking.

The only certainty was that the answer wouldn't be found in violence and death. Not anymore. He'd made his living—a damned lucrative one—capitalizing on the events that tore apart the lives of others. As long as he'd remained uninvolved, he'd been good at it, even relishing the adrenaline rushes. But after that awful day in Dublin, he'd known. Immediately. He no longer had the stomach for it.

Gordy had been too young, too full of life, too good to die. Tom regretted he hadn't told Gordy before it was too late just how true and loyal a friend he'd been and how much he, Tom, had relied on him to make the unbearable bearable.

As his mind roamed all the futile ways he'd tried to escape from himself this past year, he kept returning to a single image. The beautifully natural, trusting face of Lynn Kendall. He couldn't put his finger on exactly what it was that so compelled his attention. But he knew it wasn't so much his physical attraction to her—although that was powerful—as the quality of light—he could think of no better word—she had about her. Pure, joyful, serene.

Had he come on too strong with her? Frightened her? His impulsive behavior had surprised even him, as if he had fallen under some kind of arcadian spell woven by his renewed sense of home. But that was too simplistic an explanation. Unknowingly she had broken through years of carefully constructed defenses where the opposite sex was concerned. She was different from those women with whom he'd had fleeting relationships ever since the breakup of his marriage. What was there about her, anyway?

He veered into his driveway, pulled behind the house and shut off the engine. But he didn't make a move to get out of the cab, dumbstruck by the realization that she had something he wanted. Something tenuous, elusive. Something he wasn't sure he'd ever experienced.

Peace.

LYNN WIPED her damp forehead with her arm, then bent again to the task of pulling weeds from around the headstones. She had the Vale-family plot nearly cleared. The afternoon was muggy and overcast, but every so often there was a refreshing breeze. She liked working the earth and making orderly again that which had been long neglected. Levering the trowel beneath a particularly stubborn root system, she quietly hummed to herself. Much contentment arose from simple things like earth and wind and flowers.

Why, she wondered, do we humans complicate our world, almost as if we deliberately and willfully set out to do so? Take this morning, for instance. She didn't have to let Tom in. She didn't have to serve him coffee. Most assuredly, she didn't have to permit him to kiss her. And worst of all, she needn't have responded so enthusiastically! But she had. Deliberately and willfully.

She stopped humming. This simple, carefree vacation away from all the demands of her work had become anything but simple. On the surface she'd gone about her business since this morning, but on a deeper level she'd been counting the hours until she would see Tom Baines again.

If she chose to let anyone in Riverbend know her whereabouts, she could probably glean all kinds of information about him. Perhaps discover why he seemed, well, mysterious. But she didn't want to compromise her vacation. Besides, she preferred to judge people on their own merits, not on hearsay.

A fluttering of leaves in the nearby sycamore tree caused her to look up. The wind was shifting, coming now from the east, ruffling the dried stalks of wildflowers in the cemetery. When she glanced toward the road where her car was parked, she was surprised to see a lone figure jogging toward her, his white T-shirt and navy shorts all too familiar.

Tom. He lifted a hand in greeting, then negotiated the rise of the hill from which the cemetery had an unimpeded view of the river.

Lynn shaded her eyes and watched until he sank, breathless, on the ground beside her, a lopsided grin on his face. "You really didn't need to run all this way to tell me my bicycle is fixed," she said.

He pulled a red bandanna from his pocket and wiped the beads of sweat from his forehead. "The bike won't be ready until the end of the week. I'm out for my daily run."

Lynn gestured at the graveyard. "Do you come here often?"

"Actually I haven't been out here in years." He nodded toward a large marker topped by a Celtic cross. "That's my great-grandfather's resting place. Several members of my father's family are buried here. When I was a little kid, we used to come here sometimes on Memorial Day. But once Dad joined the State Department, my family rarely came back.''

''Why is that?''

''My father was in the diplomatic service. We lived all over the world.''

''That must've been interesting. Educational, too. No wonder you became a foreign correspondent.''

He leaned against an adjacent headstone, knees bent, his hands dangling between them. ''I suppose.''

''Wow. Such enthusiasm.'' She shook her head and grinned.

In response he smiled ruefully. ''Look, I saw stuff like the Taj Mahal and the pyramids at an early age. But I think I'd have traded all the nannies, the sights and the European boarding schools for a normal up-bringing in Riverbend.''

''But your roots are here. Did you come often?''

He nodded. ''I spent most school holidays and every summer here visiting my uncle Abe. In fact, it's his farmhouse I'm living in now. As a kid, I looked forward to those times with him and couldn't wait to get back. However, I probably acted like a jerk. It wasn't easy for me to let on that this place was so important to me. I had a reputation to protect as a worldly sophisticated—'' he grinned wryly ''—spoiled brat.''

Although he was trying to pass his behavior off as youthful insensitivity, Lynn heard in his words the yearning of a lonely boy shuttled from place to place, not feeling wanted anywhere.

She glanced at him. ''Where are your parents now?''

"They retired to the south of France in the early nineties, then died within months of each other about five years ago."

"I'm sorry."

He said nothing, seemingly lost in his thoughts. Picking up her trowel, she resumed working the earth. She sensed Tom needed space. Overhead, dark clouds were gathering and the air smelled of approaching rain. She quickened her efforts to complete her task. Tom remained where he was. At last Lynn said, "What brings you to Indiana now?"

He sighed. "That's a good question. Maybe because it's all I have left."

She sat back on her heels. "What do you mean?"

He sat cross-legged and leaned forward. "I've been all over the globe, Lynn. I've seen things I don't even want to think about." He paused. "Look around here. Death seems deceptively pleasant in a setting like this. There could be a lot of worse fates than spending eternity high on an Indiana hillside. Worse fates like starving to death, or being swept away along with your entire village by a typhoon, or having your head blown off in a border skirmish. When you've been where I've been, *seen* what I've seen, maybe a small town in Indiana is what you need to restore your faith in humanity."

Lynn laid aside her trowel and covered his hand with hers. "Riverbend is a step, then. A good one." She searched his jaded weary eyes. "I hope you find what you're looking for." She hesitated before squeezing his hand, then resumed weeding.

"I didn't mean to burden you with all that."

"No, please. It's another side of you, one I'm glad

you could share.'' Lynn could sense him struggling to dispel his somber mood.

Finally he shrugged, grinned abashedly and said, ''I wanted you to see I'm more than just a good kisser.''

She couldn't help herself. She blushed. The curse of the fair-skinned. ''Pretty high on yourself, aren't you?''

''C'mon, give me your honest opinion. On a scale of one to ten.''

Just then a huge raindrop fell on her head, followed by another and another. ''It's raining.'' She gathered up her tools.

He took hold of her arm. ''So?''

''We'd better get to the car.'' A clap of thunder underlined the urgency she felt.

He stood up, pulling her to her feet. ''I wasn't asking you about the weather.''

Rain fell softly all around them and the now-cooler air raised gooseflesh on her arms. Or was that because he was still holding her, grinning down at her? ''You're not going anyplace until I get my answer.''

''Answer?''

''Don't hold back. Probably at least an eight, huh?''

''Tom, I—''

He gave a mock sigh while the rain intensified, soaking through her T-shirt. ''Maybe I better demonstrate again.'' His lips closed over hers at the same time his arms came around her, and as he pulled her toward him, she could've been anywhere, so centered was she in the moment. When she let herself lean into him, when she moved her palms against his chest, she couldn't have said whether the accompanying lightning bolt across the river was a signal of approval or disapproval. And she didn't care.

Slowly, teasingly, he pulled his lips a bare half-inch from hers and looked deeply into her eyes. "Well?"

She breathed out her answer spontaneously. "A nine-point-five, I think."

"You think? *Think?*" He laughed huskily. "Let's make sure." And to the accompaniment of another crack of lightning, he convinced her that his kisses were worthy of a ten.

LYNN STOOD in the middle of Tom's bedroom listening to the raging thunderstorm. She had done the polite thing, of course, and given him a ride home from the cemetery. And it did make sense to follow his suggestion of changing out of her sodden T-shirt into a dry one of his, even if the faint lemony fragrance of freshly laundered cotton stimulated thoughts that would make for one heck of a detergent commercial. His shirt hung nearly to the hem of her shorts, and even though she'd toweled off, her wet hair was plastered to her head. She glanced at her reflection in the mirror over the dresser and rolled her eyes. Charming. Again.

A tap sounded on the door. "You ready for a cup of coffee?" Tom asked.

"In a minute." His footsteps retreated, and Lynn hesitated, her attention drawn to three photographs on the dresser top. The first one showed a thin-faced boy of ten or so with intense dark eyes, wearing a heavy sweater over a shirt and tie. Scrawled in the corner in childish cursive was an inscription. She picked up the frame and held it nearer to the light. "Tom, thank you, and God bless you always." It was signed "Terence Coyne." Curious. Setting that photo aside, she studied the remaining two—one of a ruddy-cheeked, unsmiling teenager in tennis whites, a racket cradled in his arms, and the other of a girl of twelve or thirteen, smiling shyly, her mouth revealing a full set of braces.

What did these youngsters have to do with Tom? He didn't strike her as the sentimental type who would collect pictures of children he encountered in his work. This was just another reminder how little she knew about this man, an insight that made her instinctive positive reactions to him all the more reckless, even irresponsible.

Making one last halfhearted attempt to fix her hair, she wandered downstairs, drawn by the aroma of coffee. Tom sat on the sofa beneath the ceiling fan, waiting. He held up her mug and motioned for her to join him. She took the coffee from him and curled up on one end of the sofa. Outside she could hear wind lashing the trees as rain pelted the large windows. Light from the lone lamp flickered, then flared, and the ceiling-fan motor sputtered before resuming its steady hum.

"Power surge," Tom muttered. "One of the hazards of country living."

"How's your candle supply?"

"Good question. I'm hoping we won't have to find out." He sent her a mischievous grin. "On the other hand, candlelight can be pretty romantic." Setting his coffee on the table, he faced her.

"Maybe, but electric light makes me downright sensible. And 'sensible' in this context means drinking up, retrieving my T-shirt and driving home as soon as the rain lets up.''

He leaned back, draping one arm along the sofa back. ''Forgive me, then, if I hope for an all-night deluge.''

Something about the wicked gleam in his eye and the *all night* flustered her. Calm, dignity, control. That was what she needed. ''You know those kisses at the cemetery?''

''The nine-point-five and the ten?''

Smugness was written all over him. She could've handled this issue more objectively had he not reminded her of the scorching ratings. ''Yes. Let's put this into perspective. I only met you yesterday—''

''Is that right?''

Was he playing with her? ''And you need to know, I don't usually act like this.''

''There's always a first time.''

''Tom, really. This is serious.''

He folded his arms across his chest. ''Okay. Serious. What do you mean you 'don't usually act like this'?''

''With men.''

''I can tell.''

''You can? How?''

''You lack…artifice.''

''Artifice?''

''Believe me, I've had plenty of practice recognizing it. Decoding feminine wiles is something of a specialty of mine.''

''Aha! The worldly journalist?''

''Your words, not mine.''

"You're saying, by contrast, that I'm a babe in the woods?"

"Something like that."

She didn't know whether to feel shame or pride. He had nailed her, though. Artifice wasn't part of her arsenal. Nor was this flirtatious conversation. The only face-saving way out was to get up and leave.

No sooner had she made that decision than the lamp flickered again, went out and stayed out. Overhead the fan blades slowed to a stop. Tom leaped to his feet. "My prayers have been answered. Candlelight it is."

His prayers. What about hers for a timely exit, an escape from the danger presented by proximity to him? Darn. The rain sounded harder than ever. She couldn't drive in that. She clenched and unclenched her fingers as she listened to him rifling through the cupboard drawers.

"Beautiful," he murmured. The next thing she heard was a match striking, and then he was back, setting two candlesticks on the coffee table. The flames illuminated his face—firm jaw, aquiline nose, deep-set dark eyes.

He sat down beside her, not touching her, watching the candles, letting the silence between them lengthen. Finally he settled an arm around her shoulders. "You think I'm just another guy on the make, don't you?"

She raised an eyebrow. "Aren't you?"

He gave a sardonic chuckle. "Ordinarily you'd be justified in coming to that conclusion, but—" he tilted her chin so she couldn't avoid looking at him "—not tonight." His fingers wound through the hair at her temple while he traced her forehead with the pad of his thumb. "Not tonight," he repeated with a sense of wonder. "There's something about you. You're…different. Not like other women at all."

Little did he know how close to the mark he was, she thought with irony. She *was* different, as several men in whom she'd been interested had been painfully quick to point out. She didn't want to be perceived as different, at least not in situations like this when, despite all logic, she found herself genuinely and powerfully drawn to someone. "No, I don't suppose I am."

With his forefinger he caressed away the vertical frown lines between her eyes. "Are you afraid?"

She drew his hand into her lap, holding it still. "Afraid?" She pondered the question. "Not for the reasons you might think. I do have to say, though, that our brief relationship seems backward to me. Usually you start by getting to know a person, then come the kisses. Not the other way around."

"Call me unconventional."

"And call me foolish."

"Foolish?" He squared his shoulders. "You poor misguided thing. Why would I call you that?"

She shot him a skeptical look, then saw how his grin faded and his eyes sobered, hauntingly so.

"Lynn—" he faltered before continuing "—you are special. Corny as it sounds, you're *not* like any woman I've ever known. And I like that. A lot." The sound of rain on the roof filled the brief silence. He leaned forward and brushed her cheek with his lips. "So before we go any further, maybe you're right. We should get better acquainted."

Her initial reaction, relief tinged with disappointment, faded in the hope of a deepening relationship.

But it would have to be an honest one, right from the beginning. On both their parts. That meant soon, very soon, she would have to tell him. And run the risk again. No man thus far had been willing to share with her the life she'd chosen. No one had even come close.

Why should Tom Baines be any different?

HE WAS ACTUALLY going to do it. Something he scrupulously avoided. Talk about himself. Why? Because of some mysterious hold this woman had over him. Bottom line—he didn't want her to leave. Was he really that lonely? Or was she really that special?

He thought he knew the answer, and it scared him. She *was* that special, and he found himself helpless to fight his need to be with her. Yet he had no right to involve another person in his private hell. Even one that, for some peculiar reason, he sensed might understand.

Lynn picked up her mug and stretched out her legs on the sofa. "Okay," she said. "Let's get started. You first. You must have quite a few friends in Riverbend."

He locked his hands behind his head and scrutinized the ceiling. Where to begin? "Once I did. There was a bunch of us that used to run around together. Or I should say, *they* used to. Because my cousin was involved, they included me whenever I visited." He couldn't let on to anyone, even Lynn, how much it had meant to him as a kid to be accepted by the River Rats gang, to feel as if he was genuinely liked just for himself. A far cry from the insidious pecking order of boarding school. "Some of them still live in the area, but I haven't looked them up yet."

"Why not?"

Why not, indeed. "I'm not ready."

"For what?"

"The demands. Country-club functions, Rotary Club speeches, family dinners."

"Family?"

"Yeah. I still have two aunts here. They own a bookstore."

"Of course, Ruth and Rachel Steele." A broad grin lit her face.

He looked puzzled. "Yes. How do you know them? I thought you were vacationing here?"

"I am. But I'm familiar with Riverbend and I love to read." He had the distinct impression she was concealing something, but before he could pursue that train of thought, she went on, "They're delightful, well-informed women." Her next question caught him with his guard down. "Who are the children in the photographs on your dresser?"

His gut tightened. The children. A decidedly difficult subject. It wasn't a part of his history he relished sharing. "The tennis player is my son Pete, and the girl is my daughter Libby."

Her breath caught. "I had no idea you were married."

"I'm not. Haven't been for a long time." He watched guiltily as her respiration returned to normal. He could have told her sooner.

"Oh." She pulled up her knees and hugged them. "Do the children live with their mother?"

He nodded. "In Chicago."

"Tell me about them."

"Pete just finished his sophomore year in high school, and Libby will be a freshman this fall." He groped for more. "Pete's the jock. Libby's more musical."

"Will they be coming to visit you this summer?"

Not if they could help it. "I don't think so."

"Are you disappointed?"

Disappointed? It was hard to be disappointed about something you'd never taken the time to know you'd miss. "They have their own friends, lots of summer activities at home."

Resting her chin on her knees, she eyed him. "None of that replaces a father."

Her tone struck him as disapproving. Well, so be it. There was no point in bucking the stone wall Pete and Libby had thrown up to insulate themselves, not that he blamed them. The list of birthday parties, school programs, holidays, sporting events, recitals he'd missed rivaled the daily market quotations for length. After all, hadn't he been doing something "important"? Covering assassinations, purges, explosions, all in the name of putting bread on the table? He looked up at Lynn, hating himself for the egocentric, insensitive bastard he was. "In this case, I'm not so sure about that. I wasn't around enough to be much of a role model."

"What do you mean *wasn't*?"

He let out a long sigh. "I might as well get this over with. Lynn, I haven't seen my children in over six months."

The shock on her face burned itself into his retinas. He'd blown it. She wasn't a woman who would understand a man's estrangement from his children. She was a woman worthy of the truth. He didn't know how he knew, but he was convinced she saw straight into his heart. The question was, would that insight disgust her, drive her away?

The shock in her eyes faded to a compassion that, if anything, was more difficult to bear than disapproval. "Tom, I'm so sorry. Something must be terribly wrong. How painful for you!"

She'd misunderstood. It was Pete and Libby who'd endured his neglect, until finally they'd more or less suggested he butt out of their lives completely. It had seemed the kindest thing to do. And if he was honest with himself, he'd kept so busy with his work he hadn't had time to miss them all that much. Ever since Dublin, though, he'd been having second thoughts. And he didn't like what he saw. Who he'd been. Was.

He was about to request a change of subject when a loud knocking at the front door saved him. He jumped to his feet. "Excuse me."

Lynn, too, rose, picked up one of the candles and followed him. When he pulled the door open, a gust of wind nearly tore it from his hand, and he saw rain coursing from the hat brim of the familiar figure of the farm manager standing outside. "Shep, c'mon in, man. You're drenched." He ushered him into the hallway.

"Thought I'd better check on you, Tom. Let you know a big maple's down across the highway. It took out the phone and power lines." He wiped his feet on the rug in the entryway, and when he took off his hat, water dripped to the floor. "Sorry." He looked around uncertainly. Then his glance fell on Lynn, who stood quietly nearby, a sheepish smile on her face.

"Let me introduce Lynn—"

"Not necessary, son. I know this pretty gal." He walked past Tom and stuck out his hand. "I thought that was your car outside. How you doin', Reverend?"

Tom blinked. He couldn't have heard right. He could've sworn Shep called Lynn "Reverend." That plain didn't make sense. "Do you know Ms. Kendall?"

Still holding Lynn's hand, Shep put his other arm around her in a protective embrace. "Know her? Son, 'course I do. She's the pastor at the Riverbend Community Church."

Lynn, her eyes shimmering like pools of rainwater, looked at Tom, then nodded tentatively as if seeking his forgiveness. "It wasn't my turn yet. I was going to tell you."

For the second time in slightly more than twenty-four hours, Tom was utterly speechless.

CHAPTER THREE

IT WAS ONLY LATER that night after Lynn and Shep had left and Tom was cleaning up the kitchen that he vented his anger. A minister? He threw the sponge against the backsplash. He'd bared his soul, for Pete's sake! And that compassionate look that had melted his heart? Chalk it up to professional concern. He supposed he should be grateful to Shep for preventing him from making a greater fool of himself. For one crazy moment this afternoon he'd even entertained the notion that this was a woman he could make a life with!

Shep, apparently oblivious to the tension in the room, had, thank God, made small talk with them until the rain stopped and they heard on the radio that the highway had been cleared. Good old Shep. He and his wife, Dorrie, had been taking care of the farm for as long as he could remember. He'd cut his teeth on Dorrie's oatmeal-raisin cookies and, as a boy, he'd found few places as comfortable as their warm, cheery kitchen.

In the minutes following Shep's revelation, it seemed to Tom that Lynn had avoided him, preferring to listen to Shep's account of the storm damage than to make eye contact with him. Why would she have wanted to look at him, anyway? She'd been caught red-handed in a monumental evasion. His jaw had ached from biting back his questions. He didn't understand. Had she lied about being on vacation? What were those responsive kisses all about? Riverbend Community Church had been his family's church for generations. His aunt Rachel even played the organ there. Why hadn't anyone told him about a lady minister?

He dumped the coffee grounds into the wastebasket, straightened, then slumped over the counter. It wasn't his aunts' fault. When had they had a chance to tell him anything? He'd made it clear that he didn't want family members disturbing him. The lifelong loner, true to form.

He flipped off the lights, which had come back on shortly after Shep's arrival, and climbed the stairs to his bedroom, stripping off his shirt as he went. What had Lynn said? "It wasn't my turn yet. I was going to tell you." Would she have? Maybe. But why had she waited at all?

Finally, just before she left to drive home, she'd laid her hand softly on his arm and sought his eyes. "I'm sorry, Tom," she'd murmured. "I'd hoped it wouldn't make a difference."

How could it not? He was barely ready to have any kind of relationship with a woman, much less with one who had other, vastly more significant...allegiances.

Without bothering to brush his teeth, he fell, exhausted, onto his bed where he lay on his back staring at the ceiling and calling himself all kinds of names until finally, more than an hour later, he fell into a restless slumber.

AFTER BREAKFAST the next morning, Lynn prowled around the house, unable to sit still long enough to read or work on her cross-stitch project. Meditation was out of the question, though that was probably what she most needed. Benedict had curled up for a snooze in the porch rocker. Why couldn't she find herself a peaceful perch, too? Someplace where she could blot out last night. Lose the disturbing memories.

She was furious with herself. When would she ever learn? Where men were concerned, it was folly to get her hopes up. Tom's reaction had been typical. What was it about her vocation that threatened them? Scared them off?

Or were most men simply unwilling to share their woman with others? With God?

From his own experience, Uncle Will, her role model and mentor, had warned her there would be times like this during her ministry. He'd also emphasized it was not only permissible but essential to be human, to question, to hurt.

Shaking her head in self-reproach, she decided she might as well do something useful. She picked up a dust cloth and began polishing the living-room furniture. If confession was good for the soul, she'd better come clean. She hadn't been forthright with Tom. She'd held back. She'd been enjoying him. She was attracted to him. She'd hoped this once...

She dabbed furiously at a water spot on top of the bookcase. Yes, she was a minister and couldn't imagine doing anything else with her life. But doctors, nurses, teachers, others were called to their vocations, too. Why should it be any different for her? She'd been created a woman, just as a female neurosurgeon or school guidance counselor is a woman. And as a woman, she had normal needs and desires—to be loved, to marry, to give birth, to nurture a family, and to love in return.

She wandered onto the porch and knelt beside the rocker, her fingers stroking Benedict's sleek fur. Sighing heavily, she laid her head against the wicker of the chair. After several moments she whispered, "Tell me, is it too much to want it all?"

WHEN TOM CAME THROUGH the door of the bookstore, Aunt Ruth looked up from the display table where she was arranging the latest shipment of bestsellers, a knowing smile crinkling the skin at the corners of her eyes. "About time. We've been wondering when you were going to show yourself. You know, Penelope only had to wait ten years for Odysseus."

Tom skirted the table and grabbed his buxom aunt in a warm hug, remembering how much he enjoyed her quick wit. "This old bear decided hibernation had to come to an end."

His aunt pulled back and studied him. "At least you haven't grown one of those scraggly beards. Rachel and I knew you'd rejoin the human race when you were darned good and ready."

Tom glanced around the shop. "Where's Aunt Rachel?"

"Over at the church practicing."

He winced at the word *church*. Then he compounded his discomfort by asking, "How *are* things at the church?"

If his aunt found his question out of character, she

didn't let on. "Simply dandy. The choir has almost as many men as women, the ladies' circle solved the problem of whose recipes to use for the annual picnic, and the next battle is heating up. Our perennial gadfly, Prentice Jewett, is agitating to keep Reverend Lynn from using the Meacham House as a community youth center. In other words, it's business as usual."

He didn't miss the acerbic tone of her last remark. "I gather you and Mr. Jewett don't see eye to eye."

She raked him with an incredulous look. "That jackass? He wouldn't know the Lord if He sat down beside him and offered him a free pass through the pearly gates."

"Sounds like trouble waiting to happen."

"Sure is. But we'll get through it. We always do."

He laughed. "As I've often said, the trouble with churches is they're full of hypocrites."

His aunt punched him playfully on the arm. "And as I've often said, what better place for them than church?"

"This new minister…Reverend Lynn…?"

"Kendall. She's a crackerjack. Best we've had in a while. 'Course, chauvinistic fools like Prentice and others had to be convinced that a woman could do the job. But Lynn's smart. She took her time. Impressed them with her efficiency, charmed them with her warmth, and preached and pastored her way into the hearts of most." She cocked her head. "I don't imagine you've darkened the door of a church lately. Why are you so curious?"

He shifted his weight to his other foot. "I'm not, really. It just seemed polite to inquire."

In a blessedly abrupt change of subject, Ruth linked

her arm through his and led him to the rear of the bookstore. "There's somebody I want you to meet." She paused at the door to the back room and looked around. "Kate, are you in here?"

An attractive young woman with a smudge of dirt on her face came out from behind a column of stacked packing boxes. "Yes, Ruth. Just doing an inventory of the delivery."

"This is Kate McMann, our indispensable manager." Ruth gestured toward Tom. "My nephew Tom Baines."

"Oh, I know Tom Baines," the young woman responded, nodding at him. "Your fame precedes you."

Kate looked faintly familiar, but Tom couldn't quite place her. "I guess you were a 'Hot Spots' reader," he said.

She grinned. "Well, that, too. No, I remember you from a long time ago."

"I'm sorry, I—"

"You wouldn't remember me. I was one of the pesky junior-high kids who thought you older kids were the gods and goddesses of Riverbend. My—" she fluttered her eyelashes teasingly "—the stories they told about you."

"Oh, puh-leeze," Ruth interjected. "No more black-sheep tales. I keep hoping my wayward nephew here has reformed."

Tom drew up to his full height. "Reformed? Who? Me?" He paused. "Be careful, Aunt Ruth. I know all about your wild youth. It must be in the genes. Besides, you wouldn't like me nearly as much if I changed my evil ways."

Ruth snorted. "I've been found out."

"Found out? About what?" Rachel breezed in the back door, stopped, did a double take, then crossed the room toward Tom, her arms outflung. "Tom!"

"Hi, Auntie. Give me a hug."

Rachel held him at arm's length. "Not until you tell me why you've been such a hermit the past week."

Ruth took a step forward. "Now, Rachel—"

"Don't 'Now, Rachel' me. Just tell me, Tom. Are you out of your self-indulgent funk yet?"

No way could he confess that not only was he not out of his funk, if anything, thanks to the Reverend Lynn Kendall, he'd sunk in deeper. "Yes, Aunt Rachel. Tom Baines has returned to life as we know it in Riverbend, Indiana."

"Praise be," Rachel intoned before giving him the postponed hug. When she drew back, she held him by the shoulders and studied him. "You look good. Rested. Maybe even ready for a serious talk with your aunts."

Something in her expression registered concern beyond the state of his health. "Sounds ominous."

She dropped her hands, averted her eyes and fidgeted with the pin on her lapel. "Not really. But Ruth and I would like you to stop by the house at your earliest convenience."

"I'll call you."

"Make it soon," both twins said at once, their synchronicity of expression causing the group to dissolve in laughter and dispelling Tom's momentary uneasiness.

"HI, GARBO. It's Kate. Do you still 'vant to be alone,' or could you stand some company?"

Lynn cradled the phone closer to her ear. "I'd love some." And who better than a best friend? Maybe Kate could help her make some sense out of her confused emotional state. "What do you have in mind?"

"The aunts are taking my twins to the carnival over in the next county and have invited them to spend the night. So...I'll bring some of my famous chicken and fixings—you know, a kind of movable feast—and we can pig out at your place. After all, I don't want to blow your cover by asking you to come to town."

"I can't think of anything I'd like better than your cooking, except your company, of course. Besides, there's something I need your counsel about."

"Oh?"

Lynn could hear curiosity in her friend's tone. "When you get here."

"Aha. The plot thickens. I can't wait."

A few hours later Kate breezed into the house bearing containers with enough food to feed six. "A hex on calories tonight," she declared as she laid out the supper.

Lynn stared at the dishes. "Are we expecting company?"

"Would I reveal the whereabouts of your hermitage?" She drew an X across her heart. "I promise I was not followed."

Lynn laughed, and the two women began to eat. After Kate regaled her with the latest antics of her twins, Lynn ventured a confession. "I'm trying hard not to feel guilty about being here near Riverbend, yet not being here, if you know what I mean."

"It wouldn't be much of an escape if you were on call. For all anybody knows, you could be in Anchorage." Kate jabbed a chicken leg in her direction. "Give yourself a break. Remember the night you stayed in the hospital until dawn keeping vigil over Iris Templeton, or the youth-group camp-out at Turkey Run State Park when it poured rain? Or how about the trip you made with the Hurtles when their daughter was arrested for—"

"Okay, okay. I get the picture."

"You won't be worth much to all those people who depend on you if you're a basket case yourself. So, my child, go in peace and enjoy your vacation."

Lynn smiled at this friend who knew her so well. For whatever reason, she had needed validation that it was permissible to spend these few weeks away. Common sense told her this was necessary R and R, but her involvement with the people of Riverbend made it difficult to turn her back, even for so short a time. Thank goodness for Kate, who brooked no nonsense. "Remember when we first met?"

"Do I? I'd never seen anybody spend as much time in both the philosophy/religion and fiction sections of the store or converse more knowledgeably about the books."

"And you guessed who I was even though I was just in town for an interview." Lynn chuckled. "I was so scared. I'll never forget Prentice Jewett saying, 'If God had intended women to be ministers, He'd never have converted Paul.' It's still a mystery to me why I was called to the church."

Kate smiled knowingly. "First, never sell yourself short. Second, never underestimate the power of people like the aunts to influence public opinion. They liked you from the first.''

''And I liked them, too. How are they, by the way?''

''Wonderful, as always. Especially after today's return of the native.''

''What are you talking about?'' Lynn forked up some creamy cole slaw and awaited Kate's answer.

''Their nephew Tom Baines is back.''

With difficulty Lynn chewed and swallowed. ''I know.''

''Lynn?'' Kate leaned forward across the table and was looking at her with keen interest. ''How do you know? He's been incommunicado ever since he returned. Wait a minute, wait a minute.'' Kate waved her fingers back and forward in front of her face. ''Don't tell me. Tom Baines is what, or rather who, you wanted to talk about tonight.''

Lynn nodded miserably. ''Dead on, Sherlock.''

''Well, you've come to the right person. I can tell you stories about Tom Baines, all right.''

''Such as?'' Lynn tried to keep the eagerness out of her voice.

''He taught all the River Rats to smoke.''

''River Rats?''

''Yeah. The gang of older kids who always ran around together. They were five or six years older than my friends and I, and we all thought they were so cool. We spent several summers being total pests, spying on them. You know some of them—Lily Holden, Charlie Callahan, Mitch Sterling, among others. But Tom was by far the most sophisticated. He'd lived in places with foreign-sounding names and went to

European boarding schools and could whip any of the others at poker. The girls were all in love with him. He was, you know, the dangerous type.''

''You don't need to limit it to past tense,'' Lynn volunteered quietly.

Kate raised an eyebrow. ''Oho. I do believe you're blushing.'' She paused, her eyes locked on Lynn's. ''How dangerous?''

''Very dangerous.'' Lynn had the distinct sensation she'd crawled far out on a particularly fragile limb.

''Start at the beginning. How did you meet Tom?''

Lynn carefully reconstructed the encounters, omitting only accurate descriptions of the—yes, there was the word again—''dangerous'' kisses. She concluded by describing the stunned look on Tom's face when Shep had called her Reverend.

She paused, watching Benedict creep closer to the table, his nose twitching. ''No chicken for you,'' she said, shooing him away before she turned back to Kate. ''I should have told Tom earlier. But the chance never seemed to come up. And although I'm not proud of it, I have an increasingly difficult time revealing my work to men. Interesting men.''

''Why is that?''

''Because the response is inevitable. They stop seeing me as a woman and start viewing me as some kind of saint. Unapproachable. Untouchable.''

''Men!'' Kate snorted in disbelief. ''Insecure little boys.''

''One of the fellows I dated while I was in seminary came right out and told me he couldn't commit to any woman who was going to be at the beck and call of a congregation twenty-four hours a day. He expected his wife to be home, period."

"Tiny minds," Kate muttered. "You just haven't met the right guy."

"Be that as it may, I need to reconcile myself to the fact it might never happen."

"And if it doesn't?"

"I can be okay with that, even if it's not my preference."

"So Tom Baines lit your fire?"

"Kate, really. That's putting it rather crudely."

Kate bobbed her head. "Oh, yeah. He did. You're pretty transparent, Rev." She leaned over and picked up both Lynn's hands. "Give Tom a chance. Based on what I know about him, I think you could be very important in his life." Her expression was sober, serious. "Very important."

"But he looked so shocked when he found out."

"Of course he did. You have to admit yours is not exactly a typical female profession. He needs time to get used to the idea."

"I suppose you're right."

"Just because you've been burned in the past doesn't mean you have to carry that baggage into every new relationship."

Her friend's words struck home, and Lynn managed a wan grin. "You mean my expectations get in the way of possibility?"

Kate smiled knowingly. "Elementary, my dear Watson."

THE NEXT AFTERNOON Tom set about his task with a vengeance. What the hell was he doing here at the cemetery, of all places? He made several passes with the gas-powered lawn trimmer, ruthlessly clearing the weeds beside the crumbling stone wall. After only a few minutes he'd worked up a sweat, but the exercise proved no more successful than had his other futile attempts to divert himself. Nothing was working. Why not? Because, if he was honest, he was cleaning up this place for Lynn.

And being here only served as a vivid reminder of her gentleness, sunny laughter and guileless eyes.

A minister.

That revelation had nearly choked him. It was one thing for her not to be his customary type of woman, but quite another for her to so completely shake his confidence in his ability to read people. The implications were clear. Adios, Ms. Kendall. He wasn't going to change his lifestyle for anyone.

He continued attacking the weeds, all the while thanking his lucky stars for the close call. Very cautiously, very carefully and very precipitately, he would back away from the trap into which, heaven help him, he'd nearly fallen.

He hacked and chopped until finally he turned the trimmer off and set it aside, then slumped against the wall. Unaccountably, it seemed vital to him to create order in this overgrown burial site. Lynn's weeding had been a start. But much more remained to be done. Something about the years of neglect made him infinitely sad. These souls deserved a better resting place.

He closed his eyes, unable to stem the onslaught of gut-wrenching images—mangled bodies lying in a rain-filled ditch, the bloated stomachs of starving infants and, despite his efforts to will it away, Gordy's blood-spattered body, sprawled on the dark, unyielding pavement.

Tom was only vaguely aware of the breeze ruffling his hair. Not much he could do for any of them, victims of man's unspeakable inhumanity to man.

But there was something he could do here, insignificant a gesture as it might be.

He grabbed the handle of the trimmer again and hoisted himself to his feet. Insignificant, but maybe, just maybe, a small step toward filling the dark void within him, healing his pain.

DURING THE NEXT FEW DAYS, Lynn found peace in taking long walks along the river, weeding the Carters' flower beds, trying a new recipe for dill bread, jotting down ideas for sermons and trying, sometimes almost successfully, to forget Tom Baines.

Late one evening she sat rocking on the screened-in porch watching the moonlight shimmering on the river, listening to the soft cello sonata emanating from the stereo and stroking the contented Benedict. She hadn't heard from Tom. Not that she'd really expected to. She'd just hoped. She had, however, come to a decision.

When he brought back her bicycle, as he'd said he would, she would take the first step. Kate had been right about her self-destructive tendencies. She set herself up with men, giving neither them nor herself a chance. It was unrealistic to expect a man, any man, to fall in with her life's plan, without allowing time for the in-depth, revealing communication upon which a solid relationship depended.

She was great at counseling others. Why was she

so blind, even pigheaded, where she herself was concerned?

Yet there were things about Tom that disturbed her. Why he preferred solitude, instead of getting in touch with his old friends. Especially the River Rats. And why he seemed evasive when she'd asked about the photographs of his children. Most men would've been boastful, but Tom had seemed somehow pained by her questions. And there was another puzzling thing. He had never mentioned the third child, the one who'd signed his photograph "Terence Coyne." In fairness, she acknowledged that Shep had interrupted their discussion. Yet she couldn't shake the feeling that, in any event, Tom wouldn't have volunteered anything about the boy.

The mournful cello vibrato pierced her awareness, emphasizing the ephemeral quality of life. Time slipped by so quickly, yet she'd been waiting for life to happen to her, expecting others to understand her and surmount her defenses.

As baffling and unnerving as it was, she had the profound sense that Tom wasn't the big bad wolf. That he was worth the risk.

THE LATE-AFTERNOON SUN filtered through leafy branches, dappling Riverbend's manicured lawns with light and shadow, as Tom drove his truck with Lynn's newly repaired bicycle in the bed. Should he call in advance, warn her he was coming over? Nah. She might interpret that as a deliberate move to see her again when, in fact, all he wanted was to deliver the bike, beat a hasty retreat and consign Reverend Lynn Kendall to the remotest corner of his memory. The last thing he needed was to imply he might have some interest in her.

He flat out didn't understand the hold she seemed to have on him. What was it about her that made it so difficult to walk away? She wasn't sophisticated or classically beautiful, and her sights were clearly fixed on a realm beyond his. Tom muttered a curse under his breath. He wasn't accustomed to things that didn't make sense. His job, hell, his entire training, was to take the nonsensical, the incomprehensible, the bizarre, and explain it, even justify it to the masses.

Almost too late he saw a collie amble out into the street. He slammed on the brakes, then sat shaking his head, his nerves jangling. Cocking his ears at him, the dog wagged his feathery tail, then ambled on. Damn. A bad day was getting worse. It had started this morning when he'd steeled himself to phone Pete and Libby. He hadn't expected the call to be any more cordial than the past ones, and it wasn't. Libby's curt response was typical.

"Can't talk, Dad. I'm on my way to swim-team practice…. Pete? He slept over at Cory's…. Gotta run." The click of the receiver and the subsequent hum on the line sent a powerful message. He was persona non grata.

If that wasn't enough, he'd had yet another call from his former editor, who was pressuring him to write a book detailing the atrocities of the final decades of the twentieth century. A cheery subject if he'd ever heard one. Now the fool dog and, next, his upcoming awkward conversation with Lynn.

All in all, he was in a foul mood. So what else was new? Even before Dublin, he'd been aware of a sense of cynicism and ennui, but during this past year, he took the prize for being a surly bastard.

Maybe that was part of Lynn's attraction. When he was with her, he almost forgot what a jerk he was. As he drove past the outskirts of town and tooled down the two-lane highway, he rehearsed his speech. "Got caught up in the moment...nothing in common...don't want to compromise your job..." *Job?* That was a lame word, surely, to describe what she did with her life.

By the time he turned onto River Road, his frown was so intense his jaw ached. Short and sweet. No prolonged explanations, no rationalizations. Shouldn't be a problem. Not that much had happened between them.

He blew out an exasperated sigh. And now nothing was going to. He rebelled against the wave of regret that swept over him.

By the time he reached the Carters' drive, he was ready, the words poised on his lips. He drew the truck up to the carport, lifted out the bike and leaned it against the side of the house. Before he reached the front door, it opened and Lynn stepped onto the porch, a smile illuminating her entire face.

Her hair was caught up with one of those scrunchy things, but tendrils of reddish gold curled beside her ears and at the nape of her neck. She wore a sleeveless navy blue blouse and one of those gauzy skirts. He swallowed hard. The way the sun was shining through the wispy material, he had no trouble making out her well-shaped legs.

But it was the killer smile that drew his eyes to

hers, bright and eager. Almost expectant. As if she had a surprise for him.

She took a step toward him. "Tom, how kind of you to return the bike."

He stood his ground. "I always finish what I begin. Besides, the truck makes it a lot easier."

"I appreciate your thoughtfulness. How much do I owe you?"

"Not a thing. It was no big deal." Was it his imagination or was this conversation stilted? Well, what else could it be, since all his senses were geared up to cut off a relationship that had never really gotten started?

"Are you sure?"

"I'm sure."

"Well, thank you very much then. Please come inside and let me fix you some iced tea by way of thanks."

He didn't want to go inside and he didn't want any iced tea. He wanted out of here. But the only way that was going to happen with any degree of grace was to follow her inside and wait for his opening. "I'll come inside for a few minutes, but I don't care for anything to drink."

He couldn't help noticing that the smile had faded from her lips, and the eyes fixed on him were puzzled. "If you have something else to do..."

"It's not that." Damn, this was uncomfortable.

"Maybe you'd rather take a walk. It's beautiful this time of the evening." She held out her hand, and the now-hopeful expression in her eyes doomed him.

"Sounds good." He took her hand, trying not to notice how perfectly her fingers entwined with his, and walked beside her through a gap in the bushes until they reached a narrow path along the river. The breeze off the water's surface and the shade from the trees lining the bank made the air here feel ten degrees cooler.

They walked quietly for perhaps a quarter of a mile, his thoughts focused on finding the right words. Yet at the same time, he felt an incongruous calm. She said nothing, but the silence between them wasn't awkward. Rather, she seemed to anticipate and accept that something was forthcoming from him, and was giving him the gift of time.

When the incessant chirping of tree frogs finally penetrated his brain, he stopped, then turned toward her, now taking both her hands in his. Looking at her, he felt like a trusted shepherd ready to butcher the spring lamb. "Lynn, I'm afraid I've done you a grave disservice, and I want you to know how sorry I am."

"A disservice?" She looked baffled.

"I took advantage of a situation. It was selfish. I like you, but I—" he could feel himself fumbling "—never should have presumed to kiss you."

"More than once I believe," she murmured, her eyes not leaving his.

"Somehow I just thought…"

"You thought I was an ordinary warm-blooded woman who enjoyed that expert nine-point-five performance."

"I guess I did."

"But now you think I'm not an ordinary woman, right?"

He stared at the ground between them, at the rich soil, at the weeds bordering the path, at the beetle emerging from under a nearby rock. He owed her the truth. Reluctantly he looked up. "You're a minister!" he blurted, inwardly cursing his tactlessness.

She clutched his hands, but said nothing for several seconds. "It doesn't have to be an obstacle, you know."

"An obstacle?"

"To our feelings."

Whoa! Where was this going? Who was in charge here? "Feelings?"

With the toe of her sandal, she made a small swirl in the dirt. "Forgive me if this sounds too forward, but I like you, Tom. And the nine-point-five?" Her face turned rosy in the twilight. "I lied. It was always a ten."

"Lynn, I—"

"Let me finish before I totally lose my nerve. I am asking you to give us a chance. Always before, I've caved in when a man has opted out of a relationship with me. I'm well aware my being a minister poses problems. And I know it's hard for you. How many men want to share a woman with an entire congregation? What kind of man is willing to take a supportive role, even a backseat, in his wife's career?" She hurtled on, while his heart thudded in concert. "Then there's the mysterious part. You know, the fact that I've been 'called.' Some men find that somehow...threatening."

Even in the cool of the evening, he was aware he was sweating. He'd had no idea this would be so difficult. He read the plea in her eyes, heard the huskiness in her voice. He felt like a cad. In the midst of his confusion of feelings, he barely registered her next question. And when he did, his breath caught in his throat.

"Tom, do you find it threatening?"

He swallowed. "Yes." He had no answer that would satisfy her, let her down easily. "Because I can't understand it."

She dropped his hands and turned away, studying the eddies in the river. "Is it necessary to understand everything? All at once?"

"I suppose not. But in my business I try."

Her voice sounded small. "Do you think you'd be willing to try in this case?"

He stared at one stray curl, lying vulnerable and exposed on her bare neck, and imagined planting his lips in that tender spot. "Try?" What was she suggesting?

She hugged her arms around her slender waist. "This is difficult for me. But I promised myself I wouldn't pretend or fool myself." He moved behind her in order to hear her. "I'm a woman, Tom, but I'm not accustomed to…coming on to a man like this, but please be honest with me. Are you attracted to me?"

Hell. He might be a cad, but he'd never lie to this woman. "Yes."

"I'm attracted to you, too. *Very* attracted."

Without thinking, he slipped his arms around her and captured her hands. "What are you saying?"

"I sense you're ready to cut and run. It's too troublesome and demanding to get involved with the Reverend Lynn Kendall." Slowly she pivoted in his arms and the invitation in her eyes and the trembling of her lips rattled him to the core. "But could you consider getting involved with Lynn, the woman?"

"It's complicated. I…"

She lowered her eyes. "That wasn't fair of me to ask. You take me, you take the whole package."

A fish leaped near the bank, falling with a loud slap back into the water. Upriver the sound of a motorboat matched the hum in his brain. "It's not you. You're a beautiful, desirable woman."

"But?" When she looked up, her expression was unflinching.

"But…I'm not a good person, Lynn."

"I don't believe that." She hesitated. "But I believe you believe it."

"You don't know where I've been, what I've seen." His stomach roiled. Death houses in Calcutta, orphanages in Romania, executions in Afghanistan. "And you don't want to know."

"Are you blaming yourself?"

The question rocked him. He knew he couldn't have stopped the carnage, the crime, the destruction. Yet he'd preyed upon it, fed off it. Could he somehow have been more compassionate? Or had he found it easier, more comfortable, to remain detached, impassive? *Was* guilt part of his problem? Part of this inertia he felt?

Slowly he became aware that her hands were resting on his shoulders, which were tensed both with anger at a universe he couldn't control and with unbridled longing for this woman who saw into the depths of his being. "Lynn, you don't understand. It's a dirty world out there."

Her eyes filled as, deliberately and tenderly, she moved her right hand and laid it over his pounding heart. "But it doesn't have to be a dirty world in here.'' Her palm warmed his entire chest and he found he had no response for her. ''Will you trust me? Give us a chance?''

No man in his right mind could have resisted. Acting against every rational fiber of his being, he pulled her tight against him and buried his face in her hair. ''You don't know what you're asking,'' he whispered raggedly.

He felt her lips moving against his ear. ''I know exactly what I'm asking. More than I've ever asked of anyone.''

He was helpless. ''What if…''

She stepped back and looked directly at him, her eyes dark with…fear? ''No *what ifs*. Just tell me I haven't made a complete fool of myself.''

His last resolve crumpled, and just before he crushed her mouth with his, he managed to murmur, ''You a fool? Hardly.''

CHAPTER FOUR

Tom COULDN'T GET enough—the softness, the yielding, the sheer femininity of her. When he finally pulled his mouth away, he held her tight, his eyes closed against the outer world and the inevitable questions. Moist smells from the river mingled with the flowery fragrance of her hair as he drew her head into the crook of his neck and felt the warmth of her breath against his skin. Why her? Why now?

The only answer that occurred to him was that, for whatever reasons, fate had tilted his world on its axis.

They stood, wrapped in each other's arms for what seemed a very long time, the only sounds the lapping of the river against the bank, the buzz of locusts, the faint rustle of the cottonwoods. Slowly, deliberately, Tom stepped back, cupping her face in his hands. "Whew. Looks as if we've taken this relationship to the next level."

Her luminous eyes betrayed a spark of humor. "'We'? You're sure I didn't push you into this?"

He gave a low laugh. "Fat chance. No wolf worth his sheep's clothing gives in that easily." He kissed her lightly. "No, I exercised my own free will."

She reached up and cupped his hands, then spoke quietly. "I'm glad, Tom. Really glad." Then she stepped away and, still holding one of his hands, began walking toward the house.

He followed, realizing he wanted her in the most elemental way, but also in another, more unfamiliar way, one separate and apart from his sexual longing.

"I SHOULD HAVE TOLD YOU earlier," Lynn said later as they lay snuggling in the Carters' hammock, "about being a minister."

"I'm glad you didn't."

"Why?"

She heard the low chuckle rumble out of his chest. "Because if I'd known, I'd have run like hell."

She moved her head, the better to see his eyes. "And now?"

The lone light from inside the house cast a glow over his face, and she could read the momentary hesitation. "Honestly, Lynn? I don't know."

Although she'd expected as much, she wasn't prepared for her surge of disappointment. This wasn't going to be easy. Much more was at stake than simple attraction. "That's fair," she whispered. "In truth, you haven't yet met the real me."

He trailed a finger over her cheek. "Who have I met, then?"

"The vacation me."

"I like the vacation you."

"But will you like the real-world me?"

He tapped her nose. "We'll have to see, won't we?"

Lynn relaxed. He was going to give them a chance. "You should know what you're getting into."

"Like?"

"Like being with someone who has irregular hours, who works on weekends, who gets her fair share of criticism…"

He smiled. "So far you're describing a foreign correspondent."

She put a finger on his lips. "Wait, I'm not finished." She paused, considering how to articulate the rest. "Who needs quiet time to prime her spiritual pump, who must love the unlovable, respond day or night to others and keep herself attuned to a higher power."

She watched him struggle for an answer. "Now we're onto shakier ground."

"So?" Her heart shriveled in anticipation of rejection.

"I've never run from new experiences. I'm not going to start now."

She could barely breathe. "But?"

"I can't make any promises. It's not just you. God and I have had no more than a nodding acquaintance for quite a few years. So I'm not exactly a churchgoer."

"That's your journey, Tom. Not one I'd try to influence—at least not directly. Let's see how things unfold. No expectations. Okay?"

He pulled her close again and his lips caressed her temple. "I can live with that if you can."

She stared dreamily at the canopy of leaves overhead, wondering if she'd made the right choice. Could Tom be the one to care enough to embrace the whole of her? Or were the obstacles too formidable?

His words came out of the night and took aim at her heart. "Hey, Rev, isn't this about faith? About stepping into unfamiliar territory?"

She relaxed into a giggle. "You *do* have a way with words."

"You know we may surprise some people."

"The aunts, for example?"

"Yeah, for starters."

It seemed like a good opening to bring up the rest of his family. "Did you know I officiated at your uncle's memorial service?"

"I figured as much."

"I'm sorry you couldn't be there."

"I was overseas when I got the word, and like I said, I'm not much for church. I prefer remembering Uncle Abe out on the farm in his baggy old clothes."

"I've never heard anyone else call him Abe."

Tom smiled fondly. "No one else did. It was just one of the ways he made me feel special."

"You must miss him."

"I do. Even though he did a lot for Riverbend, he could be a difficult person. Regrettably very few saw the mellow side of him. For instance, taking an interest in his knockabout nephew, leaving me this farm."

"Weren't you one of the River Rats?"

"A sort of honorary summer member." He shook his head. "Those were the days. It's a wonder our parents didn't disown us."

"You were *that* bad?"

"Not all of us. I was the worst, always trying to prove something. For me, it boiled down to the friendships. Something I needed then."

She bit back the obvious "Only then?" and, instead, said, "I understand from Kate McMann that several of you still live in Riverbend." She waited for him to respond. When he didn't, she went on, "Have you seen any of them?"

Shifting her so that she nestled against his shoulder, he rested his chin on her head. "No." The hammock ropes squeaked in rhythm with the swaying motion.

"As you said, I've met the vacation you. Well, you've met the hermit me, not the Riverbend me."

"So we're both in for some surprises?"

"Lynn, I don't know where I fit anymore. If I fit."

She was instantly alert to the self-doubt and vulnerability in his voice. Her heart troubled, she laid a hand on his chest. "You'll find the way home, Tom. I know it."

Just before kissing her again, he breathed out the words, "I have to, Lynn. I have to."

THE NEXT MORNING Lynn couldn't afford the luxury of basking in the shimmering, though tenuous first flush of what she dared to call love, though she had no doubt that word would inspire the same fear in Tom as it did in her. Not after Marilyn Rasmusson's call.

Her secretary apologized for disturbing her vacation, but as Lynn was quick to assure her after hearing her message, she'd had no choice. Lynn hung up the phone and emitted an exasperated sigh. Prentice Jewett, the same Prentice Jewett who had tried to block her call to Riverbend Community Church, was at it again. This time the target was the Meacham House project.

Lynn glanced at Benedict, eyeing her from the window ledge where he was sunning. "Kitty, looks like our vacation is over." Resignedly she rose and walked into Seth Carter's den, booted up the computer and accessed the e-mail server in preparation for receiving from Marilyn the text of a letter Prentice was circulating to prominent Riverbend citizens and all church members.

Why now? They'd been over this ground. Initial

objections to using Meacham House, a Victorian downtown residence adjacent to the church property and recently bequeathed to the church, as a teen outreach center had been discussed and, she'd thought, overcome. The staff was in place and a series of kickoff events was scheduled to coincide with the beginning of school only a few weeks away.

Benedict hopped onto the desk and sat on his haunches watching the screen intently as the message line scrolled up. Lynn scanned the letter and groaned. Sometimes it was darn difficult to understand human nature. She hated these "little tests," as Uncle Will called them, but accepted them as part of the challenge of working with all different kinds of people.

She hit "print" and waited. A few seconds later she held the offending page in her hand.

Dear Friends of Riverbend:
As you are aware, there are plans to use historic Meacham House as a teen outreach center. However, it is not too late to reverse that decision. I appeal to you as citizens interested in keeping our downtown viable to register your feelings immediately with the Chamber of Commerce, board members of the Riverbend Community Church and the Reverend Lynn Kendall, who has been the spearhead of this ill-conceived venture.

The young persons toward whom the program is directed are not apt to reflect the standards of public decency consistent with the positive image Riverbend businessmen work hard to project, nor is the church likely to reap any benefits from investing in such an endeavor. To the contrary, maintaining the Meacham House property, especially given the wear and tear the teen program undoubtedly will inflict, will drain funds better spent on programs with measurable, observable results.

One can only suppose what Frederick Meacham and his descendants would make of the desecration of the home on Bridge Street they so lovingly cared for and long enjoyed! Time is of the essence.

Act now!

Yours in concern,
Prentice T. Jewett

Lynn's shoulders sagged. The attack was even worse than she'd anticipated. Last spring the board had attempted to identify and deflect the objections, which stemmed mainly from those intimidated by and fearful of teenagers, particularly the teenagers whose apparel, tattoos and body piercings seemed to demonstrate a flouting of convention. However, Ed Pennington, the treasurer, had carefully worked out the figures to demonstrate the church could well afford to support the much-needed program.

It required only a cursory tour of Riverbend to see that there were few safe places for young people, particularly those economically disadvantaged. After interviewing some of the teens, Lynn had come away with the distinct impression they felt alienated by the adult community, and as she well knew, alienation was a breeding ground for trouble.

Benedict leaped into her lap and kneaded her chest with his clawless paws. "It's the pits, Ben. But you and I know those kids are worth saving." The cat nudged his nose between her neck and shoulder. "So settle down while I make this phone call."

Reluctantly Lynn picked up the phone and dialed Prentice Jewett's office. When she was connected to him, she identified herself, then got right to the point. "I understand you are the author of a letter objecting to the Meacham House project."

If he was startled to hear from her, he didn't let on. "Shouldn't come as any surprise to you. I told you last spring that you hadn't seen the end of me. You bleeding-heart women are all alike. It's unconscionable to sacrifice perfectly fine church property in the unlikely event of helping a few scraggly kids."

"I'm sorry you feel that way."

"You can be sorry all you want, but I'm putting a stop to this nonsense."

Lynn marshaled her compelling arguments, but the man wouldn't budge. Before hanging up, she asked him to discontinue circulating the letter.

His terse response was, "The die's cast. Goodbye."

After disconnecting, Lynn wilted. She felt very alone. But lifting her eyes to gaze out the window at the slow-moving river, she was encouraged by remembering the support already in place for Meacham House—Ed and Grace Pennington, Aaron Mazerik, Lily Holden, Kate McMann and, of course, the Steele sisters, who had been publicly and vocally enthusiastic. The opening would occur, with or without Prentice Jewett's blessing. But at the same time she couldn't help being disappointed that people like Prentice had such difficulty embracing those in the world unlike themselves.

The vacation had been restful, but this development meant she would have to return to Riverbend sooner than planned. She couldn't leave it to Molly Linden, the Meacham House director, to fight the battle alone. She needed to be there, too.

She shrugged in resignation. She would return in the morning after she kept her afternoon date with Tom to put the finishing touches on their cleanup efforts at the cemetery. One more day surely wasn't asking too much.

She thumbed through the church directory, then began making calls to rally support.

TOM'S JAW DROPPED. "Whoa. Wait a minute. You're telling me Aaron's my—"

"Cousin. Abraham's son."

Tom gripped the wooden arms of the antique rocker and looked in desperation from Aunt Ruth on the sofa to Aunt Rachel in the wing chair she favored for her back. The familiarity of the aunts' music room brought no comfort. It was inconceivable they were sitting here calmly saying that his uncle had had an illegitimate son. Especially not Aaron Mazerik.

"We know how upsetting this must be for you," Rachel said.

"Upsetting?" Tom launched out of the rocker and paced to the bookcase and back to the piano. "I find it inconceivable Uncle Abe would do something like that."

"That's what we thought, too," Ruth said quietly.

"My God, what will Jacob think? That makes Aaron his…half brother!"

Ruth's face fell. "I only wish we knew where Jacob was. At least we'd all be in this together."

Tom stopped in his tracks and studied his aunts, then fell on one knee beside Rachel's chair. "Oh, hell.

On top of Jacob's disappearance and Uncle Abe's death, the news you have a nephew you never knew about must've hit the two of you like a ton of bricks.''

Rachel folded and refolded the handkerchief in her lap. "It did," she said quietly.

Ruth leaned forward. "But shocking as it is, I'm grateful Abraham didn't abandon Aaron and his mother."

His mother. Jeez, Tom hadn't even stopped to consider the full ramifications. "You mean Evie?" How many times had she waited on him through the years at the Sunnyside Café?

"She never said a word." Ruth nodded in grudging admiration.

"And she could have created a scandal," Rachel added.

Tom sat back against the sofa, trying to digest all the information, process all the questions. Had Uncle Abe carried on an affair under their very noses? For how long? Had he supported Evie and Aaron? Aaron. My God, how must he feel? Had he known all those years? Harbored resentment?

"What about Aaron?" Tom asked.

"Aaron only found out after Abraham died."

"This has to be tough on him, too."

"I can't begin to imagine," Ruth said softly.

"What's he doing now?"

Rachel smiled. "That young man did a complete turnaround—went from being the town bad boy to becoming a truly fine coach and counselor at the high school. He genuinely cares for the youngsters."

"He probably knows firsthand about having a rough time growing up," Tom said grimly.

Ruth sighed. "I'm afraid so."

"What do we do now?"

Rachel looked directly at him. "We've been to see him. We assured him we consider him one of us—a Steele."

"Does he want to be?"

"Time will tell," Ruth said.

"I need a few days to come to grips with this." Tom rose to his feet. "Then I'll go talk with him."

"Thank you, dear." Rachel picked up the handkerchief and dabbed her eyes.

"Tom," Ruth pleaded, "please remember how much your uncle Abraham loved you. He had his faults, but he was a good man."

Faults? Keeping a son a secret was more than that. Sin seemed a better word. But surely, Tom thought, his uncle had had his reasons. *Let there be reasons.* "I'm grateful to you both for telling me. It can't have been easy for you. Until Jacob comes home, *if* he comes home, I'll represent the family with Aaron."

On the way back to the farm the full impact of his promise hit him. Aaron might be a high-school counselor, but that didn't mean he'd forget or forgive the injustice done him. Worse yet, what might he want from the Steeles?

Tom drew in a deep breath. God, he missed Jacob. Why had his cousin left Riverbend suddenly all those years ago, dropping totally out of sight? And where the hell was he, anyway?

ALTHOUGH TOM HAD GREETED HER that afternoon with a genuine smile and a warm hug when he'd picked her up to go to the cemetery, he seemed preoccupied as he drove. Lynn afforded him quiet by concentrating on the profusion of colors outside the window—the vivid blue of cornflowers, the cash-green of the soybean fields, the pristine white of well-maintained farmhouses. The premature end to her vacation had precipitated a chaotic morning—packing, cleaning the Carters' house, checking in again with Marilyn at the church office.

Now, however, she relished the restful steady motion of the truck, determined to milk the last few hours of pleasure from this special time with Tom before she returned to Riverbend. She turned slightly to look at him. His jaw was set, his eyes indecipherable behind his dark glasses, and his mouth, in profile, a grim line. He was a thousand miles away, but instinctively she knew his absorption had nothing to do with her.

When they reached the cemetery, he parked alongside the road, then shut off the engine and rolled down the windows. The incessant scritching of insects filled the silence. Lynn waited. As if collecting himself, Tom squeezed her hand and said, "Ready? I'll get the stuff out of the back."

Lynn watched as he collected the tools, then she grabbed the cooler and followed him up the rise to the stone wall. He hitched the lawn trimmer over his shoulder and began working on the far wall. She drew on her gardener's gloves and squatted beside a family plot in a still-overgrown corner of the graveyard and began weeding. She enjoyed the mindless repetition of pulling a handful of roots from the ground and the satisfaction of observable progress.

She glanced at Tom, moving steadily around the exterior of the wall, sweat glistening on his tanned, bare arms. The slight frown was a dead giveaway. It wasn't her imagination. Something was troubling him. She ached to soothe it away.

After an hour and a half, she sat back on her heels, surveying with satisfaction the restored order. She prayed those long gone did, indeed, rest in peace here. She stood up, putting her hands in the small of her back to ease the crick there, and watched while Tom returned the tools to the truck. A faint breeze lifted tendrils of hair off her forehead. When he returned, he carried a faded quilt under one arm, which he spread on the shorn grass. He sat, leaning his back against the wall, his legs extended, his feet crossed at the ankles. He patted the space beside him, then adopted a falsetto voice. "Come in, Little Red Riding Hood. It's only your granny."

Lynn shot him a skeptical look. "Granny, my foot!"

"Do you prefer wolves?"

She sank down beside him, kissed him on the cheek and whispered in his ear, "Infinitely."

He put his arm around her and she rested her head against his shoulder. Light from the setting sun glinted off the surface of the distant river, turning the molasses-brown water to shimmering silver. Fields dense with golden-tasseled corn surrounded them. Lynn sighed contentedly.

Tom played with her hair. Still he said nothing. Again she resisted the impulse to speak. Finally his hand dropped back to her shoulder and he said, "Ironic, isn't it? All that beauty, all that fecundity, yet in another place, another time, that scene could just as easily be a killing field."

Lynn stifled a gasp and sat very still. Finally she trusted her voice. "Tom?"

He laughed hollowly. "Sorry. I don't know where that came from."

"I think you do." When she laid her hand on his thigh, she could feel the twitch in the ridge of muscle beneath the denim of his jeans. "I'm a good listener."

"I'll bet you are. It's part of the job description." He shook his head. "Hell, I didn't mean that the way it came out. Sarcastic."

She ignored the slight. "Is it something about this place? Does it remind you of something?"

He reached up and fumbled at his shirt pocket. "Damn. I keep forgetting. I don't smoke anymore." He tilted back his head. "Does it remind me of something? Yeah. It reminds me that things are seldom what they seem. Rice paddies, mountain resorts and outdoor markets can all appear picturesque." He practically spit out the word *appear*.

"But?"

"In the blink of an eye, they can become scenes of senseless bloodshed." He removed his arm from her shoulder, got to his feet, then stood, hands in his pockets, staring at the grave markers.

"Is that what you see here?"

"Stupid, isn't it?"

His loneliness and alienation were almost palpable. She closed her eyes briefly before responding. "No. In fact, it's understandable, given what you've witnessed as a journalist. Detachment must be difficult to come by."

He shifted his weight from one foot to the other. "Impossible. That's why all this—" he waved his arm in a gesture that encompassed the cemetery and the fields beyond "—seems...phony. Superficial."

Lynn pushed herself up and sat on the wall. She raised her eyes to his, still obscured behind the dark glasses. "Trusting is that hard?"

"Especially when much of what you think is true turns out to be a lie."

"Such as?"

He turned away. "Never mind."

She stared at her lap where, in the course of the conversation, she'd clasped her hands in a death grip. This was a man with heavy burdens. A man who needed to talk. A man who couldn't be hurried.

And a man she desperately wanted to help. To love.

He turned back to her, extending a hand. She reached out and let herself be pulled into his arms. He nestled her against his chest. "I'm sorry. I didn't mean to be such poor company. My mood has nothing to do with you."

"I know that. What *does* it have to do with?"

She waited, aware of his breathing, of his hand tracing the contours of her shoulder blades. "Death."

The one syllable reverberated in her ears—bleak, ugly, final. She pulled back, still in his loose embrace, reached up and slowly removed his sunglasses. Then she sought his eyes, plumbing their depths. Cynicism, yes. But far more important—pain and confusion. "Is it anything you can share?"

He studied her for a moment, then barely shook his head. "No. Nobody who hasn't been there could understand."

"I haven't been where you've been—" she spaced out her words "—but I do know firsthand about death."

He adjusted his expression, but not before she'd seen the flicker of disbelief. With his index finger he traced down her forehead, then her nose, until, when he reached her lips, he paused as if to say, *Shh*. Then he smiled regretfully. "This is the last evening of your vacation. I don't want to ruin it. Quite the contrary." He nuzzled her neck. "I want to take you home, cook you a decadently large steak and ply you with sweet talk."

She knew better than to press him. Instead, she fell in with his change of mood by clutching both his hands in hers and drawing their locked fists to her chest. "Why, Granny, you've made me an offer I can't refuse." She lowered her lashes and gave him a calculated sultry look. "I take mine medium rare."

WITH HIS BARBECUE FORK, Tom distributed the hot coals before slapping two huge T-bones on the grill with more force than he'd intended. Damn. He was a self-absorbed ass! The worst of it was, he'd almost spilled his guts to her. Almost told her about being rejected by two children who hardly claimed him as a father. About the uncle whose recently revealed secret life made a mockery of Tom's memories. And...about Gordy.

But he wouldn't sully her idealized view of the world with his problems. It bugged him that she seemed to have all the answers, yet he recognized he needed some of her certitude, her optimism. He stopped short of calling it faith. Why was she even putting up with him? They had nothing in common.

And then he saw her. Coming down the steps, her body silhouetted in the last rays of the sun, her hair floating around her face, her smile warm, genuine, accepting. It made no sense, this tremor in his chest, this powerful need. Hell. He could no more walk away from her than fly. He held out his arms. Her smile grew more intimate and she walked without hesitation into his embrace.

"Any chance," he said, "I could talk you into by-passing dinner and settling for this?" He lowered his lips to hers and spent a long minute exploring her mouth and pulling her heated body closer to his.

When he drew away, she looked up at him with shining eyes. "It's tempting. Very tempting."

"So?" He gave her another sample kiss.

"Mmm," she hummed against his ear. "I'm a greedy woman. I want both." She nipped his earlobe. "Starting with the steak." Then she grabbed his hands playfully and leaned back, only his grip preventing her from falling. She arched her neck and laughed, a melodious tinkling sound in the twilight.

Hell, he didn't care how different they were. He didn't understand how it had happened or what he would do about it, but this woman was becoming indispensable to him. She almost made him believe in light and life.

And laughter. Over dinner, she regaled him with stories of her parishioners—the curly-headed pre-schooler who always called her "Mrs. God," the oc-togenarian notorious for the mystery meat loaf she insisted on preparing for Meals on Wheels, the church treasurer so painstaking that he spent an entire week tracking down a single unaccounted-for penny. With her flair for the dramatic, Lynn brought the characters to life for him. But it wasn't only her mimicry that made the individuals so vivid. It was the obvious love she felt for them. "And so," she concluded, "my days are never dull."

He chuckled appreciatively. "I imagine not." He toyed with his fork, aware that, with his next comment, he'd reveal his trademark cynicism. "Surely not everyone is so quaint or amusing."

She leveled a look at him. "I didn't fool you, huh?" Her lips quirked in a rueful smile. "No, some are real...challenges. People have a heavy emotional investment in institutions like schools and churches, and sometimes they can be territorial, self-righteous and judgmental. That's why I have to try to be open and, when necessary, forgiving." She picked up her napkin and wiped up imaginary crumbs. Something was troubling her.

"Like when?"

She looked up at him. "Like now."

"Trouble in paradise?"

"I'll overlook the sarcasm. Yes, trouble. Have you heard about the Meacham House project?"

"Only what I read in the newspaper. An after-school program for at-risk kids involving classes, tutoring, counseling. Does that about cover it?"

"Yes. It's desperately needed. Too many kids with absentee parents are hanging out on the streets just looking for trouble. The church will provide the facility and some volunteers, although we hope others from the community will become involved, as well. We thought we'd addressed all possible objections, but apparently not."

"Oh?"

"Prentice Jewett, who owns several downtown buildings, is launching another protest."

"And you're his number-one target."

She smiled regretfully. "How perceptive of you."

"What happens now?"

"When I go home tomorrow, I'll continue talking with supporters and we'll try to pacify Mr. Jewett. But somehow I don't see that happening."

He reached across the table and grasped her hand. "You're stepping into the lion's den, huh?"

"It's part of the job."

He rubbed a thumb over her knuckles, considering his next words. "You'll be in the public eye much more, Lynn. Have you considered the impact of that?"

"What do you mean?"

"Is it wise for you to be seen with the prodigal black sheep?"

"Who? You? I'm not worried about your past." She sighed. "But you're right. I do have to be concerned about people's perception. Are you willing to dive into my fishbowl?"

Was he? If they were publicly linked, what would that mean for her? For him? "Honestly? I don't know."

He'd expected her to be disappointed, but instead, she squeezed his fingers and said, "That's a fair answer, Tom. This is not your cause. It's mine and I'll deal with it." She hesitated, biting her lower lip. "But I need to say this. I care about you. I want to continue seeing you. If we don't do anything to raise eyebrows…"

He stood, rounded the table and pulled her up into his arms. "Like this, you mean?" Taut with desire, he sought her parted lips, felt the curves of her body melt into the planes of his. When he ended the kiss, he waited, holding her, searching her eyes.

She sagged against him. "Yes, that would do it."

The kiss had played hell with his concentration. "What?"

"Raise eyebrows." She straightened and held him by the arms. "Tom, I've told you how I feel. Now it's up to you to decide whether you can deal with the complications of my public visibility. Either way, I'll understand.''

She paused a beat as if expecting him to say something, but he was mute from the obligation not to kid himself—or her. In the uncomfortable silence, she began clearing the cutlery, stacking the dishes. ''Lynn, I—''

She turned toward him. ''I don't expect an answer tonight. This is too important for both of us. Let's take the future a day at a time. But I promise you one thing. I won't ask more from you than you're able to give.''

And what might that be? Hell if he knew. But she'd given him space. Space and time. It would take both—and more—to heal that deeper, unidentifiable need crowding his heart. He picked up the salad and followed her into the brightly lit kitchen. He set the bowl carefully on the counter, then turned to face her. ''You seem to know me better than I know myself. I don't usually let people get this close.''

She cocked her head, studying him, then said quietly, ''I know. Take your time.''

He breathed a relieved sigh. ''Thank you.'' He took the plates from her hands, set them in the sink, then led her to the front porch where, for a long time, they sat holding hands, each lost in their thoughts.

AS WAS HER CUSTOM after rehearsing the hymns and choral accompaniment for Sunday, Rachel Steele let her hands and feet automatically play over the organ keys and pedals, finding, almost by second nature, the notes of some of her favorites—''Sheep May Safely Graze,'' ''My Faith Looks up to Thee,'' ''Jesu, Joy of Man's Desiring." As she hummed and sang along, she found her glance straying repeatedly to the pulpit. Oh, the substitute clergyman's sermons had been adequate, but none had touched her the way Lynn's usually did. She'd missed Lynn and hoped her vacation had been restful. Lord knows, that young woman was a tireless worker.

As her fingers drifted over the keys, gradually her thoughts centered on Tom. She'd always worried about him. Even though Celia had been her sister, rest in peace, Rachel couldn't approve of the way she'd reared that boy. Toting him all over the globe, never settling down long enough for him to form lasting friendships. Say what you would about Abraham, beneath that gruffness, he'd always had a soft spot for his nephew and had offered the boy the only home he knew. Now Tom was back in Riverbend. Why? She and Ruth had puzzled over the question. He'd apparently walked away from a lucrative, high-profile job. And when he'd finally stopped by the other day, she and Ruth had both noticed a sadness about him. Hard to put a finger on it. Disillusionment, maybe. Ruth was right. He needed quite a few things, not the least of which was a good woman.

As Rachel swung into "Rock of Ages," a shaft of light speared its way across the sanctuary and rested on the pulpit. In that moment, the tiniest seedling of a notion took root in her mind. Ever so slowly her voice died out, her hands stilled, and she did something quite out of character. She quit playing in mid-song. Overwhelming in its simplicity and aptness, the idea grew in the silence until Rachel couldn't sit there any longer. Hastily she put her music away, turned off the organ, locked the church and hurried down Bridge Street.

Arriving breathless at the bookstore, she scurried to the office where she found her sister poring over publishers' catalogs. "Ruth, I've just had a brainstorm!"

Ruth peered over the top of her spectacles. "Dare I ask?"

Ruth, the impetuous sister, had always teased her about being the thinker of the two. But this, Rachel knew, was a good idea. Too good to keep to herself. Besides, she'd need Ruth's cooperation. "How would you like to be involved in a little matchmaking scheme?"

Ruth slowly removed her glasses and smiled suspiciously. "What are you up to now?"

"Solving our problem."

"Which problem might that be?"

"Why, a good woman for Tom, of course," Rachel said with satisfaction. "All we need to do is get them together."

"May I be so bold as to ask who 'them' might be?"

Rachel leaned on the desk, the better to observe her twin's reaction. "Why, Reverend Lynn and Tom, of course."

She was rewarded by Ruth's indrawn breath. "Have you taken leave of your senses? What would our sweet Lynn want with that brooding nephew of ours?"

"Whose side are you on, anyway?"

"Tom's naturally," Ruth sputtered.

"Then you'll see why my idea is perfect." Rachel plopped down in a chair. "She's just what he needs. Warm, optimistic, unselfish, intelligent, gregarious."

Ruth started to speak and then stopped, as if beginning to consider the idea, rather than refute it. "They're as different as night and day."

"You know the old saying that opposites attract." Rachel waited. Ruth didn't disappoint her.

"I suppose we could find a way to get them together. They could take it from there." Ruth studied her sister. "Would you do me the favor of wiping that smug smile off your face?"

"Why? I feel good."

"All right, then, gloat. See if I care." Ruth picked up an envelope from the desk and, after turning it in her fingers for a few seconds, laid it on the edge of the desk. "When you *do* feel like getting rid of that silly grin, this'll do the trick."

Puzzled, Rachel picked up the envelope and extracted the letter. As she read, she could feel a frown replacing the smile. Finally she slapped the letter down and stared, dumbfounded, at her sister. "That jackass. Prentice Jewett gives a bad name to everyone over sixty."

"My sentiments exactly."

"So what are we going to do?"

"Cook his goose, sister. Cook his goose."

CHAPTER FIVE

FROM THE MOMENT Lynn's return to Riverbend became general knowledge, she'd been overwhelmed with phone calls, paperwork and the inevitable crises. From replacing the veteran Sunday-school superintendent to reassuring Maude Haley that memorial funds would not be spent on utilities, she'd been kept on the run. And thanks to the furor generated by Prentice, she'd spent more time than she would've liked soliciting renewed support for Meacham House. However, she was cautiously optimistic their early September kickoff event would go smoothly.

Early this Tuesday morning, as was her custom each workday, she sat in a pew near the back of the sanctuary, inhaling the comforting aromas of lemon oil, candle wax and faded roses. This hushed time tended to center her for the day's demands. Today's demands, however, had begun at 4 a.m. when a hospice volunteer had called her to the Murray home where, amid his children and grandchildren, dear old Phineas Murray had left this life.

Lynn inhaled deeply, then slowly let out her breath. In. Out. In. Out. "We are but dust and to dust we shall return." The words came unbidden. Death—as complex and varied as any human event. The memory of the cemetery and Tom's haunted eyes floated into her awareness. In her heart she knew he would never be at peace until he'd overcome his demons. She also knew that helping him would require a deft and delicate touch.

She closed her eyes, concentrating on her breathing. But insistent questions pecked at her repose. Why did she feel so strongly that her destiny was linked with his? He was a most unlikely answer to her prayers. Could they find their way together? Would he ever be able to understand and embrace her calling? What could she offer him?

She sat a few more minutes before sensing someone's presence. When she opened her eyes, Marilyn Rasmusson was waiting at the side door. "I'm sorry to disturb you, Lynn, but Prentice Jewett is here. I told him he didn't have an appointment, but—"

"It's all right. This was bound to happen sometime. Tell him I'll be there shortly."

After Marilyn left, Lynn took time to formulate her approach, suspecting nothing she said would make a dent. She rose to her feet, then paused, running her hand over the smooth wooden back of the pew in front of her. "Dear Lord," she whispered, "it may be a very long day."

TOM GATHERED the sheet around him, buried his head beneath the pillow and tried—unsuccessfully—to shut out the shrill ringing. Who the hell was calling him at this ungodly hour? If he'd purchased an answering machine, there would at least be an end to the clamor. Whoever this caller was, he was determined. On the fifth ring, Tom reluctantly rolled over, sat up and swung his legs over the side of the bed. Stifling a yawn, he fumbled for the phone, noting that the bedside alarm read 7:22 a.m. "What?" he barked.

"And top of the morning to you, too. Are you hung over?"

So much for amenities. But then, Harry Milstein hadn't made a bundle in the publishing business because of his bedside manner. "Jeez, Harry, did you ever consider that some of us actually sleep?"

"Hell of a way to spend time when you could be writing."

Slumping over his knees, Tom put a hand to his forehead. A hangover would be a relief compared to sidestepping an insistent editor. "What do you want, Harry?"

"I wanna know how far along you are on the book."

"The book? What part of *no* don't you New York types understand?"

"Tommy, Tommy, listen to me. It's a natural. Who else is better equipped to write the definitive volume about the last quarter of the twentieth century? 'Hot Spots' in depth. Eyewitness history."

"No."

"No? I've got a sweetheart of a contract here you can't refuse."

"Watch me." Tom swallowed the sourness in his mouth. There wasn't enough money in the world to induce him to catalog those heinous scenes or revisit the rapacious acts of power-hungry despots. But therein lay his problem. He was a journalist. A reporter of events. He corrected himself. *Had been.* Now he was merely a writer with no material. *Nada.*

"Listen, I'm gonna send you the contract. Won't hurt ya to look at it. You're my man, Tommy. It's got *New York Times* bestseller written all over it. I'll check with you later."

Tom stared at the dead phone. A wake-up call in more ways than one. How long could he avoid examining his future? What the hell *was* he going to do? Money wasn't the problem. He'd socked plenty away in sound investments during his overseas stints, and he took care of his kids generously. But a man had to have worthwhile work. He wasn't such a deadbeat that he didn't understand that. Trouble was, he no longer had a clue what *worthwhile* meant for him.

He set the receiver in the cradle, struggled to his feet and headed for the shower. Not an auspicious beginning for the day he'd set aside to go see Aaron Mazerik.

Soaping up under the steady stream of hot water, he tried to project the meeting. The last encounter he remembered with Aaron was one summer in high school when they'd had a knock-down-drag-out fight over some girl whose name he couldn't recall but whose claim to fame was a figure made to drive adolescent boys wild. Aaron, cocky and defensive, never took guff from anybody. Tom winced. The characterization sounded remarkably like himself. What had the intervening years done to the two of them? And, in light of Aaron's newly revealed parentage, where did they go from here? Damned if he knew.

He drained the mug, then set it on the counter before moving decisively to the wall phone. As long as he was doing something about Aaron, maybe today was the day to do something more about his kids. Deep down he admitted he didn't like the wad of guilt he carried around. He didn't want to be the kind of father who ignores his children.

He dialed the kids' number and listened to the ring, trying to ignore the beating of his heart.

"Hello." Libby. Her voice sounded faint, petulant.

He glanced at his watch. Eight-forty-five. "Did I wake you?"

"Who's this?"

"Your dad."

"Why are you calling so early?"

"I *did* wake you."

"Duh."

He worked hard to keep his irritation in check. "We haven't talked in a while. I wanted to see how you were doing."

"Now?"

"Is something wrong with now?"

"Dad, it's the crack of dawn."

"I guess I'd forgotten how teenagers sleep in, especially in the summer." He paused, groping for a topic. "How's the swim team doing?"

"Fine."

No old-time prospector ever had more trouble locating the mother lode. "I thought I'd come see one of your meets soon."

"You're kidding, right?"

"Why would I be kidding?"

"Like you've been so interested before?"

He guessed he had that coming. "You're right. I haven't been much of a father." He paused uncomfortably. "But I want to do something about that."

"What?"

"Maybe I could come visit, and you and Pete and I could spend some time together. What do you think?"

"When?"

"How does next weekend sound?"

"So soon?"

"Libby, are you trying to avoid me?"

"I thought it was the other way around."

The arrow found its target. "Hey, I know it must have seemed that way. But I'd like to try to change things. I'm asking you to give me a chance."

No answer. He waited. "Okay," Libby said in a tight voice.

"Is Pete there?"

"No. He's gone to the lake with a friend."

"Would you tell him I called? Tell him I'm coming?"

"Yeah. Sure."

"Great. I'll talk with your mother about all this."

"Okay. Bye."

"Libby? Wait." He closed his eyes, aware his fingers had tightened around the phone. "I love you, honey."

After a long interval, he heard her say, "Yeah, well, see ya."

Slowly he hung up and stood listening to the quiet. In the past he'd have been discouraged and given up. But today something was different. Today he was determined to give his kids his best shot. And today at the very end of the conversation, he was nearly positive he'd heard his daughter choke back a sob.

TOM STOOD on the sidewalk early that afternoon studying the Riverbend High School gymnasium, hearing in his memory the rabid fans stomping and cheering as Jacob and Mitch Sterling helped put the town on the map in the only way that counted in rural Indiana—basketball. When he used to visit his uncle for winter break, Tom envied Jacob not only his star quality, but the solid security of attending the same school, growing up with the same friends, being accepted, no questions asked. Of course he hadn't articulated it that way then. Rather, those feelings had found expression in a gnawing hurt he'd tried desperately to mask by spouting off about his adolescent adventures and conquests. And that obnoxiousness was exactly what Aaron would remember about him.

Tom started up the walk toward the gym. Well, that was okay. Aaron hadn't exactly been a Dale Carnegie clone himself with that giant chip on his shoulder. Entering the lobby, Tom paused, letting his eyes adjust to the dimness. Trophies crowded in the glass case reflected dull points of light. Tom made a frame of his hands and peered through the panes in the locked doors to the basketball court. Championship banners hung from the walls, and it took little imagination to conjure up the blare of a pep band and the *thump-swish* of basketballs.

How could it have been over fifteen years ago? Tom shrugged, then started down the corridor toward the offices. He didn't even know if Aaron would be here. He'd thought about calling ahead of time, but had rejected the idea. This was awkward enough without having the initial encounter take place over the phone. He stepped around textbook cartons stacked in the office entryway and nodded at the receptionist. "Aaron Mazerik in?"

"He's with a student. Have a seat. He'll be with you shortly." She resumed the filing he'd interrupted. Tom sat on the bench she'd indicated and waited, resenting his uncle's secret indiscretion and wondering how the hell he would begin this conversation.

Before he could script the encounter, a tall, lithe, dark-haired man emerged from the office, an arm around the shoulders of a scrawny, pimple-faced teen. "Remember, Josh, if you want to take physics, you're going to have to do your best in that advanced math class whether or not you're crazy about Mr. Zachary."

"Okay, Coach. I understand." The boy nudged his glasses up on his nose. "Thanks."

Tom rose to his feet as the boy turned to leave. Which was when Aaron, with a lift of an eyebrow acknowledged him. "Aaron." Tom nodded his head in greeting.

"Ruth Steele said you were back in Riverbend." That was it. No word of greeting whatsoever.

"In a funny kind of way, it's always been home."

"You've been gone a long time." Aaron, his weight balanced on the balls of his feet, hadn't moved. "Seen the world, I guess."

"Some of it I'd rather not have seen."

"I made it as far as Indianapolis," Aaron said tonelessly.

Tom could feel the sweat gathering in his armpits. His cousin wasn't making this easy. "Is there, er, someplace we could talk?"

Aaron handed the receptionist a manila folder, then glanced at Tom's feet. "I see you're wearing running shoes. How about we toss the ball around a little in the gym?"

Was this the modern-day equivalent of throwing down the gauntlet? Tom hadn't picked up a basketball since boring stretches on assignment in Saudi during the midnineties. "Sure."

Their footsteps echoing in the eerily empty corridor, Aaron led the way back to the gym, where he unlocked a door, then retrieved a basketball from an equipment closet. "Here." He rifled the ball to Tom, who made a head feint, dribbled around Aaron and went in for a layup. Muscles he hadn't used in months protested. Aaron grabbed the ball, jumped, then floated a two-handed overhead shot into the basket.

For the next five minutes they grunted, dribbled, pivoted, jockeyed for position and tacitly competed in a grueling game of one-on-one. Finally Tom, panting, held up his hands in surrender. "Time-out."

Aaron tucked the ball into the crook of his arm. "You're not bad. With a little coaching, we'll get you there."

Tom plucked his handkerchief from his jeans pocket and wiped his forehead. "I'm way out of shape."

"I didn't mean to take advantage of you."

Something in Aaron's voice caused Tom to look at him closely. The man was giving no quarter. "Didn't you?" Tom inquired mildly.

Aaron bounced the basketball twice. "Maybe," he conceded. "I don't give in easily."

"Are we still talking about basketball?"

"Probably not." Aaron gestured to the one section of bleachers pulled out from the wall. "Okay, let's get this over with." Aaron rolled the ball in the general direction of the closet and walked toward the seats.

Tom sat lounging back, his elbows resting on the row behind the one where he was sitting. Aaron straddled the seat. Only the hum of a distant floor polisher somewhere in an exterior hallway broke the silence. "So did you ever get into Rhonda Marley's pants?" The shadow of a smile played over Aaron's lips.

"She of the 42 D's? Nah." Tom chuckled. "Thanks, I've been trying for years to remember her name."

"But you obviously didn't have any trouble remembering the equipment."

"Endowments like that are unforgettable." Tom paused, looking intently at Aaron. "Seems like you beat me then, too."

"Probably."

Tom moistened his lips. "If Jacob were here…"

"Yeah, I know. He'd be the family representative, coming to see how the bastard son is taking the news."

"So? How *are* you taking it?"

Aaron placed a hand on each knee and arched his back, then stared over Tom's head. "How do you think? Out of the clear blue sky I discover that the wealthy, beloved town patriarch never had the guts to acknowledge he fathered a second son, a son whose mother worked her fingers to the bone as a waitress and still lives in a dump. That all the clothes, golf clubs, tennis rackets, boats and cars I coveted could have been mine." He lowered his head and looked straight at Tom, his jaws clenched. "That instead of being Aaron Mazerik—punk, misfit, outsider—I could have been Aaron Steele—privileged, admired, accepted." He rolled his tongue around inside his mouth. "How do I feel about all this? It's a helluva jolt, that's what."

Tom waited, sensing Aaron needed to say more.

He did. "And you know what? Here's the irony. Even if I could, I wouldn't change a damn thing. I love my mother, and although I don't understand it, I admire her for what she's been willing to endure. I've learned a lot from butting my head up against life, and I know that things are just that. Things. And in the big scheme, they don't matter.''

Aaron stood up and began pacing in front of the bleachers. ''But I've got to tell you, Tom, I'm angry. I'm angry that my mother had to raise me by herself, I'm angry that she had to struggle for so long, and I'm angry that, instead of continuing to be Aaron Mazerik, good-guy counselor and coach—a position I've worked damned hard to achieve—for the moment the only way this town views me is as Aaron Mazerik, bastard son of Abraham Steele.'' He stopped and looked down at Tom. ''Put yourself in my position. Hell, how do you think I feel?''

Tom eased forward, considering his words. ''I've got no argument with you. You're entitled to all those feelings.'' He leaned over, his elbows on his knees, his head hanging, wondering how to ask the next question. Finally he straightened. ''Did my uncle help you at all?'' he asked, hating the raw edge of pain in his voice.

Aaron slumped down beside him. ''He tried, I guess.''

''In what way?''

Aaron, his voice expressionless, told Tom how Abraham had used Dr. Julian Bennett as an emissary to help Evie and Aaron financially and to keep tabs on them, and how Abraham had always treated him with interest, even kindness, right up until he died. ''But under the circumstances, that's small consolation.''

''He robbed you of a father, didn't he?'' His stomach lurched. For all intents and purposes, he hadn't had a father, either. Nor did his own kids.

Aaron gave him a puzzled sidelong glance, apparently hearing something different, mellower in Tom's voice. "Yes, he did."

"So where do we go from here?"

"Damned if I know." After an awkward silence, Aaron abruptly stood. "If you don't mind, I've had enough for one day." They started walking toward the door. Pausing to lock up, Aaron spoke again. "Your aunts have been decent about this. Please thank them for me."

"I will." Tom hated to end the conversation negatively, but it was his responsibility to say the rest. "Aaron, if there are any legalities we need to discuss—"

Aaron wheeled around and faced him. "Like what?" he demanded.

"Claims or—"

Aaron's eyes narrowed and his words came out in a hiss. "There is nothing the Steeles can give me that I don't already have. What kind of man do you think I am, anyway?"

Beneath the anger, Tom recognized a sudden kinship in Aaron that had nothing to do with bloodlines, but rather with life experience. "I think," he said slowly, "you're a man I would very much like to get to know."

PETE BAINES threw his gym bag in the general direction of the closet and slumped down at his desk. He knew he should unpack his wet swimsuit before his mother threw a hissy fit, but that could wait. Here he'd had a great time at the lake with his buddies and had even succeeded in getting better acquainted with Polly Bridges, to the point where she'd let him kiss her

Saturday night. He grew hot just thinking about her in that skimpy bikini of hers.

And then Libby had to ruin it all. He'd been all set to ask Polly out for next weekend. But no. His absentee father was actually going to put in an appearance, and they were expected to drop all their plans and do what? Act like it was a big deal? Pretend they were a regular family?

Fat chance! He was getting along very well, thank you, without the interference of his father, whose rare visits simply served to screw up his life. Maybe it had been different when he was a dumb little kid and a trip to the zoo with his dad seemed like a really neat idea. He knew better now.

He brushed his hand across the globe sitting on his desk and set it rotating, frowning at the colored pins he'd stuck in it—back when his mother had suggested he could keep track of his dad that way. Sure enough. A red pin in Afghanistan, a blue one in Singapore, a green one in Croatia, a yellow one in Iraq, along with several others. Like a friggin' pin would somehow make up for always having to tell his friends his father was on assignment and couldn't come to—you name it—the Webelos ceremony, his eighth-grade graduation, the club tennis tournament.

Abruptly he knocked the spinning globe onto the floor. He was tired of all this! Either he had a father or he didn't. And at this point, it would be easier just to forget him. His dad had this weird habit of showing up every time Pete started to feel good about his life. Like this upcoming weekend. Screw it. He had no intention of falling all over himself just because Tom Baines had decided to spend a few hours with him.

Never mind that his stupid sister seemed to think

otherwise. Oh, she did a pretty good job of not letting on to their father that she missed him, but Pete hated that girly hope in her voice when she'd told him their dad had called about the weekend. Didn't she get it? Dad just showed up when it suited him.

Disgusted, Pete leaned over and scooped up the globe. There it was looking at him—the latest pin. Stuck smack-dab in the middle of Indiana. Riverbend. At least Kuala Lumpur sounded exotic. And before, he'd been able to brag about his dad, flash around some of his "Hot Spots" columns. Now what?

Libby had been all excited when she'd learned their dad would be living for a while so close to Chicago. Maybe she'd pictured one of those sloppy sentimental family reunions like you see in movies. Maybe even that their parents would get back together. Yeah, sure.

He stood up and stared at the open closet door, where dirty clothes and shoes littered the floor. Then, defiantly, he threw the globe into the back corner where it came to rest on top of a pair of muddy hiking boots.

Okay, so he'd get through the weekend somehow. But he wasn't going to make it easy for his dad. No way.

TOM PULLED into a parking place in front of his aunts' place, climbed out of the truck and ambled to the door. After yesterday's disturbing encounter with Aaron, he was looking forward to a quiet dinner with Ruth and Rachel.

As if dealing with Aaron wasn't enough, there was the unsettling matter of Lynn. When he'd gone into seclusion, he hadn't counted on meeting a woman who, by quiet example, challenged many of his as-

sumptions. It had been several days since he'd seen
her. He'd been caught off guard by how much he
missed her. He'd call her after he left the aunts, see
if he could visit her later. The little dinner get-together
would break up early, so surely he wouldn't scandal-
ize Lynn's neighbors if he stopped by for a while.

Aunt Ruth flung the door open before he raised his
hand to knock. "Come in. You're late."

He planted a kiss on her cheek. "Don't tell me
you've started the cocktail hour without me."

She linked her arm through his and sent him a sly
glance. "No, but you've kept three beautiful women
waiting."

"Three?"

"Think you can handle that many?"

"If they're beautiful? A piece of cake."

Ruth drew him into the formal parlor where, sitting
on the sofa, was the Reverend Lynn Kendall, her eyes
dancing. "Lynn, may I present my nephew Tom
Baines." Lynn nodded her head and smiled demurely.
"Tom, this is our pastor, Lynn Kendall."

He started to confess he already knew Lynn, but
Ruth and Rachel's expectant looks stopped him. He
and Lynn had clearly been set up. Because he didn't
want to spoil his aunts' pleasure, he'd play along, at
least for a while. He crossed the room, leaned over
and picked up Lynn's hand, then winked by way of
soliciting her complicity. "Pleased to meet you."

She signaled acquiescence by squeezing his hand.
"Likewise I'm sure. I've been hearing a lot about
you," she said coyly.

He straightened and faced the aunts. "From these
two?"

Ruth bustled forward and ushered him to a large overstuffed chair. "I only told Lynn the good parts."

Perched on a hard-backed chair, Rachel added, "We wanted at least her initial impression to be positive."

"And it is." Lynn's low voice trembled with concealed amusement.

Ruth sat down beside Lynn, a smug expression on her face. "We'll save the truth for another day."

Tom feigned a put-upon look. "You malign me, Auntie dear."

"We love you, anyway," Rachel said, turning to Lynn. "You'll have to forgive us. We're rather partial to our nephew. We tend to spoil him."

"As well you should." Lynn assessed him. "He looks like he could use a little feminine attention."

Tom's pulse quickened. He knew exactly the kind of feminine attention he needed, but the aunts' formal parlor was hardly the appropriate venue. He spread his arms expansively. "Bring it on, ladies. You won't find me resisting."

"I'll start, then, by taking your drink order. I already have Lynn's." Ruth rose. "Rachel, could you bring in the hors d'oeuvres?"

While the two were out of the room, Tom whispered, "Did you know about this in advance?"

Lynn shook her head. "I was as surprised as you. Eventually, however, honesty is going to compel me to confess we've already met."

"Not yet. They're enjoying this too much." Then, hearing Rachel returning, he grinned and put a finger to his lips.

Rachel had just set down the tray of cheese and crackers when Ruth brought the drinks. "Lemonade for you, Lynn.'' She handed Lynn a tall crystal goblet, then turned to Tom. ''Your scotch and water, Tom.''

''Are the two of you still drinking sherry?'' He pointed to the wineglasses the aunts held.

Rachel held up her wine. ''It's good for the digestion.''

Ruth laughed. ''That's as good an excuse as any.'' Then, as if she was commenting on a prize rose in a horticultural show, Ruth proceeded to sing Lynn's praises, touting her many accomplishments during her time in Riverbend.

Finally Lynn held up her hand and laughingly protested. ''Oh, dear, Ruth. Enough. Heaven help me if I have to live up to that list of virtues. We don't want to mislead Tom. You both know I have many flaws, too.''

''I know no such thing,'' Rachel said indignantly. ''I can't name one.''

''I can,'' Lynn said. ''For instance, I seem to have totally misjudged Prentice Jewett and his reaction to Meacham House.''

''Oh, *that*.'' Ruth's chin quivered indignantly. ''Prentice is a first-class fool.''

''An influential one who's causing quite a stir.'' Lynn's voice sounded strained. ''I had a tense meeting with him yesterday.''

Rachel glanced quickly at her twin as if checking for permission, then smiled enigmatically. ''Don't you worry. Ruth and I have a plan.''

Tom noticed Ruth's eyes light up. ''Watch out, Lynn. The aunts are noted for their nefarious schemes.''

''Nefarious! The idea,'' Ruth snorted. ''You know

very well we have always been quite successful in influencing public opinion.''

''I'm not questioning your success. It's your methods.'' Tom grinned. ''You two could put the CIA to shame.''

Lynn looked from Ruth to Rachel. ''I have to admit I'm curious.''

Rachel took a sip of her sherry. ''You'll see, Lynn. You have right on your side, as well you should.''

''And if these two are involved,'' Tom offered, ''*might* as well.''

He listened while Lynn and his aunts explored the Meacham House subject more seriously. Some downtown business owners were objecting on several levels—the teens would make too much noise with their loud music, their coarse language and disreputable appearance would offend potential customers, and the house would degenerate into a gathering place for drug users, turning the downtown into a commercial wasteland. Tom grimaced. He hated the thought of bigoted busybodies interfering with what was clearly a project close to Lynn's heart.

At dinner Tom watched with interest the interplay between Lynn and his aunts. They clearly adored her, and she impressed him by holding her own admirably in a discussion of several bestselling books. Ruth had been right. He was in the company of three beautiful women.

Over dessert, the conversation took a turn when Ruth abruptly put down her fork and said to Tom, ''Perhaps now we can talk about your visit with Aaron.''

Tom frowned. Was this an appropriate topic for Lynn? Before he could find a tactful way to pose the question, Rachel anticipated it. "It's all right, Tom. As our pastor, Lynn knows about the situation. Ruth and I would like her to be a part of this discussion. Perhaps she can help us find a way to make peace with it all."

"I'll do what I can," Lynn said, folding her napkin and carefully setting it next to her empty plate. "But in the long run this is something you will have to work out among yourselves. And it will take time."

"Lynn, do you know Aaron?" Tom asked.

"Not well, but he's been helpful in talking with the Meacham House volunteers about the teenagers and their problems."

"He and Lily Bennett Holden make a striking couple," Ruth said.

"An odd pairing, though," Rachel added.

"At first glance they might appear mismatched," Lynn agreed, "but you only have to be in the same room with them a few moments to feel their connection. It's positively incandescent."

Ruth nodded. "Aaron has been looking for someone like Lily all his life."

"We're straying from the subject," Rachel reminded them. "How did Aaron react to you, Tom?"

"Given that he hasn't seen me in years and we were never friends, about what you might expect. Minimal civility with a healthy dose of hostility."

"Some bitterness would be understandable," Lynn suggested softly.

"After we found out about Abraham's role in Aaron's life, we called Aaron," Ruth said. "He was polite. Very controlled. But he did say he had no hard feelings where we were concerned."

Rachel leaned forward. "In fact, he said we'd been

among the few folks in Riverbend who'd always treated him with respect.''

"He was pretty hard on Uncle Abe yesterday.'' Tom winced, remembering the hot waves of Aaron's anger.

"I'm sure our brother did what he needed to do,'' Rachel said.

"We're biased, sister. From Aaron's viewpoint, it wouldn't necessarily appear that way.''

"No, it doesn't,'' Tom said. "In fact, I wouldn't blame him if he never gets over his resentment of us.''

Lynn looked from one to the other. "Abraham isn't here, so Aaron can't confront him. It's natural he might take his anger out on the family.''

"Oh, dear,'' Rachel murmured. "That puts you on the front line, Tom. How did you feel about him?''

Tom finished the last of his pie, then said, "Believe it or not, I liked him.''

Lynn sought his eyes across the table. "I can believe it,'' she said softly. She turned to Ruth and Rachel. "Find the small openings, look for the good and build a bridge.''

Ruth raised her brows hopefully, then responded, "I pray it will be so.''

Just as Tom knew that Aaron's angry words were justified, he also knew that healing the family breach wouldn't be easy. Not for the first time, he wished like hell Jacob was here. If and when he returned, there'd be another huge hurdle to leap with Aaron. He and Jacob were half brothers, after all. Tom leaned back in his chair, determined to change the subject. "Thank you, Aunties, for a delicious meal.''

Lynn stood and began clearing the dessert plates.

"Quit that,'' Rachel said. "Ruthie and I want our

guests to be exactly that—guests. We'll take care of this later."

"Meanwhile, why don't you two run along? We old ladies turn in early, you know." Tom could swear there was a conniving gleam in Ruth's eyes.

"Lynn lives only two blocks down on East Hickory. But it's dark out. Do you think you might drive her home?" The affected innocence of Aunt Rachel's question almost made Tom laugh out loud.

Lynn demurred. "I can walk by myself."

Tom gallantly presented his arm. "I wouldn't hear of it." Warmth spread in his chest as Lynn tucked her hand through his arm.

Ruth patted them both on the shoulders. "You make such a nice couple, don't they, Rachel?"

Beside him, Tom could feel the giggle welling up in Lynn. "Is that what my devious aunties are up to? Matchmaking?" he asked.

The aunts looked flustered. "I...we..." Ruth, rarely at a loss for words, was tongue-tied.

Lynn withdrew her hand and turned to embrace the women. "Remember when I told you I have flaws? Well, I've been guilty of one tonight. I—" she looked at Tom "—we haven't quite been truthful with you."

"You haven't?" Ruth sounded incredulous.

Tom moved to put an arm around each aunt's waist. "It's my fault. I led Lynn astray. I was having too much fun."

Rachel cocked her head to look up at him. "Whatever do you mean, Tom Baines?"

"We've already met," Lynn, looking abashed, volunteered.

"You have?" Rachel sounded both confused and pleased.

Tom pulled the aunts closer to him. "Yes, and while I appreciate all your elaborate machinations this evening, I have to tell you—no matchmaking is necessary." He found Lynn's eyes, warm with affection. "We've already taken care of it." He kissed each aunt, released them and grabbed Lynn's hand. "Thanks for a great time. I'll talk to you soon. Meanwhile I have a beautiful woman to escort home."

Lynn murmured thanks as he whisked her out the door, leaving the aunts speechless. But he took satisfaction from their expressions. No doubt about it— they were delighted by his revelation.

"I LIKE YOUR HOUSE," Tom said as he walked around the living room, studying the watercolors displayed on the garden-green walls. "It has a cozy feel."

"It should." Lynn laughed from the kitchen where she was making coffee. "It's tiny. These Victorian cottages aren't known for spacious rooms."

He sank onto a chintz-covered sofa with a rounded back. The lace curtains, potted ferns, wicker rocker, glass-enclosed bookcase and antique chest that served as a coffee table showed her knack for making a room welcoming. None of the pieces matched, but somehow it all worked.

Draped across the high back of a wing chair, the large black cat she'd introduced as Benedict stared at him unsettlingly. "Invading your territory, am I?" Tom challenged. The cat merely closed his eyes, yawned and resumed his scrutiny. "Could you at least give me a chance, fella? I kind of like the lady of the house."

"Talking to yourself?" Lynn entered the room with a tray, two mugs and a coffeepot.

"No, Ben and I were just having a man-to-man chat."

"About?" Lynn sat beside him and served him a cup.

"Staking my claim."

She raised an eyebrow. "To?"

He set his coffee aside and stilled her hand before she could pour her own cup. "You." He gathered her in his arms. "You," he repeated against her ear.

"And what did Ben say?" she asked softly.

"I believe his exact words were, 'Go for it, dude.'"

Lynn chuckled against his neck. "No way. Ben's far too possessive for that."

"What do you say we give him something to be possessive about?" He raised her chin and kissed her, first lightly, then with increasing pressure. He could feel her fingers clutching his head, sense the same urgency in her body that thrummed in his. Reluctantly he pulled back and cleared his throat. "Um—" he nodded at the windows "—the lights are on and those lace curtains aren't exactly opaque."

"Why, Mr. Baines, are you embarrassed?"

She constantly surprised him with her wonderfully earthy flirtatiousness. "The last thing I want to do is compromise you."

She laughed. "Why is it I don't believe you?" She picked up her coffee and moved to the rocker. "But I do see your point. You stay there—" she pointed to the sofa "—and I'll sit here."

Tom threw a baleful look at the cat. "Help me out here, Ben. Next thing you know, she'll want me to leave my calling card in a silver tray and politely withdraw." Ben regarded him with what was clearly disdain.

Lynn rocked back and forth. "I told you so."

"What?"

"That this wouldn't be easy." She paused. The delicate chime of the clock on the mantel rang nine. "I'd like nothing better than to sit on that sofa and neck with you."

"Neck?" The old-fashioned word amused him. Besides, he definitely had something more in mind.

"We have to be sure, Tom, both of us, before we take this much farther. And—" she blushed "—you need to know there's a point beyond which I can't go." Her eyes signaled a silent appeal.

Of course. Why hadn't he thought of that himself? She had a moral example to set. It wasn't as simple as two adults satisfying their mutual needs. She was drawing the line. And to step over the line meant commitment. "Hey, I understand." He laughed self-consciously. "You were right. It isn't easy." He swallowed, then cleared his throat and found himself saying, "I want you." The words ricocheted around the room, bald in their truth. "Before. Now. Tomorrow." His body was tense with desire.

She had stopped rocking and was clutching the arms of the chair. Finally she spoke. "I want you to know it is taking every bit of willpower I have to stay in this chair."

Her full breasts rose and fell with her breathing, and he felt the evidence of his own desire. He cast about for a way to defuse the moment, then again turned to the cat, who had crawled down the back of the wing chair and now sat curled in the seat. "I guess I should take some comfort from that, huh, fella? But it's not easy for us tomcats, is it?" He looked back at Lynn, whose luminous eyes and flushed cheeks betrayed her emotions. "Lynn, you told me the other night you wouldn't ask of me more than I can give. I want to make the same promise to you."

She raised her fingers to her lips and tenderly blew him a kiss. "Thank you," she whispered.

"I think maybe it's time I was going." He managed a grin before rising to his feet. "While I can still keep that promise."

She followed him into the small entry hall, where she put her arms on his shoulders, reached up and brushed his lips with hers. "When will I see you again? I want to, you know."

He held her by the waist, not tempting himself by moving any closer. "I'll be out of town this weekend."

"Weekends aren't good for me, anyway."

"That's right. You're on duty then."

She chuckled. "That's one way of putting it."

"What about Monday? I'll pick you up and take you to my place."

"It's a date." She kissed him again. "Have a good trip. Where are you going?"

There was no reason not to tell her. But if things didn't go well… "Chicago."

"Oh." She waited.

Hell, this was stupid. Surely it wouldn't jinx anything to confess the truth. "I'm going to see my kids."

He could swear she was looking through his eyes and into his soul. Her hands relaxed on his shoulders and the smile she gave him put light where before there'd been none. "Good."

That was all she said. But the way she said it was like a one-word benediction.

He turned to leave. She followed him out and stood on the porch watching him depart, her arms snugged protectively around herself. When he was halfway to his truck, she called his name softly. He stopped and turned to face her, relishing the way the interior lamp backlit her golden hair. "What?"

"Thank you for giving Ruth and Rachel such delight and especially for telling them we've done our own matchmaking." He almost bounded up the steps, heedless of his promise, but before he could move, she smiled and waggled her fingers at him and said one last thing that warmed him all the way home. "You're a good man, Tom Baines."

CHAPTER SIX

"A GOOD MAN"? Tom slammed shut the drawer of the motel-room dresser and stuffed his dirty clothes into his overnight bag. Thank God Lynn hadn't witnessed this weekend's debacle with the kids. The "good man" would've died on her lips.

He grimaced. Not that he'd expected a warm, fuzzy Brady Bunch-type reunion. No. For Pete and Libby, a piranha might have been a more welcome weekend companion. It wasn't merely that he didn't speak their language, know any of their friends or behave in a "cool" manner. Their hostility went beyond that, as if they were determined not to permit him a way back. Hell, why should they?

The truth was, he'd known even at the time that part of his eagerness to globetrot in the name of work derived from his fear that he had no notion how to be a father. Bottom line, parenthood scared the crap out of him. Certainly his own father had been too busy to be much of a dad; and for Tom, committing to staying in one place had felt frighteningly confining, even though for a time he'd tried. So what had he done? He'd run. There. He'd said it. No wonder Selena had finally, though reluctantly, given up and divorced him. Who could blame her? Maybe it would be easier on everybody if he simply faded out of the picture instead of trying to win his way back into his children's good graces.

He zipped up the bag, tossed the card key on the dresser, then doused the lights. Easier for them? Maybe. But not for him. Guilt and need clawed at his guts, reminding him that *easy* demanded a painful price.

THE AIR HELD a hint of fall Wednesday noon when Lynn joined Kate outside the church for their customary triweekly walk. "Sorry I couldn't come Monday," Lynn said as they turned the corner onto East Oak, "but I had a few things on the front burner."

"Like Meacham House?"

Lynn nodded.

"The aunts are in a tizzy over Prentice Jewett. They're spending hours plotting his downfall."

"Although it would be uncharitable of me to hope for their success, I do wish he'd give up his opposition."

"Lots of folks are behind you on this, Lynn. It's the right thing to do."

"I know." They stepped up their pace, passing showcase Victorian homes with sweeping lawns where ancient trees shaded wide front porches.

"That's not all the aunts are in a tizzy about lately."

Lynn could feel it coming. "Oh?" she asked innocently.

"No." The two paused at the corner of Adams Street to let a delivery truck pass. "I understand Tom made their day by playing one-upmanship in the matchmaking game." Kate shot Lynn an amused look, then grabbed her arm and started off across the street. "So what's going on in the romance department?"

"Hmm. A cautious courtship, maybe?"

"That doesn't sound very exciting."

"Prudent, though. I wouldn't tell anyone else this, but if I'm not careful, this could become a lot more exciting than either Riverbend or I am ready for."

Kate laughed. "Aha! He turns you on, then."

Lynn felt her face flush, maybe from the exertion. "More than that." Her brows knit. "There's a deeper part of him that intrigues me."

"Sure you're not simply trying to save him?"

Now it was Lynn's turn to laugh. "You know me too well. That, too, I suppose. But a lasting relationship has to be built on more than rescue."

"And so?"

Lynn waved to one of her parishioners who was out sweeping her front walk. "We've agreed to move slowly and see where it goes."

"When did this happen?"

Lynn decided to come clean. "I had dinner with Tom Monday evening at his farm. The seclusion there keeps us out of the public eye. Once I get him talking, he's a great conversationalist, and I love hearing him reminisce about Riverbend." She stopped short of admitting how troubled she was, however, by the topics he'd avoided discussing—his work and the details of this past weekend in Chicago with Pete and Libby.

Kate nudged her with an elbow. "Surely good conversation isn't all that went on."

"You're relentless, you know that?" Grinning, Lynn slackened the pace. "Okay, true confession. Being alone with him is pretty heady, and 'moving slowly' requires every last ounce of my willpower."

"Are you worried about the reaction of people at the church?"

"That's a consideration, but in the long run I have to follow my heart."

"Good girl," Kate said. "I have to admit I'm a bit envious. The twins are wonderful and keep me more than busy, but a love life would be a welcome novelty. Guess I'll just enjoy yours vicariously."

Lynn's sympathy welled up. She admired her friend for her upbeat attitude, but she knew her marriage had been a disaster and that, as a single parent, Kate struggled—although her five-year-old twin daughters, Hope and Hannah, were the light of her life. Lynn almost felt guilty for the way her heart expanded every time she said Tom's name. She wanted Kate to be able to feel that rush of love and desire for a man, too. Surely someday the right one would come along for her.

"Kate, I can't tell you what a relief it is to be able to talk about Tom." There it was again—that flood of well-being. "I don't know how this could happen so quickly, but I can't stop thinking about him."

Kate stopped dead in her tracks and framed Lynn's face with her hands. "It's called love, honey. And you're as entitled to it as the next woman." Then Lynn felt herself enclosed in a warm embrace. "I'm happy for you," Kate whispered.

Lynn's eyes misted with gratitude and with the knowledge that she, too, was happy.

FRIDAY NIGHT Tom rested the latest John Sandford thriller on his chest and closed his eyes. Even the intriguing plot twists weren't holding his attention. His mind kept returning to two subjects—Lynn and his kids. He'd planned to take Lynn out tonight—until she'd called from the hospital to say she needed to stay with a family whose father was having emergency surgery. When his plans had been thwarted, he'd experienced a twinge of resentment. Not good, he reminded himself. That was the part of her life she'd warned him about. The part he'd have to accept if he wanted her.

Earlier in the evening he'd worked on a letter to Pete and Libby. Twice he'd torn it up. Once because it sounded pathetically like begging, and the second time because the caustic tone spoke all too clearly of his irritation at their indifference. Over dinner Monday night Lynn, in her tactful manner, had suggested he keep trying with them. As she'd reminded him, the relationship hadn't fallen apart overnight and it wasn't going to be mended overnight, either. But for a man accustomed to action, patience was difficult.

He tossed the book aside, left the easy chair and stood for a moment listening to the moody Dave Brubeck number playing on the stereo. Smooth jazz and a good book—his usual antidotes to loneliness, and neither had worked worth a damn this evening. Might as well go to bed. See whether insomnia was lying in wait—or worse, bad dreams. He turned off the stereo and dimmed the lights.

Before locking the front door, he paused, staring out at the cloudy, moonless night. Beyond the line of trees at the edge of his property, where usually there was no sign of life, he thought he saw a flame flicker. He looked again. Nothing. He rubbed his eyes, chalked off the illusion to exhaustion and hauled himself off to bed.

Around one-thirty he became aware that the staccato pops and high-pitched metallic bursts he was hearing were not part of the Gulf War nightmare from which, with difficulty, he finally emerged. He grabbed a T-shirt, pulled it on over his briefs and stumbled to the front porch. From there, it was clear someone was shooting fireworks from the same general area where he'd earlier seen the flame—an area all too near the cemetery so dear to Lynn.

He returned to the bedroom, hurriedly donned jeans and shoes, then set off in the truck to investigate. Nearing the cemetery, he could hear the thrumming bass of a car radio or boom box. *Brmm. Brmm.* The steady rhythm jolted his psyche. As he rounded the curve right at the cemetery, he encountered at least a dozen pickups and souped-up cars. He jumped from the truck and started up the hill. The heavy-metal music was deafening. Just then another set of firecrackers exploded, punctuating the night with bursts of sound followed by raucous shouts and laughter.

Son of a bitch! If anyone had desecrated that cemetery… And there they were, fifteen to twenty teens, some dancing drunkenly around a campfire, several huddled against the wall drinking beer and smoking God knew what, and a couple sprawled in the shadows so engrossed with each other they were unaware of his presence. Locating the boom box, Tom hit the off switch and wheeled on the group. ''What the hell do you think you're doing?''

A chorus of protests rained on him. One of the smokers looked up blearily and said, ''Piss off, man.'' A long-haired, black-clad youth with a pencil-thin brush of facial hair on his upper lip said to the others, ''Lemme handle this.'' A cocky sneer distorting his mouth, he took his time sauntering over to Tom and stopped just short of crowding Tom's space.

"I want you off this property right now," Tom said.

"Think you can scare us? You don't own this bone dump." The teen postured for his friends as if to say, *Get a load of this guy.*

Tom stood his ground. "If you don't pack up and get out of here, you'd be well advised to be scared."

"We got as much right to be here as you do."

"You're trespassing on private property, drinking illegally, not to mention desecrating a graveyard."

"You musta aced your ACT test." A big-breasted redhead in tight jeans ambled over. "'Desecrating'— I'm impressed," she said, her blue eyes ice-hard.

"Lemme straighten you out, man." The ringleader poked a finger in the direction of Tom's chest. "We're not leavin' here, and there ain't nothin' you can do about it."

"If you're not out of here in ten minutes, I'll call the sheriff."

"Who made you boss?" the girl challenged.

Tom winced. The hell of it was, he could picture himself at their age doing exactly the same thing these kids were doing.

"Okay, okay." He held his hands up in a conciliatory gesture. Others who had been on the fringes of the conversation now massed behind their spokesman. "Look, I worked my butt off helping to get this cemetery looking nice again. You don't need to party here. Plus, the fireworks are disturbing the peace." He decided against mentioning the music.

The redhead rolled her eyes. "Like there are so many places to have fun in this hick county."

"Let me put it this way," Tom said. "You leave here now, I won't call the sheriff. But if I ever catch you out here again, I won't even hesitate."

Some of the girls started gathering up blankets and snacks, and Tom heard one of them say, "My folks would kill me if we got caught."

Tom pointed to the empty beer bottles and fireworks boxes. "You need to clean up this mess."

The young man with the mustache glared at Tom, seemingly oblivious to the grumbles and preparations going on behind him. "I got only one thing to say to you, man." Then, in explicit street language, he told Tom precisely what he could do with himself.

"You've got quite an attitude, son."

"And you ain't improving it. And just for future reference—" he pronounced it ree-fur-ence "—nobody tells Damon Hudson where to party."

"I don't care where you party, so long as it's nowhere near this cemetery." Tom started toward the truck, then turned around. "Ever consider using that mouth of yours to accomplish some good?"

"Oh, yeah. Right." The kid spread his arms in disbelief.

"You hear of Meacham House? You might give it a try when it opens."

Damon laughed derisively. "I got a news flash for you, pops. You'll never catch me in that place. I don't need no reformin'."

"Who said anything about reforming? You might find it's an okay place to hang out."

"Screw it." Damon started to walk off.

"You afraid?" At Tom's words, the youngster stopped in his tracks. "Afraid your buddies'll think you're a wimp? Afraid you might like it? Why don't you bring them and come see? The center opens the Monday after Labor Day.''

The kid whipped his head around, sending his dark hair flying. ''You really think those church—'' he almost spit the word ''—ladies want us hangin' around?''

''Yeah, I really do.'' Tom thrust his hands in his pockets. ''I dare you to give it a try.''

The redhead moved closer to Damon. ''It might be a kick to let them see what teenagers are really like.'' For all her attitude, Tom could swear he saw in her eyes a flicker of vulnerability.

The boy seemed to consider the idea. He looked from side to side at his cohorts. ''Whaddaya think, guys? Wanna give Meacham House an in-ter-est-ing send-off?'' Mean-spirited laughter and exchanges of high fives greeted the suggestion. Damon held up his hand and the group quieted. ''Tell ya what, big shot. We'll come under one condition.''

Tom waited. ''What's that?''

''You come, too.''

''Me?''

''Yeah,'' Damon drawled.

By no stretch of the imagination was he a youth worker, Tom thought, and he had zero desire to encounter any of these yahoos in the future. ''Deal. I'll see you there September eleventh. For now, though, pack up and get out of here.''

Tom strode quickly down the hill, and as he got into his pickup, to his chagrin, he heard the boom box blast the night again. His words had apparently made little impression. All he'd succeeded in doing was recruiting a bunch of kids who very well might sabotage the opening of Meacham House.

Beyond that, the smart-ass kid had succeeded in manipulating him. The very last thing he wanted was to get involved with a bunch of misguided teenagers. He already had his hands full with his own two.

He reached down to press in the cigarette lighter before he caught himself. Damn. Meacham House.

"I MAY AS WELL tell you," Tom said the following Monday evening as he sliced the tomatoes Lynn had set out on the small counter in her tiny kitchen. "I hope I haven't ruined the Meacham House opening."

She glanced up from the pot she was stirring. "Really? Single-handedly?" He looked so serious it was almost comical. "How?"

"You may have more teens opening night than you counted on. Not model citizens, either."

She crushed some basil between her fingers and threw it into the stew. "And this is a problem?"

"They're wise-ass troublemakers with big mouths and no desire to be rehabilitated."

"Good." Lynn thumped the ladle on the rim of the pan and set it in a spoon holder. "They're exactly who the program was designed for."

Tom set down the paring knife and frowned at her. "But—"

"Are you trying to protect me? These are the very kids we want to reach. We know they'll be defensive and resentful to begin with."

"That's putting it mildly." Then Tom filled her in on his confrontation with Damon and his gang at the cemetery. "So," he concluded, "they may set out to defy you."

Pushing up the sleeves of her sweater, she smiled

at him. "And defy you, too, from what you're telling me." She couldn't help it. The chuckle erupted.

"It's not funny, Lynn."

"You're right, it's not funny. I'm well aware their appearance en masse may fuel Prentice's objections and create some challenges for our staff. But it's still worth doing. If it's trial by fire from the very first, maybe we'll be all the more successful sooner."

He placed his forehead against hers. "Are you always such a Pollyanna?"

She circled his waist, hooking her hands behind his back. "Always."

"Isn't that a bit unrealistic? You know, there are some bad people in the world."

She raised her head and looked into his troubled eyes. "I know that. I can be optimistic without being blind or uninformed. In the long run, though, I believe people are inherently good. Our job with these kids is to give them a chance to prove it."

"Then we have our work cut out for us."

She smiled. "I like the sound of that 'we.'"

He nuzzled her neck. "Me, too."

"I think the aunts do, too," she whispered.

He paused in his ministrations long enough to say, "Oh?"

She could hardly concentrate for the insistent sensations warring with rational thought. She molded her body to his. "Rachel found me after church yesterday and very discreetly but obviously—" He shushed her with a toe-curling kiss. She struggled to continue. "Your aunt voiced her opinion that you had finally exercised some good sense."

"I was merely waiting for the right woman." He

kissed her again in a way that left her feeling she was that woman.

His hand was straying from her shoulder to the button at the neck of her sweater when she heard a popping noise from the stew pot. More than just their supper was coming to a boil. She pulled from his grasp and removed the pot from the burner. "Saved."

He moved away, then with the tip of the knife, pushed the tomato slices from the cutting board onto a plate. "What? The stew or you?"

"The stew, of course." To herself, though, she admitted she was learning a great deal about temptation. Tom was a very male, very sexy kind of guy who easily made her forget she needed to exercise caution.

Later, over fruit, cheese and coffee, Tom again made passing reference to his disappointment concerning the weekend in Chicago with his kids. Lynn decided to press him. If she was serious about him, she needed to be serious, as well, about his son and daughter. "Please tell me more about Pete and Libby. About what's happened between you and them."

His lips thinned, and for what seemed a long time he didn't say anything. "You're not going to like it," he said finally.

"How do *you* know?"

Picking up a section of apple, he traced circles on his plate. "They couldn't care less if they ever saw me again."

"I don't believe that!"

He held up his hand. "Let me go on. I don't blame them. It's hard to relate to an absentee father, especially one who hasn't given them the time of day for years on end."

"Why, Tom?"

He dropped the apple slice, then rocked back in his chair. "Several reasons, none of which qualifies as an excuse. First, I didn't know how to be a parent. Second, the lure of journalistic achievement, even glamour, was powerful. Third, I suppose Selena and I should have realized early on we were ill suited. She's a great person, but a homebody by nature. She never understood my wanderlust."

He linked his hands behind his head and stared at the ceiling before going on. "I cared nothing about diapers, potty training, nursery schools—all the stuff that consumed her. Even when the kids were older, I didn't seem to know how to talk to them, how to understand what was important in their lives. And I can't say I made much of an effort. It was easier to turn from the uncomfortable to the comfortable. I was a damned good reporter with an ego the size of a small country. I enjoyed thinking of myself as 'our man on the scene.' When you're halfway around the world and gain a good deal of attention from important people, it's hard to get excited about the first time a kid rides a bike without training wheels or learns to do a back flip in gymnastics class."

"And now?" Lynn could feel his pain as if it was her own.

He lowered his hands, then shook his head wearily. "I don't know. Pete just looks at me with this mocking sneer as if daring me to prove something to him. Damned if I know what or how. And Libby? She's taken eye-rolling to an art form and acquired an unlimited supply of words like 'gross' and 'embarrassing' to describe my every move. That makes it darned difficult to pull off the hey-kids-I'm-back number."

"Their actions are understandable, given their history. But not insurmountable."

"Easy for you to say." The words were laden with irony, but Lynn concentrated on the sadness in his eyes.

"You can never retrieve the past, but you have years in front of you to be a father." She smiled warmly. "Even a grandfather. It's important that you keep trying."

"I'm not sure I can."

She experienced a surge of irritation, which she quickly squelched. Anger on his children's behalf would not be a productive response. "I think you have to, Tom." The air crackled with tension and she remained silent, watching hot wax form ribbons down the stem of the candle burning in the middle of the table.

Finally he shrugged. "We'll see."

She worked to mold the wax to the taper before it dripped onto the table surface. "What about the other one?"

His brow furrowed. "Other one?"

"The boy in the photograph in your bedroom. Terence."

Tom raked his hand through his hair, and Lynn didn't know if the candlelight was playing tricks, but she could have sworn his eyes filled. "Ah, Terence." He sighed heavily. "That's another story."

When he didn't elaborate, she suggested they move to the living room where they'd be more comfortable. Apparently still lost in thought, he picked up his cup and drained it.

She blew out the candle, then stood and led him to the sofa. A small Tiffany table lamp spread a rosy light. He sat down, then pulled her across his knees, cuddling her against his shoulder. For a time the only sounds were their quiet breathing and the creaks of the old house, bending to the stiff wind outside. "Terence is all that's left of a time in my life I don't talk about." He stopped as if gathering his words. She didn't move, sensing that whatever was coming was critical for him.

"First, I have to tell you about Gordy Maxwell, the toughest, bravest man I ever met. He was my cameraman for eight years. He ventured into places the hounds of hell would've fled. And his photos? What can I say? He was a genius. He had a talent for capturing faces that gave war a hauntingly human dimension, in a way my most eloquent words never could." Tom rubbed a hand up and down Lynn's arm as if buying time. "He was also the best friend I ever had. We got our asses shot at, closed down more pubs than I care to think about and joked around like brothers."

Lynn raised her head slightly. "*Was,* Tom?"

His hand stilled on her arm and she watched his eyes narrow. "The bastards blew him up." His controlled anger was more jarring than if he had screamed the words. "It was a terrorist bomb in Ireland," he went on tonelessly. "We were in the wrong place at the wrong time."

"Go on," Lynn encouraged.

Tom told her the whole miserable tale, finishing with, "I found a boy, still breathing, underneath Gordy's body." Tom paused. "Gordy had saved him."

"Terence?"

Tom nodded. "Yes."

"So you saved him, too."

"Don't make me a hero, Lynn. I was still on the sidewalk when that bomb went off."

Lynn reared up. "What became of Terence?"

"His wounds were superficial. He was more traumatized than hurt. He and his parents wanted to do something for me. *Me?* I was so angry about Gordy, I could hardly be civil. But it wasn't the kid's fault he survived and Gordy didn't. So I told him to send me a picture, write occasionally if he wanted to."

"And?"

"Faithful as clockwork. I've been sending him my address changes, and every month I get a letter from him."

Lynn clasped his hands in her lap. "Do you think it should've been you, instead of Gordy, who got killed?"

He pulled his hands away. "What's this? Are you playing shrink now?"

"*Do* you?"

He stood and paced to the far side of the room, where he stopped, gripping the back of a desk chair. His voice filled the room. "Hell, yes. Gordy was worth a dozen of me. Nothing about it makes any sense."

"No, it doesn't."

He turned around and fixed his eyes on her. "I thought you'd have all the answers."

"Well, I don't."

"I'll bet you could come up with some platitudes if you tried." She bit her lip, trying not to take his attack personally, knowing he needed to vent. "How about 'Everything happens for the best' or 'Ours is not to wonder why'? Then there's my personal favorite. 'God has His reasons.'"

"You're asking a mighty big question," Lynn said.

"So why aren't you answering it?"

At times like these, Lynn felt her inadequacy especially keenly. And what she said now could be significant. She slowly rose and went to him. She touched him lightly on the shoulder. "Because my answers might not be your answers. At this moment I can be either your counselor or your woman. Which do you need from me?"

He crushed her to him. "Right now? Just hold me."

She reached up, feeling the rigidity of his shoulders, then ran her hands up and down the tense muscles of his back. "I can do that." Then softly but firmly she repeated the words. "I can do that."

CHAPTER SEVEN

OVER THE NEXT FEW DAYS, in addition to her regular duties, Lynn was swamped with details concerning the opening of Meacham House. Molly Linden, a nurse new to Riverbend who had agreed to direct the program, had already put in an unprecedented number of hours cleaning the property, scrounging furniture donations, laying in a supply of food and training the adult volunteers. Lynn didn't know which was her bigger fear—that few if any kids would show up, or that there would be so many they would feel overwhelmed and quit participating before giving the program a chance.

The volunteer staff had decided food, music and a nonjudgmental atmosphere were key to hooking the teens. After that, they'd promote activities, tutoring and a peer-counseling group. It would all take time, and Lynn prayed Prentice Jewett would cut them enough slack to prove to doubters that Meacham House could succeed.

At the end of a particularly grueling afternoon, Lynn wandered out into the church garden and sank gratefully onto a stone bench facing a large flowering crepe-myrtle bush, its lush magenta blooms brilliant against the lawn.

She closed her eyes, waiting for her interior monitor to stop hounding her with uncompleted tasks.

In a few days she'd learn if this grand experiment would fly. At times she'd questioned whether she should attempt such a large-scale outreach project so early in her Riverbend tenure, but she'd concluded Meacham House would be a boon for many and a genuine blessing for some. If she was wrong? She clutched the edge of the bench and leaned back, exposing her face to the sun. She'd cross that bridge when she came to it.

If Tom was correct about the group of rebellious teens he'd encountered at the cemetery, she'd have her answer sooner rather than later. She recalled his concern that he'd sabotaged the opening. Ah. That evening.

She straightened and stared past the crepe myrtle into space. She hadn't known how to help him. He wasn't ready for the usual pastoral responses. She hadn't found the right things to say to him. Not about his children, not about his friend Gordy and not about the cosmic "Why?" that had erupted from the depths of his anguish.

Then had not been a time for words, only for reaching out with the best-known antidote for fear and loneliness—connection to another human being. He had held her so fiercely she knew he'd been unaware of the strength of his grasp. His pain had been forged in the white-hot flame and fueled for a very long time under crisis. It would not be assuaged overnight.

She rose to her feet and approached the crepe myrtle. She cupped a blossom in her palms, awed once again by the beauty, variety and fragility of nature's gifts. If only she could wrap her hands around Tom's hurt and soothe it away. When he was ready, *if* ever he was ready, she could perhaps help him. But only in his time. Only if he asked.

Meanwhile, if she wasn't very, very careful, she would watch his spirit curl into itself and wither just as, with the first hint of cold, the flower she cradled in her palms would.

Somehow she had never expected that loving a man would be this difficult.

THE FIRST MONDAY evening after Labor Day, an eclectic group gathered on Washington Street in front of Meacham House. Its gabled two stories spoke of another era; however, signs over the large wraparound front porch announcing music and food were strictly contemporary. Lynn watched nervously as a few stray teenagers loitered on the lawn, looking distrustful. Molly, a smile wreathing her face, her bright red curls bobbing, hurried to greet the young people. If anybody could charm them up the walk and into the house, it was the effervescent director.

From the backyard, Lynn heard the music begin. One of her parishioners led a five-piece band, which was donating two hours tonight, and beyond that, the leader had agreed to offer weekly guitar lessons. Molly had been scrupulous in securing permission from town officials to forestall neighbors' objections to the music, and most of the property owners contacted had been cautiously receptive.

Lynn wasn't quite so optimistic about Prentice Jewett and others like him. She hoped he wouldn't show up. But she had a sinking feeling that nothing would keep him away.

Off in the distance she noticed Ruth and Rachel Steele making their way toward Meacham House.

Wally Drummer, the retired high-school coach, and Mary, his wife, were already on duty dishing out pizza and soft drinks to the five or six kids Molly had lured inside, and now several other kids, attracted by the music, were walking around to the back of the house.

Lynn felt someone touch her arm and turned to see Aaron Mazerik. He had been a tremendous help when the idea for Meacham House had first been broached and had taken a genuine interest in the project. "How's it going?" he asked.

"Slowly. But I guess that's par for the course with something like this."

"Don't be discouraged. It's early yet. I overheard some of the kids talking at school today. It's a peer-group thing. Nobody wants to be the first to arrive, to appear uncool. Then there are others who think the idea is dumb. Of course, those are the very ones who could profit most from what you're offering here."

Lynn sighed. "I know you're right. I'm trying hard to be optimistic."

"Atta girl."

"Where's Lily?" One of the town's recent hot topics of conversation had been the announcement that Lily Bennett Holden, a young widow who had recently come back home to Riverbend, and Aaron were soon to be married.

"She'll be over later. We thought it might not be so great to overwhelm the kids at first with too many adults."

Lynn inclined her head toward the group of on-lookers, mainly adults, standing near the street. "Good thinking. I'll suggest to them that they make themselves less conspicuous."

"Okay. Meanwhile, I'll see if I can snare that

bunch.'' He pointed toward the corner where a group of teens dressed mostly in black milled around, smoking. ''I know those kids. Some of them are real pieces of work. But Meacham House is exactly what they need. Wish me luck.'' Shoving his hands into his pockets, he sauntered casually toward the group.

Meanwhile, Lynn made her way to the adults, mainly interested church members. ''Thanks for coming. We appreciate your support. However, it's been suggested the kids might feel freer to join in if there weren't so many of us hanging about.''

Grace Pennington looked around, then grinned. ''It does come across as running the gauntlet, doesn't it?''

''Why don't you visit with the kids inside?''

At her invitation, some of the adults made their way toward the house while others dispersed. Out of the corner of her eye, she saw Aaron talking with the group on the corner. One young man with shoulder-length black hair and a scraggly mustache kept gesturing. Finally Aaron left the teens and moved back to Lynn. ''Got any idea who promised to meet them here? Damon Hudson, the kid with the attitude, said he wasn't coming near Meacham House unless this dude showed up.''

''Tom.'' Lynn's heart sank. Where was he?

''*Tom?* Tom Baines?''

Lynn nodded.

''He's the last person I can imagine being involved with that bunch.''

''It's a long story.''

Aaron leaned over and studied Lynn's face. ''You look worried. Is he supposed to be here?''

''He said he'd come.'' Before she could say anything further, they were interrupted by a voice coming from a loudspeaker. In moments a flat-bed truck rounded the corner. Banners hanging from the bed read Save Our Square, Say NO to Meacham House, Protect Your Property. The voice emanating from the speaker was unquestionably Prentice Jewett's.

"Citizens of Riverbend, what do you want in this historic neighborhood? Deafening rock music, drug transactions, public indecency? Many of you have worked hard to build your businesses, rehabilitate these fine old homes, improve your properties. You enjoy a peaceful quality of life. Are you going to let a bunch of teenagers ruin all you've built up?"

Lynn felt a knot forming in her solar plexus. The band stopped playing, and out of the corner of her eye she saw the formless group of kids on the corner ambling closer. One of the boys, who sported spiked purple hair, shook his fist and shouted an obscenity in the direction of the truck. Wonderful. A confrontation in the making. Prentice would undoubtedly call it a "rumble" and enjoy every minute of being proved right.

Volunteers clustered on the porch, and Aaron and Molly hurried to join Lynn. By now the truck was slowing in front of Meacham House, and Prentice's rhetoric was becoming more impassioned. "It doesn't take much, folks, to turn a decent, God-fearing neighborhood into a slum. Take a look at these kids! Do you really want the likes of them lounging on the sidewalks presenting that kind of disreputable image to visitors? I urge you to talk to the town council and…"

Before he could finish, the boy Aaron had identified as Damon stepped in front of the truck and stood defiantly, arms outstretched, daring the driver to hit him.

Lynn watched Prentice, jowls quivering, lean out of the window of the cab. "Whatsa matter?" Damon challenged. "You afraid of us, pops? Afraid we're too 'disreputable' for this town? I got news for you. We belong here as much as you do."

About this time, to Lynn's everlasting relief, Tom, who must have been on the other side of the street obscured by the truck, stepped forward and put his arm around the shoulders of the belligerent teen, who shrugged him off. Then Tom said something to him. The boy frowned, seeming to consider the words, then turned back to Jewett. "You ain't seen the last of us, grandpa."

As if deliberating his next move, the youth stared at Meacham House. Then, shooting Tom a cryptic look, he gestured to the other teens, who followed him and Tom up the steps and onto the porch, where they all turned to witness Jewett's reaction.

About this time Ruth and Rachel arrived on the scene. Lynn saw the two of them look at each other, nod triumphantly and approach the truck. "Get out of there, Prentice," Ruth said in a peremptory voice, audible to the entire group.

"Now," added Rachel.

"Why should I?"

"Because if you don't, sister and I have a little surprise for you that won't be particularly pleasant," Ruth said.

Anticipating additional fireworks, the few bystanders remaining on the sidewalk edged closer to the truck.

"Remember old man Fenter's outhouse?" Rachel prodded.

His face flaming, Prentice stepped down from the truck. "What are you two up to?"

Ruth withdrew a handful of photographs from her handbag. "Would you like these to be made public?" She handed them to Prentice, who quickly shuffled through them.

"You wouldn't dare."

"Wouldn't we?" Rachel linked her arm through his. "You of all people ought to understand the mischievous ways of young people when left to their own devices. The trouble they can get into."

Ruth commandeered his other arm, and together they propelled the hapless Jewett up the walk toward the porch. "Just think," Lynn heard Ruth say sotto voce, "if there had been a Meacham House back in our day, certain obstreperous young men in Riverbend wouldn't have gotten into so much trouble."

"But then," Rachel went on, "those days are gone. And we certainly wouldn't want those former, er, indiscretions to affect anyone's judgment about all the good some of those youths have subsequently done, now would we?"

Between them, Jewett sputtered, but when Ruth tightened her grip on his arm, he must have reconsidered his position, because he didn't say a word.

Lynn was rooted to the spot. Unbelievable. The sisters were blackmailing Prentice. And the price? The answer came swiftly.

"Rachel and I ask only one thing. That you spend some time at Meacham House, see what these folks are trying to accomplish and then make your judgment. Give them some time to prove themselves. We have a store downtown, too. But we think Reverend

Lynn and the others deserve a chance to make this work. Now, what do you think?''

Trailing them up the sidewalk, Lynn stifled a grin when she heard Prentice mutter, ''There never was any getting around the two of you. I suppose I could give it a look-see.''

TOM HAD DEBATED about even coming this evening to the Meacham House kickoff. He hated being snookered by some punk of a kid. He studied the living room, set up with folding chairs, beanbag chairs and huge floor pillows, the walls festooned with colorful posters. The teens clustered in groups of two or three taking full advantage of the food still piled on the dining-room table. Others drifted in and out of the backyard or took up a spirited game of Foosball in the downstairs bedroom, now a game room. A few were upstairs using the computers. Most of the adult guests had gone home, including Prentice Jewett, who had stayed only long enough for the most cursory of tours. However, Ruth and Rachel were involved in an animated discussion with Damon's well-endowed female companion, Keri Mellon. Tom smiled indulgently. His aunts seemed totally oblivious to the girl's nose ring, tattoo and pseudo-sophisticated expression. Ruth caught his eye and gave him a triumphant wink.

Aaron materialized beside him. ''I didn't expect to see you here.''

''Believe me, neither did I.'' He shrugged. ''Somebody has to protect the aunts.''

''I think there's a little more to it than that.'' Aaron inclined his head toward Lynn, who was talking to a younger boy who watched her intently. ''You can't take your eyes off Reverend Lynn.''

Tom mentally groaned. So much for discretion. "She's quite a woman."

Aaron scrutinized his expression, then lifted an eyebrow. "That she is." They stood quietly in the doorway until Aaron spoke again. "What did you say to young Hudson out in the street to get him in here?"

"I told him if he wanted some fun, he could stay and watch a pair of old ladies put the screws to Prentice Jewett. Then I reminded him of his promise."

"Promise?"

"Yeah, a little deal between him and me. He's the main reason I came, though I wouldn't have bet he'd show up. Nor that if he did, he'd actually come in."

"Hudson could use someone to take an interest in him. His mother died when he was six, and his alcoholic father works the night shift at the foundry. Kid's basically been on his own for years."

An edge in Aaron's voice reminded Tom that Aaron hadn't had it so easy, either, and they both knew why. Was this Aaron's way of sticking it to him about Uncle Abe?

About that time Damon sauntered in from the kitchen, his dark eyes sweeping the room, a curl on his lips.

"Know anything about photography?" Aaron's question to Tom seemed completely out of the blue.

"By osmosis. Hard not to pick up some stuff as a journalist."

"You might mention that to Damon. He's a bright enough kid who doesn't care a thing about school, but the art teacher told me he's shown a real talent for photography. There's a darkroom in the basement. Could be the hook we need with him." Aaron walked away as abruptly as he'd come.

Tom gritted his teeth. He didn't know all that much about photography, and what he did know he'd learned mainly from Gordy. Those memories were still painful. And clearly he didn't know squat about kids. But what could it hurt to sound Damon out?

"Hey, kid." He jerked his chin at Damon. "Seen the darkroom?"

For just an instant the boy's features relaxed before his mask of indifference slipped back into place. "Didn't know there was one."

Tom didn't give him a chance to say no. "C'mon, I'll lead the way." Aaron had said the darkroom was in the basement. How hard could it be to locate it?

As they started toward the cellar steps, the younger kid, not more than ten or eleven, who'd been talking to Lynn, stood up. "Darkroom?"

Lynn rose and put her hand on the boy's shoulder. "Tom, I don't think you've met Mitch Sterling's son, Sam. Sam, this is Tom Baines and his friend Damon Hudson."

Son of a gun, Tom thought. Mitch's kid. Tom noticed that Lynn made a point of facing the boy as she spoke. Was he hearing-impaired?

"Pleased to meet you, Sam. Your father and I were good buddies when I used to visit Riverbend a long time ago."

"Really? Were you a River Rat?" The boy formed his words deliberately, enunciating with care.

Tom nodded. "Sure was."

"Cool." Sam looked at Tom, then at Damon. "I like cameras and stuff. Could I come with you?"

Damon shrugged. "It's a free country."

From behind Sam, Lynn smiled at Tom, then discreetly cupped her hand to her ear. The smile was almost sufficient reward for taking these two unlikely kids in tow.

Tom easily located the darkroom, and both boys found it a source of endless fascination. Damon became almost civil when Tom offered to lend his expensive camera to Meacham House for use by the participants. Sam seemed interested both in the camera and in Damon. In fact, if Tom wasn't mistaken, when Sam looked at Damon, incipient hero worship lit up his face. What would Mitch think of that? Well, it wasn't his worry.

When they went back upstairs, the volunteers were cleaning up. Only Keri, Damon, a few of his sidekicks and Sam remained. Lynn, her arm around Keri's waist, approached them, a satisfied expression on her face. "Damon, I hope you and your friends will come back. On Wednesdays we're serving supper at six-thirty. We'd love to have all of you."

Damon's eyes flickered to Keri. He shrugged indifferently. "Maybe." He paused as if waiting for something.

"You gonna bring the camera on Wednesday, Tom?" Sam's eyes were shining.

Damn. He'd made his one token appearance. He hadn't counted on getting roped into another. He'd intended to lend the camera to the center, not become involved himself. He looked away from the approval he saw in Lynn's eyes. Unjustified. "Are both of you going to be here?" Sam nodded enthusiastically and Damon gave another shrug. "Okay, guess I'll see you then."

"Unless something more important comes up," Damon said skeptically, as if recognizing Tom's reluctance. "Let's blow this joint, Keri." They started toward the door, then Damon turned and addressed Lynn. "Did that Jewett prick back off?"

Tom opened his mouth to suggest that "prick" wasn't a word used in conversation with a minister, but when he looked at Lynn, she was unperturbed. In fact, she was smiling at Damon. "Thanks to you and the Steele ladies for standing up to him, he seems willing to give us some leeway. I hope we can win him over."

"We gotta," Sam said, looking admiringly at Damon. "Him and me can help."

"Runt, I ain't makin' no promises. I do exactly what I want. It's just a question of *if* I want. Got it?"

Sam turned his gaze to the floor. "I guess."

Damon gave a grunt of approval, stared around the room as if memorizing it, then grabbed Keri's hand and stalked out the door.

Lynn looked at Sam. "We'd better call your dad to come get you." She started toward the phone.

The boy nodded. Tom waited while Lynn dialed, then mouthed to her, "Later?"

She shook her head. "Not tonight. I'm bushed." Then she spoke into the phone. "Mitch, Sam's ready for you to come get him…. How did it go? Generally speaking, it was a positive beginning."

Tom, his arms hanging at his sides, stood there feeling useless. He had mixed feelings about the whole evening—about his awkward conversation with Aaron, about this odd alliance with Damon, about Lynn's unwillingness to see him later. He supposed she *was* tired, but on the other hand, wouldn't she want to share tonight's success with someone she professed to care about?

Molly, her fair face flushed, came in from the

kitchen and put a hand on his arm. "Thanks for all your help, Tom. We could sure use you on a regular basis."

He hoped his answer didn't sound churlish. "I'm not really into kids."

She smiled as if his comment hadn't fazed her in the least. "They'll win you over. You'll see."

After he made his farewells, he walked down the darkened street toward his truck, troubled by his mixed emotions. Why was he getting involved with other people's children when his own would barely speak to him? It was nuts.

LYNN HAD BARELY time enough over her lunch hour the next day to dash into the bookstore. Kate greeted her with a hug. "Congratulations! From what I hear, the opening was a great success."

Smiling, Lynn returned the embrace. "I wouldn't go that far. We did have a fair turnout, although clearly some of the kids came primarily for the food. The proof will be how many come back regularly."

"They'll be there. You'll see."

"I hope so. Are Ruth and Rachel here?"

"They're in the office."

"I want to thank them for their help with Prentice Jewett."

"They've been pretty hard to live with this morning. They are *very* pleased with themselves." Kate chuckled. "They've had so much fun plotting his comeuppance."

"What in the world did they say to him?"

Kate took her by the arm. "Come on. You need to hear it from the horses' mouths."

When the two slipped into the office, Rachel looked

up from the computer, and Ruth, who'd been writing a letter, set down her pen. "Welcome, Lynn," Ruth said. Rachel smiled sheepishly.

"Is this Command Central?" Lynn joked.

Ruth eyed her smugly. "The brain trust assembled here."

Kate excused herself. "Somebody has to tend the store, after all."

Lynn pulled up a chair. "Okay, ladies. I'm dying of curiosity. Out with it."

"My, the Lord does work in mysterious ways," Rachel offered, her eyes twinkling behind her glasses.

"His wonders to perform," Ruth added.

"I'm not so sure about the Lord," Lynn said. "In fact, I think He might have some serious reservations about your methods." She grinned. "But I'm delighted with the results."

"It was an inspired plan," Rachel said. "Sometimes the end does justify the means."

"I'll bet you didn't know Prentice Jewett has a questionable past," Ruth explained. "One he hoped no one remembered."

Rachel pursed her lips. "One he has tried very hard to live down. But with the help of some of our contemporaries, we were able to reconstruct some of the notorious incidents Prentice was involved in as a youth."

"Turns out we weren't the only ones who had photographic evidence," Ruth crowed. "Axel Morrison and several other boyhood accomplices of Prentice's had recorded his escapades for posterity."

"Like?" Lynn couldn't wait to hear what they'd cooked up.

"Like the time Prentice stole a farmer's outhouse,

broke into the school and put it in the high-school principal's office. Like the time the old-maid geometry teacher walked out on her porch only to find it covered with cow patties. We could go on, but you get the drift." Ruth sat back in her chair and crossed her arms, the picture of satisfaction.

"Prentice was a wild one in those days," Rachel continued. "He had more scrapes with the law than you can shake a stick at. A real doozy, that boy!"

"So we rounded up a few of our classmates who still live here, put our minds to it and the rest is history." Ruth continued to wear her tickled-pink smile. "The photographs showed Prentice digging a new latrine for the outhouse. That was part of his punishment."

Rachel erupted in a laugh. "We figured the least we could do for the youth being served by Meacham House was to remind that jackass Prentice that he needn't come off holier-than-thou so long as we're around."

Lynn shook her head in a cross between disbelief and admiration. "Even though I'm risking moral compromise by approving of your scheme, I want you to know I think you two are something else! Thank you so much for defusing what could have been an ugly confrontation."

"If it saves one youngster," Rachel said, "it will be more than worth it."

"I only hope nobody remembers any of my youthful escapades," Ruth said with a mischievous grin.

"There's always one person who will," Lynn suggested.

Both she and Ruth turned to Rachel, who adopted

a superior smirk. "Rest assured, I've got the goods on her."

Lynn rose to leave. "I'll see you both in church on Sunday?"

"As always," Ruth said. "Besides, we need to get ourselves right with the Lord."

Lynn smiled, then gave each of them a hug. "A prudent course, always."

TOM SHOVED his chair back from the computer, re-reading what he'd written about last night's Meacham House opening. Not his usual stuff at all, yet not half-bad. Just the act of putting words on paper filled him with a sense of purpose he hadn't had since Ireland. Returning to international journalism wasn't in the cards, nor was that morbid book proposal of Harry Milstein's. For the moment he'd write whatever came into his mind. Later he could worry about trying to sell again.

He stood up, stretched, then wandered around the living room, thinking on his feet, frustrated about Lynn. She had a lot of people looking to her for support, advice and encouragement. The last thing she'd needed was for him to dump his past on her. At least she hadn't tried to "fix" him.

When the phone rang, he pulled himself together and answered it.

"Hi, Tom. This is Lily. Where have you been keeping yourself, anyway?"

"Even after I've seen Paree, I still like to come back to the farm."

"Consensus is you've holed up long enough. As you may have heard, Aaron and I are getting married a week from Saturday, and we'd like you to come.

We're having a small church wedding, followed by a reception at our house. Most of the old gang will be there. Please say yes.''

Tom hesitated. ''You've cleared this with Aaron?''

''I'll admit you weren't at the top of his list, but he's trying, Tom, really trying to come to grips with the past. He knows Riverbend is a small place. It's going to take time for him to adjust to the news that your uncle was his father, with all the implications of that fact. But avoiding the issue or hiding from the Steeles isn't Aaron's style. Since you and he have already had a couple of encounters, I think your coming to the wedding will help others see that Aaron doesn't want to foster ill will.''

''What *does* he want?''

''I'm not sure he knows yet. But this is a step, Tom. Please say you'll come. It would mean a lot to me.'' She paused. ''In the long run, I think it will be meaningful to Aaron, too. And perhaps to you.''

Lily Bennett had always been difficult to refuse. ''All right.''

''And just in case you're interested, Lynn Kendall will be performing the ceremony and attending the reception afterward.''

''What are you suggesting?''

''Maybe you'd like to escort her to the reception.''

Jeez, the town was full of matchmakers. ''I'll think about it.''

They concluded the conversation and Tom hung up. Before he could change his mind, he called Lynn and made the date. At the very least he'd get a reading on Riverbend's reaction to his interest in Lynn.

Maybe, too, he could get a reading on his own emotions, not only about Lynn but about being back in Riverbend. About whether he could ever fit in.

CHAPTER EIGHT

TOM WAS A FEW minutes late to the first Wednesday-night dinner at Meacham House, but the aroma of garlic and tomato sauce had him mounting the front steps two at a time. He was starving. Three teens sat at the porch table wolfing down platefuls of spaghetti. One of them deigned to look up and raise a forefinger. "Hey, man."

Tom stopped and laid a hand on the back of the youth's chair. "Looks good. Save any for me?"

"Better hurry," a listless-looking girl with stringy blond hair said, motioning with a fork toward the kitchen.

Not a smile in the bunch, and wariness blanketed their eyes. But they were here. That was the main thing. And the food was clearly a hit.

Inside, six or eight kids had found perches and were balancing plates on their knees. He looked around, searching for Lynn. Molly, who was dishing up the pasta, waved and smiled. "Soup's on," she mouthed.

He had to step over a long-legged kid who was sopping up tomato sauce with a crust of French bread. "'Scuse me." By way of response, the boy moved his leg a scant three inches. Tom set his camera down on top of a bookcase and headed for the dining room.

Molly extended a plate of steaming spaghetti. As he took it from her, he jerked his head toward the living room. "The dinner looks like a real draw. I don't think you'll have to worry about leftovers."

She smiled. "I just hope we have enough. Several who still need to eat are upstairs on the computers, and that doesn't count any others who walk in off the street."

He couldn't help himself. "Where's Lynn?"

"She'll be here later. She had a meeting at the community food bank. She's on the board, you know."

He didn't know, but he wasn't surprised. "Damon?" he asked, looking around.

Molly's smile faded. "Not yet. Several of his buddies are here, but he's still a no-show."

He felt someone tug on his sleeve. "Tom, come eat with me, okay?" Sam Sterling looked up hopefully.

Tom turned to pick up a piece of French bread. "Sure, kid, just a minute."

"Tom, please? Come eat with me. The big guys don't want me."

What was the matter with the youngster? Hadn't he heard him the first time? Molly set down her spoon and took hold of Tom's elbow and turned him to face the boy. "Now tell him."

He'd forgotten. Sam read lips, so of course he hadn't "heard" Tom's response. He felt like a heel. "Hey, Sam," he said. "Get your plate and we'll find us a place." He nodded at the soft drinks. "Root beer okay with you?"

"Sure."

Tom grabbed two soft drinks, then found seats on the stairs. Both of them dug into the food. After a few minutes Tom tapped Sam on the shoulder to get his attention. "What makes you think the big kids don't want you?"

"I'm not a teenager. But I heard they have art and photography and stuff here. I like to draw. Reverend Lynn said if I wanted to try it, I could come."

"But you're not quite sure?"

"Most of 'em don't pay any attention to me, but I liked that Damon kid. I saw him at the square yesterday after school. He said, 'Hi, runt. See ya tomorrow night.'" Sam twisted a fork through lank strands of spaghetti. "But I guess he forgot or something."

Poor Sam. He must be very lonely if a *hi* from the likes of Damon Hudson made his day. "Maybe he'll come later."

"Maybe."

"Meanwhile, when we finish, I'll introduce you to my camera."

Sam shifted and moved a few inches closer. "Cool."

After dinner a few of the teens left, but most stuck around, some heading for the computers, others taking seats in the art room where a local artist was offering instruction in watercolor painting. Molly steered a few of the boys to the basement rec room, now converted to a music room where the bandleader from Monday was setting up to teach guitar. Several hung out in the living room studying or talking.

Just before he and Sam got down to business, Lynn breezed in carrying a large box. "Look, guys. We have a present." Some of the teens quit talking and stared at her. "The owner of the office-supply store donated a printer. Now we'll be able to put out our own newsletter. Who likes to write?"

The listless-looking blonde held her hand up tentatively. "I prob'ly wouldn't be any good, but I'll help."

Several others shrugged as if to add their willingness to hers. Lynn winked at Tom by way of greeting, then rushed on, "Okay, then." She set the box on the coffee table and sat on the floor amid the kids. "Let's start brainstorming. Who needs to receive a newsletter and what do we want it to say?"

Tom and Sam found a quiet corner in an upstairs bedroom set up as a study hall. Tom removed the camera from the case and was starting to explain the various parts when they heard a loud racket from the stairs.

"Whaddaya mean, no smoking? What kind of stupid place is this, anyway?"

Tom recognized Molly's cool, objective tone as she explained.

Then another outburst. "Look, lady, you can't tell me what to do. Nobody tells Damon Hudson where to get off."

Tom walked quickly to the head of the stairs. "Need some help, Molly?"

"Ooh, here comes the big man with the muscle." Damon stood at the bottom glaring up at him.

Tom leaned against the wall, folding his arms across his chest. "No muscle, Damon. But if you're going to hang around here, you need to remember you're expected to behave courteously."

"Hey, man," Damon said in a whiny voice, "she told me I couldn't smoke here."

Tom nodded to Molly to indicate he'd handle Damon from here on. "You'll get no big lecture from me about the dangers of tobacco. I used to smoke, and we both know it's not good for us. But give Molly a break. I'm sure the fire marshal had something to say about the rule."

Damon's eyes narrowed, as if considering the logic of Tom's argument. "Where's the kid?" he said in an abrupt change of subject.

"Up here with me. We're looking at the camera. You're welcome to join us." Tom turned away and walked slowly toward the study hall, his ears cocked for the sound of feet on the stairs. Nothing. A tough nut, that kid.

"Okay, Sam." Tom leaned forward, making sure his lips were in Sam's line of vision. "This is the F-stop. Let me explain how it works." Several minutes passed before Tom became aware that Damon was leaning against the doorjamb, listening.

Tom beckoned to him. "Pull up a seat." Then he went on with his explanations. "You missed the spaghetti," he said offhandedly as he pulled off the lens cap.

"So? I thought the runt here would be home with mommy eating his supper."

In a voice louder than usual, Sam said, "I don't have a mommy."

"Everybody has a mom, stupid."

"Do you?" Sam challenged.

Damon's cocky attitude underwent a subtle shift. Tom waited. Something important was going on. "Used to."

Sam stared at the floor. "Me, too. Used to."

Where was Lynn now that he needed her? Tom thought. She was the one with the expertise. How was he supposed to make anything right here? Before he could intervene, Damon clamped Sam on the shoulder. "But look, kid, we're doin' okay, know what I mean? Who needs a mother, anyway?"

The answer to the question was apparent in the

weighted silence that ensued. "Maybe, well, maybe—" the hopefulness in Sam's voice was heart-breaking "—we could be like…buddies."

Damon withdrew his hand. "I dunno, runt."

"I don't see why that wouldn't be a good idea," Tom interjected.

Damon jerked to his feet. "Hey, man. This is between the kid and me. Ain't none of your business, got it?" His eyes were hostile. Clearly this conversation had struck a nerve.

Tom held up his hands in surrender. "No problem. Do it your way. Now do you or do you not want to learn anything about my camera?"

The youth stood silent, as if weighing the cost. Then he slumped into his chair. "Might as well. I'm here, ain't I?"

THE DAY OF AARON'S WEDDING, Tom shifted uneasily in the pew, watching dust motes dance in the shafts of late-afternoon light streaming through the tall stained-glass windows. He was barely aware of Rachel's organ prelude, the hum of anticipation as ushers seated the guests or Ruth's presence beside him. However, the tattoo of his heart and the shallowness of his breathing were all too apparent. It wasn't merely that he hadn't been in church for a long time—it was the anticipation of seeing Lynn in her clergy role. It had been easy enough to avoid the reality, as long as they kept her profession and their personal lives separate. He had no idea how he would react this afternoon or what such an innocuous event as a wedding might imply for their future.

The music stopped and a rustle of expectation spread through the nave. When the organ resumed,

Aaron, tall and erect in his dark suit, escorted his mother down the aisle. Evie wore a pink dress in some sort of satiny material, and her eyes were fixed with pride on her son's handsome face, as if looking at the guests, many of whom she'd served as a waitress, would incite their disapproval of her and Aaron's changed status in the community. After Mrs. Bennett took her place in the first row of the bride's side, Rachel began to play Clark's "Trumpet Voluntary." Tom scarcely took in the bridesmaids who passed his pew in a pearl-gray haze. Because he had eyes for only one woman. While everyone else turned to watch the bride start down the aisle escorted by her father, he stared at Lynn, who had emerged from a side door and stood at the altar steps, clothed in a lace-trimmed white alb and stole, a welcoming smile radiating from her face. He didn't know when he had ever seen a more beautiful woman. He swallowed the lump in his throat.

When Lily reached Aaron, Tom noticed Aaron's usual guarded look vanish. In its place was a kind of awed joy. Two of the unlikeliest people in the world to find each other, and yet watching them, Tom sensed the depth of their love and commitment. And on a level that disturbed him, he found himself envying them.

"Dearly beloved," Lynn began in a clear, pure voice. And from that moment, Tom was lost. He didn't believe in angels, but he'd swear one was performing this ceremony. It was as if the three—Lily, Aaron and Lynn—were enveloped by an aura, setting them apart. With a sinking sensation Tom realized he was intensely uncomfortable. This couldn't be the Lynn who teased him about being the big, bad wolf, the Lynn whose laughter had a rich, earthy quality, the Lynn who responded so enthusiastically to his kisses. The woman before him was…untouchable.

Beside him, Ruth dabbed her handkerchief to her eyes and sighed with pleasure. Tom clasped his hands between his knees and bent forward, blotting out the scene. Yet the words Lynn spoke were inescapable. "We come together as a community of family and friends to witness the vows of Lily and Aaron, whose union is a beautiful example of 'amazing grace.' Each of them would admit that in their own ways, they were 'lost.' They rejoice today in the fact that they now are 'found,' and have found in one another a future filled with promise."

She went on speaking, but Tom had stopped listening. He, too, was lost. And finding himself was proving damned difficult. Would he ever be man enough to stand before a congregation and pledge his undying love for Lynn? He knew, beyond the shadow of a doubt, that he could do so only when he could offer her a whole man, one worthy of her love. His heart contracted. That was a tall order.

The rest of the ceremony passed in a blur. Only when he heard Lynn's delighted laughter did he look up. Her amusement was because Aaron was kissing his bride in a manner that left no doubt as to how he felt about her. In a curious way, the laugh gave Tom hope. Most angels didn't have such an uninhibited manner of expression. At least he didn't think so.

The triumphant chords of Handel's "Water Music" filled the church, and the beaming couple, with eyes only for each other, made their way down the aisle. Ruth nudged Tom with her elbow. "Did you ever see a more beautiful bride? That ice-blue sheath is perfect on her. And the flowers…simply exquisite.'' She continued prattling about the details of the service while Tom stared at the front of the church, where Lynn, head bent over the Bible clasped in her hands, walked from the sanctuary.

This new Lynn had given him serious pause for thought.

"REVEREND LYNN, it was a lovely ceremony. Thank you.'' Lynn stood at the punch table beside Eleanor Bennett, Lily's mother, both of them watching the bride and groom make the rounds of the guests. The usually serious Aaron was grinning from ear to ear.

"They're a wonderful couple, and they deserve happiness. I'm glad I could be a part of this special day in their lives.''

Eleanor cocked her head, a smile teasing her lips. "Didn't I see you come in with Tom Baines?''

To Lynn's relief, the smile looked encouraging. "Yes, you did.''

"Lily has always been so fond of him. We all hope he'll stay in Riverbend.'' When Lynn didn't respond, Eleanor went on, "Judging from the way he looks at you, dear, I think you might have a great deal to do with his decision.'' With a nod of her head, Eleanor indicated Tom, who was standing across the room.

Lynn felt a quickening of her pulse as his eyes found hers. "I take it you would approve?''

The bride's mother gave a knowing chuckle. "Approve? I'll dance at your wedding.''

She and Tom were a long way from that eventuality, but it was gratifying to know that at least one denizen of Riverbend would entertain the notion. "Now if you'll excuse me, I need to circulate.''

Lynn took a tentative sip of the refreshing punch and was about to go join Tom when Genevieve Potts, one of her more cantankerous elderly parishioners snatched at her sleeve. "Reverend Lynn. Lovely ceremony."

"Hello, Genevieve. Nice to see you."

"I was Lily's piano teacher," she said by way of justifying her inclusion on the limited guest list. "Such a talented, refined young woman."

"Yes, she is. I'm glad to see her so happy."

Genevieve's nose quivered. "It won't last, you know."

"I beg your pardon?" Lynn was dumbfounded.

"Not with that Mazerik fellow. He's way beneath her."

Lynn set her cup on the edge of the table. "I'm sorry, but I can't agree. Aaron is a fine man, and the two of them deserve all of our good wishes."

"Humph. We'll see." The woman smiled smugly. "And as for couples, didn't I see you come in with Ruth and Rachel Steele's nephew?"

Lynn bit her tongue. "Yes, you did."

"Well, you can't be too careful, my dear. You have to remember your position in the community." She leaned forward confidingly. "That man has sown his share of wild oats, you know."

Lynn straightened to her full five foot six. "I, for one, believe there is good in each of us. And I see a great deal of good in Tom Baines. I hope you will look for it, too."

Genevieve's mouth dropped open and she stammered a reply. "Well, er, I suppose that is what we're taught, but—"

"Forgive me for ending our conversation, but I

haven't congratulated the groom, and he's coming this way right now." Lynn greeted Aaron with a warm hug. "Much happiness to you both," she said to him.

"Thanks." Aaron then nodded toward Tom, in conversation now with Beth Pennington and Charlie Callahan, whose recent unexpected reunion, much to everyone's delight, had rekindled their love. "And may I say the same to you?"

Blushing, Lynn found Aaron's twinkling eyes. "I think those sentiments are a bit premature."

"Maybe. I'm only now getting to know my cousin." The word came out with forced familiarity. "He and I have had our differences in the past, but he's not a bad fellow."

"No," Lynn murmured, "he's not." She patted Aaron gently on the cheek. "You're neglecting your bride. Go."

After linking her name with Tom's in her own mind for these past few weeks, Lynn found it odd to hear them linked on the lips of others. During today's ceremony, she'd focused solely on the bride and groom, but afterward, while she was unvesting, she had become aware of her ongoing and all-too-human desire. Like Lily, she wanted to be married to the one true love of her life. And despite the odds, it was Tom, only Tom, who fit that definition.

He had seemed unusually quiet on the drive from the church to Aaron and Lily's house. She hadn't asked him why. Perhaps they were both a bit on edge about making their entrance as a couple, knowing that they would be greeted by reactions as varied as Eleanor's and Genevieve's. Upon their arrival, Lynn had been swept up by guests wanting to discuss the wedding, Meacham House or other church matters, but she had noticed Tom seemed content to stand against the wall in the corner of the dining room, visiting with those who approached him, but making no effort to mingle.

Beth and Charlie had moved away, and he stood there now, his arms crossed over his chest, his eyes making a slow circuit of the room. She smiled to herself. Ever the observer. A journalistic attribute, she supposed. That was one difference between them— she plunged into things, while he studied them. She accepted people at face value; he appraised them before forming an opinion. Yet, she reminded herself, even in her own premarital counseling sessions, she talked with couples about valuing such complementary traits and understanding they had the potential to strengthen a relationship. She certainly hoped so.

Just then Tom's eyes stopped on her, and a lazy grin spread over his features. He walked slowly across the room toward her. The whirl of color, the hum of conversation and the high-pitched laughter of a woman ladling punch seemed to be coming from another place. Lynn waited, hands at her sides, until Tom, his eyes riveted on her, put an arm around her waist. "How are we doing? Am I behaving myself?"

"Let's see." She made a pretense of checking off numbers on her fingers. "By last count, only a half-dozen guests have bolted the reception to run through the streets to announce that we're an item."

"Seriously, you're sure our being together isn't putting you in an awkward position?"

"I'm proud to be with you, Tom. Please don't feel you have to walk on eggshells. The people who matter will understand. As for the rest—" she shrugged "—it'll take them longer, but they'll come around."

"That's my girl. Ever the optimist." He ran a finger under his shirt collar. "I could sure use some fresh air. How about you?"

She smiled up at him. "I thought you'd never ask."

As they strolled toward the porch, she couldn't help overhearing a murmured comment from a woman she'd never seen before. "Isn't that the pastor? Who is that man with her? I thought she wasn't married."

"She isn't," her companion responded. "And I doubt Baines is the man for her."

Lynn glanced up. Tom must've heard, too. His jaw was working. She poked him playfully in the ribs with her elbow. "What do they know, anyway?"

"Only what I've been thinking."

"Tom?" She stopped dead. "Give yourself a break. When the time comes, the only person who will decide who's right for me will be me. And the very last criterion I'll use is what other people think. So there."

He pulled her closer and through clenched teeth muttered, "That's easy enough to say, but other people *do* matter."

"Not as much as you do," and with that, she stood on tiptoe and planted a quick kiss on his cheek, an act accompanied by the indrawn breath of Genevieve Potts, who was lurking behind a flowering plant.

"ALONE AT LAST," Tom gloated, throwing his suit jacket over the back of a chair and extending his arms to offer Lynn a bear hug.

Lynn snuggled into his embrace, rubbing her cheek against his shoulder. "Not exactly," she said, jerking her head toward the window ledge where Benedict surveyed them with seeming utter disdain.

"I'll take my chances with him," Tom said just before capturing her lips with his. It had been too long since they'd been alone, too long since he'd felt his body come alive in response to the smell and feel of her. With every fiber of his being, he longed to scoop her up, transport her to the bedroom and learn every intimate detail of her body. But much as he might want to, he couldn't. That right would not be his unless...until...

She disengaged her lips and laid a gentle palm on his cheek. "Mmm, good," she murmured. "Can we try that again?"

He gladly obliged. But just as he was getting with the program, his blood near the boiling point, the incongruous image of Lynn officiating at the wedding came to him. He stiffened. Sensing the change in him, she pulled away, then gazed at him quizzically. She looked as if she wanted to say something, but instead, turned and headed toward the kitchen. "I'll put on some coffee. Make yourself at home."

He stripped off his tie and rolled up his shirtsleeves before sinking onto the sofa. From the kitchen he could hear the faucet running, the clatter of a canister lid. Because of the startup of Meacham House and a series of pastoral emergencies, they hadn't been alone together—really alone—for more than a week. He'd missed her. The kisses tonight were nice, but he could no longer pretend everything was hunky-dory. Before seeing her officiate at the wedding, he hadn't fully realized how improbable this whole thing was. They needed to talk. Now.

When Lynn returned, she set the mugs on the coffee table, kicked off her shoes, then perched beside him, tucking her legs up under her. "Okay, something's on your mind. Out with it."

It was disconcerting that she read him like a book, but the time for sidestepping the issue was long past. "I met the vacation you, I've gotten to know the Riverbend you, but today I saw another you."

Smiling wistfully, Lynn twisted a strand of hair around her finger. "The reverend me?"

"Yes."

"And?"

He rubbed his palms on his thighs. "I don't know what to think. You were…something else. It was as if I was seeing you for the first time." He threw his head back on the cushion and stared at the ceiling.

"It scared you?"

This was harder than he'd expected. "That's putting it mildly. You are so loving, so perfect, I—"

"Here we go again."

"What do you mean?"

Lynn clutched the hem of her skirt. "The mistaken notion men get of me as, I don't know, Lynn the Madonna. Tom, I am graced by having the ability to help others on occasion. That does not overwhelm who I am as a woman or diminish my need to love and be loved."

"But your example is pretty hard to live up to."

"How many times do I have to say it? I am far from perfect. In fact, at the reception I very nearly lost my temper with Genevieve Potts. I can be as petty, selfish and mean-spirited as the next person. And until you see me as that flawed human being, I don't know how to reassure you."

Tom reached for her hand, aware of the depth of her distress. "Help me understand, Lynn. What you do isn't anything I've had much experience with." He looked intently into her eyes, filled with longing and something else. Desperation?

"Maybe if I tell you about my upbringing, it will help." She looked away as if gathering her thoughts, then turned back to him. "My father died when I was five, and my mother took my older sister, Pam, and me to live with her widowed mother. Nana was a powerful influence on me. In fact, I'm named for her—Elizabeth Lynn. She was full of life, never called anyone a stranger and was generally loved by everyone she met. She believed we should live each day as if it were our last, and that it's our duty to leave the world a better place. My mother's brother, Uncle Will, was a minister and the closest thing in my life to a father. From the time I was tiny, I've always known that his ministry is simply part of who he is. Integral, natural, if that makes sense. Not something separate, or an acquired or cultivated behavior."

She looked pleadingly at Tom, but he simply nodded for her to continue.

"When you grow up without a father," she said, "there's a yearning that's never quite satisfied."

He averted his face. "Or when you grow up with an absentee father."

Benedict diverted them from the painful silence when he leaped from the ledge and padded down the hall. Lynn continued. "Couple that need with the wonderful ways in which Mother, Nana and Uncle Will cared for me, and it's little wonder I always wanted to help people. Especially help them to discover where they belong and to understand how much they are loved. When I was a girl, my favorite pastimes were playing church and doctor. And since blood isn't my favorite thing…'' She smiled self-deprecatingly.

He decided he needed to lighten the tone. "And here, all along, I thought you had to be struck by a thunderbolt."

"Heck, no. That's the easy way. And I never do anything the easy way." Her eyes mellowed. "Like falling in love with my doubting Thomas."

His throat constricted, and he choked out his disbelief. "Say again?"

She pulled his hand from her lap, grazed his palm with her lips, then glanced up at him, her beautiful gray eyes swimming with affection. "I love you."

He was sure she could hear the rattling of his heart in his chest. How could he possibly respond? He had the capacity to make her life more complicated than she could imagine. Rather than risk saying the wrong thing, he simply pulled her to him and held her, running his fingers gently through her hair. He knew she was waiting for him to speak. His mind rioted with exhilaration and fear. And with the realization she might get hurt because of him.

The shrill of the telephone startled them both. Lynn sent him a searching look before crossing the room to pick up the phone. He couldn't help overhearing her end of the conversation. "Calm down, Mae…. You say he's left…? What about the children…? Don't say that, honey. Stay where you are, and I'll be right over…. No, it's no trouble. I wouldn't think of having you be by yourself tonight." She concluded the conversation, then turned to Tom. "I'm sorry, but I have to leave. Now."

He stood and took a step toward her. The timing couldn't have been worse. There was so much left unspoken. "Lynn, please. Do you have to go?" He was aware his tone sounded accusatory. The room was charged with tension.

She walked past him, slipped her feet into her shoes and picked up her purse. Before she turned around, he saw her swipe a finger across her eyes. Then she faced him, a reproachful look on her face. "Yes, I do. Don't you understand, Tom? It's who I am."

They left the house together, neither saying another word. What was there left to say except, "I love you, too"? And *that* he couldn't bring himself to utter.

IT WAS AFTER FIVE the next morning when Lynn wearily let herself into her house. Benedict, waiting in the entry hall, rubbed against her legs and purred madly. She scooped him up, draped him over her shoulder and nuzzled his neck. "Oh, kitty, it was not a pretty sight." Mae's tearstained face, hollow eyes and defeated sag of the shoulders weighed heavily on her heart. When Lynn had arrived at the run-down old ranch house, the tiny porch light had done little to illuminate the way. She'd nearly tripped over the bikes, plastic toys and gardening tools littering the lawn. She wasn't surprised. She'd only seen Merlin Farrell a couple of times and never in church. He had struck her as the kind of man who feels entitled to a good time and views his family responsibilities as unwelcome burdens.

Unfortunately, tonight, that impression had proved correct. He had stormed out of the house, telling Mae he was leaving her for good. Mae, a dependent sort, was beside herself. How could she provide for the children—three under the age of ten? Where could she go? What could she do? Beyond that, she was further devastated by the news that her husband had found another woman, one who, in his words, "knows how to make a man happy in bed and out." The poor woman had been frantic.

Lynn carried Benedict into the living room and sank gratefully into the rocker. She'd done what she could to calm Mae. They'd talked, prayed and finally, after a cup of warm milk, Mae had said she was exhausted and should go to bed. Lynn had promised to put her in touch with a social worker and Legal Aid. The destruction of a marriage was always a sad event and, regrettably, all too common.

Lynn leaned her head back and closed her eyes, too tired even to attempt to crawl into bed. Besides, today was Sunday and she was due at the church for the early service at eight. She'd curl up here in the living room for an hour or so, then take a bracing shower to prepare for her day.

Setting Benedict aside, she moved to the sofa, unfolded an afghan and stretched out gratefully. She turned on her side, scrunching a decorative pillow under her head. Then her heart sank. From the street lamp casting light through the lace window curtains, she could just make out the two mugs sitting on the coffee table. Untouched.

Helpless, she stared at them through tears that seemed to come from nowhere. She could rationalize that they arose from her exhausted state. But she knew better. She'd bared her soul to Tom. For once, she'd risked putting her feelings out there. And had been rejected.

She raised herself on one elbow, retrieved a tissue from the end table, blew her nose, then fell back, unable to stem the sobs. She'd told him. Said the words she'd never uttered to any other man. And they were as true right this moment as they'd been then. She loved Tom Baines. Deeply, everlastingly. Hopelessly?

Yet at some almost subconscious level, she understood he'd been fighting the connection between them, holding back in ways that had more to do with him than with her. It was as if they were involved in some complicated dance figure—approach, connect, withdraw. Painful and difficult as it would be, if she loved him, she would have to wait. After all, she'd stated her feelings. It was his turn now. If he chose to take it.

Benedict jumped on her chest and made himself a nest. Even though she was exhausted, Lynn lay for a long time, staring into space. "Oh, Sir," she finally whispered, "have I fallen for the wrong man?"

SUNDAY AFTERNOON Tom planted the tee in the grass, then stood gazing down the fairway, lining up his shot.

"Since you last played here, they've put a trap on the left about sixty yards from the green," Mitch Sterling said.

Tom nodded appreciatively, gave one last glance down the fairway, then whacked the ball, which took a good bounce and landed just right of center.

"Nice shot." Mitch stepped forward, took a couple of practice swings, then hit his drive.

As they rode down the fairway in the golf cart, Tom experienced a tug of satisfaction. He'd learned to play on this course, and although he'd golfed on some of the finest courses in the world, there was something in the smell of the grass, the familiar tree markers and undulations of the terrain that spelled home. He'd been pleased yesterday at the reception when Mitch had suggested today's outing.

Beside him, Mitch chuckled. "Remember our famous River Rats tournament?"

A memory came to Tom, one he hadn't had in years. "You mean the time we wouldn't let the girls play? Told them it was a guys-only event?"

"That's the time." Mitch slowed the cart a few yards from his ball. "Lily and Beth somehow convinced the pro to let them in the bag room."

"That's right. And they took all our clubs except for a driver and a putter."

Mitch laughed again. "Made for an interesting round, didn't it?"

"I can still see Lily's triumphant look when they met us afterward in the grill room for hamburgers. And how Jacob stuck her with the bill. Those were special times."

"Yeah." Mitch left the cart, hit his second shot, then returned and steered toward Tom's ball. "You know, I hope my kid can have some of those good times."

Tom sensed a sadness in his partner's voice. "Sam? I've met him at Meacham House. He seems like a fine youngster."

"He is, but he has a lot to deal with."

Tom had heard the story about Mitch's wife leaving him and her hearing-impaired son. "He has some challenges, all right, but from what I've seen, he's handling them well."

"He's a good kid, but I wish…" Mitch shook his head. "Never mind." He didn't have to say anything further.

"How's Caleb doing?" Tom remembered Mitch's grandfather with great fondness.

"Thank heaven for him. He's been a godsend with Sam, an ideal sitter and companion. Until lately. He's recovering from hip surgery now. Slowly."

In his friend's face, Tom saw the worry lines deepen. Knowing Mitch, Tom figured he'd handle whatever came his way. But he was facing a lot. Alone.

Mitch parked the cart on a path near the green, but made no move to get out. "I'm grateful, too, to Lynn Kendall for taking Sam under her wing and letting him participate at Meacham House even though he's only ten. With Caleb being out of commission and my store manager quitting, I'd have been in a real bind without her." He smiled ruefully. "Small-town neighborliness. You can't beat it."

When they reached the twelfth hole, they were held up by a foursome playing in front of them. Mitch tipped back his hat and spread his arm across the back of the seat. "Have any plans to stay around here?"

Plans? There was that ugly word again. "I don't know, Mitch. I'll have to make some decisions soon. The only thing I know for sure is that I'm not going to be a foreign correspondent anymore."

"There are quite a few of us who hope you'll find a reason to stick around." Mitch turned and looked at him challengingly. "But maybe you already have."

"What are you talking about?"

"Another characteristic of small towns—gossip. Tongues are already wagging. Maybe Lynn will provide you reason enough to stay. She's a quite a woman."

"Tell me about it," Tom muttered as he jumped

from the cart, grabbed his driver and strode to the now-empty tee box. No way was he going to tell Mitch he'd lain awake half the night cursing himself for being such an insensitive, indecisive ass. What was so damn difficult about telling Lynn he was crazy about her? About telling her how, more than anything, he wanted to make a life with her?

He teed up, and in a burst of anger swung hard and let the ball fly. "Fore!" he shouted, as helplessly he watched the ball land a mere yard or two behind one of the men in the foursome, who turned and shook a fist at Tom.

Mitch strolled up beside him and laid a friendly arm around his shoulders. "You don't have to take it out on the ball, buddy. It was me who asked the wrong question."

Tom drubbed the head of his driver into the grass. "No. You asked the right question. But the hell of it is, I don't seem able to answer it."

Mitch slid his own driver through his fingers, then set up his ball. Before he hit, however, he said something else. "Love's a lot like golf, Tom. A game of patience." And then Mitch hit a perfect drive right down the middle of the fairway.

Some guys are just in the groove, Tom thought with envy.

SUNDAY EVENING after the golf game, Tom stared at the draft of his column about Meacham House. He needed to do more with the unlikely cooperation between Sam and Damon and the developing chemistry between the adult volunteers and the kids. Volunteers like himself. He groaned. Not only had those two kids gotten under his skin, demonstrating real talent in photography, but they'd convinced him to show up every Monday, Wednesday and Friday. And he'd done it all last week, when things were going well with Lynn.

But last night had been a disaster.

He shuffled the papers on his desk. Lying there to further complicate his life was the contract Harry Milstein had sent him. Harry was many things, but a liar he wasn't. The six-figure advance was very attractive. Tom knew he could write the book. Even do a creditable job of it. And make a mess of himself in the process. The day might come when this was a subject he could revisit. But not now. Maybe not ever. In his mind, the cries of children echoed too loudly, too hauntingly.

Abruptly he turned to the computer and typed his rejection of Harry's offer. He knew the editor wouldn't understand, but that was tough. Some things were beyond the reach of money. This was one of them.

The printer was clacking out the letter when the phone rang. He picked it up. "Hello?"

"Tom?" He'd know that voice anywhere. "It's Selena."

She rarely called him unless it was an emergency. "Is something wrong with the kids?"

"No." She paused. "It's my mother."

"Lila?"

"She's had a major stroke. Right now my sister's in Trenton taking care of her, but we need to make other arrangements as soon as it's practical."

"I was always fond of your mother. I'm sorry to hear about this."

"I've located a nursing home. A patient is moving

out at the end of the month.'' She hesitated. ''I was wondering if…well, if I could send Pete and Libby to stay with you while I get Mom settled.''

An immediate objection occurred to him. ''What about school?''

''They're good students. They could miss a few days. Besides, three of those days they'll be out of school, anyway, for the teachers' conference break.'' She sounded anxious. ''It would only be for a week or ten days.''

A week or ten days! What would he do with two teenagers for that long? Particularly when they had so little use for him? ''I don't know how Pete and Lib will feel about that arrangement.''

''More important, how will you feel about it?'' There it was, the subtly put, but familiar challenge to his parenting skills.

''I'm okay with it,'' he lied smoothly. ''In fact, it might give us a chance to establish some common ground. My weekend with them wasn't a rousing success. Maybe it was too short a visit.''

''Maybe.'' She hesitated, then went on, ''Actually, Tom, they could stay with friends. But I don't think that's best. They need time away from the social whirl here. Frankly, some of their friends are a bit too sophisticated for my tastes. And they need time with you. For what it's worth, your weekend in Chicago wasn't the disaster you seem to think it was.''

''It wasn't?''

''No. Of course, they wouldn't give you the satisfaction of telling you they enjoyed it, but the trip to the Navy Pier was a big success. Libby wears the T-shirt you bought her so often I can scarcely get it off her back to wash it. Give them a chance, Tom.

They're teenagers, after all, and their behavior reflects it. If you say yes, I'm not planning to give them a choice."

Tom recognized that his ex-wife was handing him a golden opportunity. One that might never come again. One that scared the hell out of him. He raked a hand through his hair. What the heck? "Sure, Selena, send them on. I'll handle it somehow. Let me know the details. Oh, and when you see your mother, give her my love."

"I will. And, Tom…thanks. I don't think you'll regret having the kids. I appreciate your willingness to help out."

"Sure thing. Call me when you know something more." He hung up and sat staring at the phone, feeling more inadequate than he had in years. His first instinct was to call Lynn and solicit her help.

But after last night, that was out of the question.

PETE SLAMMED his bedroom door, cranked up the volume on his CD player and tried to lose himself in the vibrating rhythm of Mötley Crüe. Sweeping the magazines, books and dirty clothes off his bed, he flopped down, then threw an arm over his eyes, determined not to cry. He wouldn't give either of his parents the satisfaction. Besides, he was too old and too angry to cry.

His mother had broken the news right after dinner. She was actually going to send him and Libby to stay with his father for a week in that hick town in Indiana. He'd only been there once. The place had these spooky-looking houses with steep roofs and gaping windows, kind of like that Addams-family house he'd seen on TV reruns. Some of the kids there even wore boots and overalls. It was a wonder they didn't have straw and manure sticking to their feet.

Most of the time, he could manipulate his mother. This time nothing he said got through. She just kept talking about how he and Libby needed to be cooperative, that this was the best way they could help Grandma. Bull. They could help a lot better if they stayed right here with friends, but no. Mom just kept saying, "The best place for you is with your father." Right. Like the famous Tom Baines had ever given them the time of day. Like letters from places with names he couldn't pronounce would make a difference. Other guys had dads who helped with that stupid Pinewood Derby in Cub Scouts, actually took them to watch the White Sox, and not only showed up at soccer practice, but put in a good word with the coaches. Hell, he might as well be an orphan. At least then he wouldn't have to talk about his dad to all those gaga adults who seemed to think being in the middle of a war in Bosnia was some big deal.

Libby had pulled her you're-ruining-my-life-and-it's-not-fair routine, complete with big tears and the grand finale, "Mo-ther, how could you do this to me?" Zilch. His mother was like someone he'd never seen before—what was that new vocabulary word they'd just learned for the PSAT? Yeah, "obdurate." That got it.

So now he had to pack up and leave just when he'd gotten Polly Bridges all warmed up and on the verge of letting him cop a feel and who knew what else? Crap. Riverbend. What kind of a dumb name was that, anyway? About as original as Treestanding or Browndirt.

No way was he going to tell his friends where he

was actually going. Let 'em think he was on some cool trip with his famous journalist father. And contrary to what Dad might have in mind, no way was he going to be caught dead with any of those rubes in that butt-ugly town. He'd hole up in that stupid farmhouse and play Nintendo till his eyes bugged out first.

That settled, he sat up on the edge of his bed, grabbed the phone off the desk and dialed Polly's number. Might as well start laying it on about his ''exciting trip'' and how much he'd miss her and all that other mushy stuff girls grooved on so that maybe when he returned home, she'd let him get beyond first base with her.

CHAPTER NINE

TOM LEANED his elbow on the desk, cupped his chin and stared at the words on the computer screen. It was no use. His mind wasn't on the work. Monday was Lynn's day off, although she'd probably show up tonight at Meacham House. All he had to do was call her. Pick up the phone, dial the number and talk. And say what?

"I know I hurt your feelings"? "I'm sorry I can't commit"? Hearing her say she loved him had knocked the pins out from under him. There'd been no game playing, no coy flirtatiousness, no expectations. And because of that, he'd believed her.

Rubbing his tired eyes, he rocked back in the chair. An "I love you" deserved some kind of response. She'd told him she wouldn't ask more than he could give, yet, at this moment, he wasn't sure she hadn't. Even without the complication of Pete and Libby's pending visit, he and Lynn had issues to work out, not the least of which was how he really felt about her being a minister.

Still. He couldn't simply pretend nothing had happened. He stood up and paced to the window, staring out at the sunny September day. His need to see her warred with his confusion about what he'd say when he did. Hell, he'd faced SCUD missiles, mud slides and firebombs more easily than he could brave Lynn. But he had to.

That decided, he switched off the computer, picked up his keys and left the house before he could change his mind. She was either home or she wasn't.

It turned out she wasn't. He rang the doorbell several times, all under the scrutiny of Benedict, who glared at him from his perch in the living-room window. Disappointed, Tom decided to stop at the cemetery on his way home. He hadn't been back since Damon and his pals had partied there. Maybe he should check to see if they'd cleaned up their mess. He'd hate for Lynn to find the site trashed.

After parking the truck, he strolled up the knoll now covered with crimson sumac and mustard-tufted prairie grass. Then he saw it, half-buried in the tall vegetation. A bicycle he'd know anywhere. He hurried the last few yards, then stopped, holding his breath. Lynn sat with her back to him, her arms wrapped around her drawn-up knees, gazing out over the scene before her, now a riot of brilliant yellow-gold and wine-red foliage bordering fields of browning cornstalks. Wisps of her strawberry-blond hair lifted in the breeze. So still. So lost in thought. He felt like an intruder.

As if sensing his presence, she slowly turned her head. "Hi," she said softly, as if she'd been expecting him.

He started toward her. "Hi, yourself." He stood over her. "Mind?" he asked, indicating a spot by her side.

"Not at all." She hugged her knees even closer to her chest.

He settled beside her and joined her in studying the

distant river. Finally he spoke. "Am I disturbing your day off?"

Without looking at him she said, "You're never a disturbance."

"I'm glad." He couldn't judge her mood. She wasn't rejecting him, nor did she seem angry as most women would and as she had every right to be. She just seemed...pensive, sad maybe.

Moments passed during which he tried to formulate words to tell her why he'd sought her out today. To tell her of the love he felt for her, to say how much he longed to gather her in his arms and stay isolated in this place always. But his reluctance to commit, which he knew he couldn't justify, stopped him.

Finally she turned her head, smiled wistfully and said, "I've made things difficult for you, haven't I?"

Her clear gray eyes arrested any glib response he might have made. "Not you, exactly."

"I did come on pretty strong."

"Lynn, I—"

"I meant every word."

"I know." Just when he thought he could no longer bear the hope he read in her face, she lowered her gaze.

His eyes narrowed as he stared at a man fishing from a small boat in the middle of the river. "I want to be able to give you the sun, the moon and the stars." Beside him, he heard her sigh. "But I can't right now."

"It's okay. I'll wait."

His heart expanded, nearly breaking out of his chest. He disengaged one of her hands, cool to the touch, and enfolded it in his. "Until I get my life straightened out, it would be unfair to make any promises.''

''I understand,'' she murmured before laying her head on his shoulder.

He was afraid to move, afraid to break the spell that her acceptance of him had woven. It was as if they were suspended in a time and place the real world couldn't touch, although he knew it would intrude soon enough. God willing, one day he would be worthy of her.

''What brought you here today?'' she asked.

''Thought I'd better see if the kids cleaned up the cemetery. I didn't want you finding a mess after all the work you've done.'' He glanced around. ''Looks like they did a pretty good job.''

''Except for that beer can.'' She nodded toward the wall.

''What about you?''

''Me?''

''What made you come?''

She withdrew her hand and shifted position so that she faced him, her legs crossed. ''I'm still training for a charity bike ride in West Lafayette. But why here? Why today? It's the anniversary of my grandmother's death, and this seemed a comforting place to be.''

''Your nana?''

''Yes.'' She rested her hands on her knees. ''She taught me so much about living. But ironically, perhaps her most important lesson was about dying.''

''In what sense?''

Lynn turned and gazed at a nearby headstone. ''See that? When I was a child, I thought cemeteries were spooky and death was scary.''

''It is.''

"It can be. But it can also be beautiful."

He shot her a skeptical look. There had been nothing beautiful about Gordy's death.

Without reacting to his expression, she continued, "When Nana was diagnosed with cancer, I had just graduated from college. I made up my mind to go home and help care for her for as long as it took. She faced the chemo, the hair loss, the pain, everything, as she had faced the rest of her life. With optimism and faith. Caring for her, I got to know her in a way I never would have otherwise. Time was short, and she still had stories to tell, wisdom to pass on, love to give. She made the most of every moment. Toward the end she kept telling me I shouldn't be afraid for her. She pictured death as a journey, much like birth, into a bright, promising new world."

"What happened?"

"Her actual passing was apt. Beautiful. My mother, Uncle Will, my sister and I were all gathered at her bedside. Her labored breathing eased. Then she held out her hand and, one by one, we held it. It felt warm and her grip was stronger than it had been for many weeks. She looked at us with recognition, a tiny smile hovering around her lips. Then we all became aware of a presence in the room…or a quality of light or something. It's hard to explain. She simply smiled and said, 'Verne,' my grandfather's name, then her eyes closed and she was gone. Oddly I've never felt a greater sense of peace. All of us in the room knew we had shared in a mysterious and lovely rite of passage."

Though tears stood in her eyes, she seemed to glow with inner joy. "That's how I know there's more,

Tom, much more than we have any glimmer of. For Nana and for Gordy and all the others.''

"I'd like to think you're right."

"But you don't?"

"I just don't know, Lynn. I really don't."

A cold breeze ruffled his hair, and he stood up, unsure how to conclude such an intense conversation. He studied the sky. "Not much daylight left. You'd better be getting back to town. Would you like a lift?"

She got to her feet, brushing dirt off her fanny. "Thanks, but I need the workout." She checked her watch. "If I leave right now, I can make it fine."

They started down the hill together. When they reached her bike, she straddled it. He stood holding the handlebars, reluctant to let her go. "Thanks for giving me space."

A tiny smile lit up her features. "Patience is a virtue, we're told." She sobered. "Besides, I know you have a lot on your mind with your kids and all."

"Speaking of the kids, they're coming to visit."

"For the weekend?"

"No." He explained Selena's situation. "I'm not sure what I'll do with them."

"They'd be welcome at Meacham House."

"Somehow I can't visualize Pete having much in common with kids like Damon."

She brushed back a wayward lock of hair. "You might be surprised. Will I see you there tonight?"

He let go of the handlebars. "Sure. Be careful."

When she started pedaling down the road, he stood watching until she was a speck in the distance. Pete and Damon? *Surprised* wouldn't begin to describe it. *Flabbergasted* would be more accurate.

Not for the first time since Selena's call, he felt his

gut clench. He had no idea what to do with a pair of teenagers, especially when his whole future with them might hinge on these next few days.

ALTHOUGH THE CONVERSATION at the cemetery this afternoon had changed nothing, Lynn was relieved she hadn't had to come to Meacham House tonight amid a crowd of teenagers and face Tom for the first time since her declaration of love. And a crowd was what they had. Three kids huddled around a coffee table, their math homework spread in front of them. Two girls sprawled in the armchairs barely looked up from their books to acknowledge her. Hoots of laughter erupted from the dining room where Molly was supervising the construction of posters advertising a community open house in October. The beat of rock music reverberated from the basement. Lynn sighed contentedly. So far, so good.

Upstairs she found Keri and the skinny blonde, Angie, working on the layout for their first Meacham House newsletter.

"Hi, Reverend Lynn," Keri said. "How's it going?" She might be a pretty girl if she smiled, but her expression conveyed perpetual boredom.

"Great. Need any help?"

Angie's lusterless hair fell over her face obscuring her eyes as she answered, "Not really."

"When you finish, why don't you print out a copy to show me? I'm eager to see it."

"It'd be better if we had a scanner," Keri complained.

"Then we could print photos," Angie added.

Lynn leaned against the doorjamb, considering. "That's a great idea. Some of the kids are getting into photography. We could use their pictures. Maybe we can get someone to donate a scanner.''

Keri squinted at the monitor. "Don't hold your breath on the photos."

"Why not?"

"Damon's not coming back." In her tone Lynn sensed both triumph and regret.

"Why not?"

"He says he don't care about the stupid darkroom. Says it's no big deal and he's got better things to do."

"Like what?"

Angie looked up with a cynical smirk. "Don't ask, Rev. You don't wanna know."

Lynn stepped forward. "But I do. Is he in trouble?"

"When hasn't he been?" Keri said.

Lynn struggled to remain calm. "Do you know where he is?"

Both girls shrugged. "Beats me," Angie said.

"Would you tell me if you knew?"

"No," Keri said, as if Lynn's question was incredibly naive.

Lynn had known all along there would be rough spots. Apparently they'd hit their first one. And there was only one person who might have a chance with Damon. "I'll be downstairs if you need me," she said. Nodding toward the monitor, she added, "I'm really excited about what you're doing."

Back on the main floor, she looked in vain for Tom. Had he stayed home, after all? She stepped out onto the front porch, gathering her sweater around her. On the swing sat Sam, one toe dragging along the cement as he pushed himself to and fro. She stood in front of him. "Mind if I sit down?"

194   HOMECOMING

He shrugged. It was the evening of shrugs, it seemed. She hitched one leg up and sat so she could see his face. He was not happy. She tapped his knee. He turned to look at her. "What's wrong?"

"My friend didn't come."

"Who?"

"Damon."

"What about some of the others?" She nodded her head toward the living room.

He swung back and forth a couple of times. "They don't want me."

"Oh?"

"They think I'm a baby." His face flushed with the epithet. "Only Tom and Damon want me here."

"I want you here."

He didn't say anything, just shrugged again. Her heart ached for the little guy. She knew from Mitch that he was desperate to belong. He was convinced his hearing impairment made him unacceptable. The fact that he hung around here, instead of with his peer group, revealed the degree of his isolation.

"Sam? That you?" The familiar voice sent shivers through her. Dressed in a maroon jogging suit, Tom strode up the walk.

Lynn moved closer to Sam and cupped his head to turn it toward the steps. Sam's shoulders straightened. "Tom? I thought you weren't coming."

"Well, here I am." He smiled down at the boy. "Better late than never."

"Sam, why don't you go on down to the darkroom? Tom will be there in a minute." She laid a restraining hand on Tom's arm and waited to speak until Sam was inside. "I need your help."

"How's that?"

"Damon."

Tom let out an exasperated sigh. "Trouble?"

"I'm afraid so. Keri and Angie said he isn't coming back. I'm worried for two reasons. First, the girls indicated he's up to no good. Second, Sam seems to have developed quite an attachment to him. One thing that young man doesn't need is further rejection."

"And what exactly do you propose I do about it?"

"Find Damon. Talk to him."

Tom hooted. "Me? I'm the guy who can't even communicate with his own kids."

"Will it hurt to try?"

He stood there frowning for a minute, seemingly at war with himself. Then he shook his head helplessly. "Jeez, lady. The things I'm willing to do for you. I'll go work a while with Sam, then I'll set out. Damned if I know where to look."

No way could she stifle a chuckle. "Given what I hear of your checkered past in Riverbend, I'll bet you know *exactly* where to look."

He put an arm around her. "Well, since you put it that way, perhaps I do have a few leads."

She smiled up at him. "Thanks, Tom. I—"

The front door opened and Keri Mellon stood observing them. "Rev, what're you doin' out here with the party Gestapo?"

Lynn nearly choked. "The party Gestapo?"

"If you'll excuse me, I have something developing in the darkroom," Tom said, beating a hasty exit.

"Yeah, he busted us." Keri studied Tom as he brushed past on his way into the house, then turned back to Lynn. "You know what? He was putting the moves on you just now." Before Lynn could pick her chin off her chest, the girl went on. "He's not my type, of course, but for somebody older like you, he could be okay, I guess.''

Lynn composed herself, hoping her blush wasn't visible in the dark. ''Are you ready to show me the newsletter?''

''Anytime.'' Keri stood aside to let Lynn pass through the door. Then, for the first time, the girl smiled, adding quietly, ''Maybe he's even more than okay.''

AFTER HELPING SAM develop his picture of two boys playing hoops at a playground, Tom sent him upstairs. He lingered in the darkroom fingering the edges of a photograph of Damon's he'd just printed. The remarkable picture depicted one of his long-haired buddies playing a guitar. The use of light and shadow forced the eye to the guitar. The grace and power in the long fingers poised on the strings drew the viewer's attention from the hard, cynical features of the performer. The photo made a statement: Even a streetwise, alienated youth can find solace and meaning in music. Damn. How could Damon drop out of this program? He had such talent.

Tom flipped off the darkroom light and, as an afterthought, tucked the photo under his arm. Where the hell was he supposed to find the kid, and if and when he did, what was he supposed to say to him?

Although he knew it was fruitless, he started by driving to Damon's home, if you could call it that. A garage apartment with rickety wooden stairs in a neighborhood whose best times had occurred long before the Great Depression. The place was dark, and his vigorous knocking on the scarred door produced no response. From there he tried the neighborhood pool hall, a used-car lot where gangs of kids often hung out and finally the park alongside the river. Nothing. He turned the truck around and started back through the now-deserted downtown. Out of the corner of his eye, a flicker of light caught his attention. The flare of a cigarette from the alley behind the Sunnyside Café.

It was worth a try. He parked a little farther down the street and started back up the sidewalk. As he approached the alley, he could hear two voices, one louder than the other. "*'Scuse* me? You think *that*'ll buy you a score? Not tonight, dude. This is high-grade stuff."

"I'm not made of money, you know," Tom heard Damon say.

"I've got a news flash for you, sonny. I don't take no charity cases."

Tom stepped into the entrance of the alley, wondering belatedly if the pusher was armed. "Damon," he called forcefully. "What's going on here?"

At the sound of his voice, the guy who was obviously a dealer turned and ran out the other end of the alley. Propelled by the adrenaline pulsing through his system, Tom raced toward Damon, who had hesitated a beat before trying to run away himself. What in hell was the kid into? He outran Damon and, grabbing him by the arm, whipped him around so that they were eye to eye. "You got mush for brains or what?"

"Get your friggin' hands off me!"

The boy twisted away, but was no match for Tom's iron grip. "You're not going anywhere until we have a little talk."

Damon's cold, implacable eyes fixed on Tom. "I'll yell for the cops. Tell 'em you're molesting me."

"Go ahead." Tom stared back. "That'll save me the trouble of notifying them myself about your failed transaction. They'll watch you like a hawk from now on."

There was a brief flicker of fear in Damon's eyes. "So what's new?" Tom had to hand it to the kid. He wasn't backing down. "I don't know what's with you, man, but you're a pain in the ass. Leave me alone. My life's none of your damn business."

"You're the one who's the pain in the ass. And, believe me, I'm sorely tempted to leave you alone, but I'm not going to. You know why?"

Damon didn't blink, nor did he answer.

"Because, besides the fact that you're determined to ruin your life before you even hit eighteen, you're one damned talented guy, and I have a peculiar aversion to seeing talent go to waste. So that makes your life my business." Still holding Damon by the arm, he turned him around and propelled him toward the street. "I want you to see something. And if, after you do, you still want to smoke and snort your brains out, that's your decision."

Although the teen kept trying to jerk away, Tom marched him resolutely toward the pickup. For Lynn as much as for the kid, he'd give this his best shot. After that, he was through. Let someone else do the saving. When they reached the vehicle, Tom swung open the door and jerked his head at Damon. "Get in."

"You gonna make me?"

"If I have to." Apparently something in Tom's tone of voice or stance proved persuasive because, with an insolent smirk, Damon climbed into the passenger seat. Tom kept his eyes on the youngster as he rounded the pickup, then opened the door and took his place behind the wheel. He picked the photograph off the dash and handed it to Damon. "Hold that while we go for a short ride. What I want you to see is at my house. When we're finished, I'll take you home."

Hostility emanated from the boy, and neither of them said a word until Tom pulled to a screeching halt at the farmhouse. "This'll only take a few minutes. If you're as smart as I think you are, it may change your life. C'mon." He didn't give the boy a chance to argue, but started toward the house.

Behind him, he heard the passenger door open and close. When Tom reached the front door, he turned and studied Damon, who had stopped on the bottom porch step, the photo clutched in his hand. The boy scowled at him. "What are you up to anyway?"

"Judge for yourself," Tom said, opening the door and holding it wide for Damon. "Ever hear of Gordy Maxwell?"

The boy didn't move. "No."

"How about Gordon Parks? Ansel Adams?"

"They were photographers."

"Bingo." Tom turned on an interior light. "If you like photography, I've got a real treat for you."

With a sideways glance, Tom took in the boy's indecision, the genuine temptation he'd placed before him. Maybe there was a glimmer of hope, after all. He moved briskly toward the bookshelves in the living room, laying his hands immediately on the volume he wanted. Once again he heard footsteps behind him. Damon had made it as far as the entry hall.

Tom laid *Collected Photos of Gordon Maxwell* on the library table and switched on the table lamp. Damon edged closer. "Take your time. Look all you want while I get us a couple of sodas." Tom left the room, mentally crossing his fingers.

Tom breathed a sigh of relief when he returned with the drinks. Damon had pulled a chair over to the table, set aside the print and was slowly turning the pages, examining each photograph intently, seemingly oblivious to Tom's presence. He waited, drinks in hand, until Damon reached the final page, then started across the room. "What do you think?" He set Damon's soda on a coaster.

Damon looked up, his usual sneer gone. "Awesome," he said.

The word, not just the throwaway teenage comment, but a heartfelt reaction, required no response. Tom dragged a straight chair to the table, straddled it and draped his arms over the back. Damon had turned to the beginning of the book and was starting back through the pages. "I agree. Awesome."

"This guy signed your book. Do you know him?"

"Yeah, I knew him." Tom struggled to keep his tone neutral. "We worked together for eight years."

Damon flipped back his dark mane of hair, leaving his face exposed. "What happened to him?"

Tom took a swig of his soda and swallowed slowly. "He was killed in a bomb blast."

"Oh."

"At thirty-two. Too young."

"Yeah," Damon muttered, then continued turning pages. At last he reached the photo Tom was waiting for. "Hold it." Tom laid his hand in the middle of the page. When he withdrew it, there was Gordy's picture of the tank commander standing in the turret of the metal monster. A human being encased by heavy armor, a modern warrior invincible in his steel skin. Until you looked into the soldier's face. Again Gordy had managed just the right angle. In the officer's expression was courage, but also a vulnerability, a fear, that rendered the portrait haunting.

"Now," Tom said softly, "give me your photograph." Damon looked up, puzzled. When he carefully handed over the print of the guitar player, Tom placed it beside Gordy's photo of the tank commander. He paused to allow Damon time to see what he saw. "Gordy was killed before he had a chance to live up to his full potential. Why are you trying to kill yourself before you even begin to live up to yours?"

The only sound was the hum of the refrigerator. Tom waited. Damon swallowed. "What do you mean?" he finally asked.

Tom scooted his chair closer and dared to put an arm around the boy's shoulders. "Don't you see it?"

"What?"

"You could be every bit as good a photographer as Gordy was."

The boy shrugged, as if loath to admit the possibility.

Tom pointed to the pictures. "See the similarities? You have the same concern for light and shadow, the same commitment to bringing out the soul of a subject."

"You think?" Tom heard the suppressed longing in Damon's voice.

"With training and experience, you could be as good a photographer as he was. But there's an even more important question."

"What?" Damon was moving his finger over Gordy's photo, tracing the lines of the tank.

"Can you be half the man he was?" Tom stood up and moved the chair back to its normal position. Damon remained motionless. Tom hoped he'd gotten his attention. "I'm going to answer that question for you. Not unless you decide to make something of yourself. Gordy didn't have a bed of roses as a kid, either, so you can't use that as an excuse. But that's a story for another day. Bottom line, you've got talent. Loads of it. Now you can either piss it down the drain or you can do something with it. Booze and drugs aren't part of that picture, understand? So you've got a decision to make." He leaned over and flipped off the table lamp. "C'mon. I'm taking you home."

Damon stood up, his face obscured by his hair, one finger still trailing over the cover of Gordy's book.

It was probably an impulsive thing to do, but Tom couldn't stop himself. "Would you like to borrow the book for a few days?"

Damon looked up, the rigid set of his face momentarily betrayed by hunger. "You wouldn't mind?"

"Not if you bring it back when you come to Meacham House next time." Tom watched the boy struggle with his thoughts. "And you will come, right?"

Damon picked up the book, inserted his own picture between the covers and finally looked evenly into Tom's eyes. "Yeah. I'll come."

LYNN HAD JUST CRAWLED into bed when the telephone rang. She glanced at the clock. After eleven. In her business, it was rarely good news at this time of night. As always, her heart thudded as she picked up the phone. She took a deep breath to relax before she said hello.

"Hi, it's me." Hearing Tom's calm voice, she exhaled and settled back against the pillows. "I thought you might want the Damon report."

"I do. Please tell me it's good news."

"Okay, then. It's good news. But it still won't hurt to cross our fingers or, in your case, send up a prayer or two."

"I'm already doing that," she murmured.

"Figured you might be." Then he launched into the story of his evening with Damon and concluded by saying, "So photography is the motivating force."

"I think there's more to it."

"Like what?" Tom sounded puzzled.

"Like attention from a man who won't let him off the hook and who believes in him."

"Wait a minute." She could hear the oh-no-not-me in his voice. "This was a one-time deal."

"Not if you really want to rehabilitate the young man." She scooted to a sitting position. "You're the key, Tom. He desperately needs you to monitor him, to help him restore his self-esteem."

"All this because I lent Meacham House a camera?"

"Just another example of God's mysterious ways," she said innocently.

"Easy for you to say." She could almost see the frustrated frown on his face.

She smiled. "Yes, it is."

"I've got my own responsibilities. The kids arrive Friday night."

"You said Damon would come back Monday evening."

"Yes."

"Without you there?"

His silence signaled big-time hedging. Finally he answered. ''Probably not.''

''In that case, we'll all look forward to meeting Pete and Libby then.''

''What if they won't come?''

''There's only one reason they won't.''

''What's that?''

''If you give them an out.'' She wondered if she should go on and finally decided to risk it. ''They're looking for direction from you, Tom. Remember, you're the parent. They're the kids.''

''I haven't had much practice with that.''

''Then it's time to start.''

''You don't give a man much wiggle room.''

''Not about this, I don't. But on some other things...''

His voice dropped. ''Yeah, I know. You might wait a long time. I wish—''

''Shh. I'll take my chances.''

''You're something else, you know that?''

''Thank you. But be on your guard. I'm holding out for 'happily ever after.'''

''You drive a hard bargain.'' The need in his voice, so clearly echoing her own, sent a shimmer of warmth through her.

''We're worth it,'' she whispered before saying good-night and gently replacing the receiver.

She lay back down, pulling the blanket around her bare shoulders and plumping her pillow just so. Her body told her she needed him now, her head reasoned it wasn't time, and her heart promised that somehow, someday, they would be together.

Benedict, as if sensing her aloneness, padded into

the room, leaped onto the bed and curled up by her head. "Ben, I wish you could help me. I said I'd be patient. But it's not easy." The cat purred as if in sympathy. "Not when I want him so much."

CHAPTER TEN

PETE KICKED a puke-green hedge apple ahead of him down the dirt lane. He had to get out of that stuffy old farmhouse, away from his jerk of a father whose idea of entertainment was to shoot clay pigeons and fish in that yucky river. His friends at Weymouth Prep would bust a gut laughing if they could've seen him out there in that stupid cornfield target-shooting. His dad had acted like it was some big-deal father-son thing to handle guns. The whole time they were out there, he was missing the World Tennis Association match on TV.

And dumb Libby had acted as if she'd been given special status or something. A girl asked to shoot. She'd looked like a klutz trying to shoulder the heavy gun. Worse, now she was complaining about a bruised shoulder. Well, duh. If she'd have done what their father told them to, she wouldn't have a problem. That was just like her, thinking she knew stuff she didn't.

Spotting a pair of large blackbirds ahead of him, he sent the hedge apple flying toward them, dispersing them amid a grating series of cackles. Corn, cows and crows. Man, this was the middle of nowhere.

Only two good things so far. The warm oatmeal cookies Dorrie had brought them and the visit to his father's aunts, Rachel and Ruth. At first he hadn't wanted to visit the two old ladies. He'd met them before the one other time he'd been in Riverbend. But he was a little kid then and couldn't remember much about them, except that one of them smelled like gingerbread. He forgot which.

So he'd been surprised when the plump one made him laugh and took him into the bookstore, even though it was closed for Sunday, and let him pick out any two books he wanted. He'd gotten one with all these pictures of tennis stars and then a sci-fi adventure by his favorite author.

Damn. Those retarded crows had landed again right in his path. Again he kicked the hedge apple at them, and again their outraged squawking erupted.

Oh, one other good thing. Today was Monday and he wasn't in school. He could picture his classmates bent over their smelly biology-lab stations, hear them in French class repeating parrotlike those artsy-fartsy phrases like "*Je m'appelle Pierre*," and falling asleep after lunch while old man Hazelhorst droned on about supply-and-demand.

He reached the end of the lane and looked up and down the country road. One tractor going about negative-five miles an hour. That was it.

Reluctantly he turned around and headed for the house. Tonight would be the worst. His father had made a big deal out of telling them about the Mitchum House, whatever it was. He was supposed to be excited about meeting some other kids. Retards, prob'ly, if they lived in this place. Besides, he couldn't picture it. His father with a bunch of teenagers?

He felt a tightening in his stomach. Why would his dad be interested in going there? He hardly had time to come visit him and Libby in Chicago. It made him mad just thinking about it.

He stopped, staring down the road with disgust. This time he picked up the hedge apple and flung it with everything he had at those creepy birds.

IF SHE HADN'T SEEN IT with her own eyes, Lynn wouldn't have believed it. Ruth and Rachel Steele huddled at the dining-room table at Meacham House surrounded by several teenagers who defined the word *grunge.* Neither of the women seemed remotely perturbed by the purple fingernails, pierced lips and noses and weird hair. Keri scooted her chair closer and watched over Ruth's shoulder as she flipped the black pages of a photo album.

"This is the old high school." Ruth pointed to a black-and-white photograph.

"Whaddaya mean 'old high school'? You're telling me our rattrap of a school is new?" A skinny boy with a pimply face and head shaved but for the ponytail popping out of his crown, looked at his peers for approval. One snickered, but several of the girls had the grace to look embarrassed.

"It's all relative, I suppose," Ruth said. "It seems like yesterday we graduated from Old Main—" she gestured at the photo "—but to you it must seem like ancient history."

"What happened to the old school?" one of the girls asked.

Ruth shook her head sadly. "Burned to the ground right after we graduated."

"Good riddance," a surly-looking, heavily made-up girl with orange hair muttered.

"Now, you don't mean that." Ruth adopted a serious tone. "Education is very important."

The girl rolled her eyes. "It's boring."

"Let's see what we can do about that," Rachel suggested. "Why don't you bring some of your assignments and let Ruthie and me help you? Maybe it's boring because you don't feel very successful."

"Yeah, Kala," one of the boys taunted. "Those D's ain't gonna get you on no honor roll."

"Tell you what," Ruth intervened. "Sister and I will spend forty-five minutes helping you each Monday and Wednesday night, and then for fifteen minutes we'll tell you some of the secrets of Riverbend."

"Oh, right," the orange-haired girl said, tossing her head dramatically. "Like there're so many."

Unperturbed by her skepticism, Ruth went on, "So you don't want to know how the school burned down?"

There was silence. The fellow with the ponytail seemed to be considering. "Forty-five minutes? That's all?"

"That's all," Rachel echoed.

He looked around at the others. "What else have we got to do? Hey, it'd be worth it to see Fleerbaum's face if we all passed one of her tests."

Lynn chuckled when Rachel threw her twin a triumphant look over the rims of her glasses. One of Lynn's hopes when she had suggested the program was that it would become intergenerational. Thanks to the Steeles, she hadn't had long to wait.

Speaking of waiting, Lynn glanced nervously at the door. Damon had already been upstairs twice ostensibly to get something to drink. The first time he'd sauntered to the front window and had stood for several minutes sipping a root beer and gazing at the sidewalk. The next time he'd sidled up next to her, his hands hidden in his baggy trousers' pockets. "Tom coming?" She'd told him as far as she knew he was, but from Damon's increasingly nervous mannerisms, she had the uneasy sense he was ready to cut and run. And even if—*when*—Tom came, he'd have Pete and Libby with him. It was anybody's guess how Damon would react.

Even though she usually left the chore to the kids, Lynn walked around picking up empty plates and soda cans. She shared Damon's edginess. She had no idea what to expect from Tom's children. He'd called late Sunday night fit to be tied. With the possible exception of a visit to Ruth and Rachel's, nothing he'd done to make them feel at home had succeeded. He said it was as if they were determined not to like anything. Knowing it would be cold comfort to tell him these things take time, Lynn kept silent.

Besides, the more she'd pondered the situation, the clearer it became that a large part of what was going on with Tom was tied to belated desire to connect with his kids. Even though she recognized that step as a significant one in his healing, there was a personally important aspect. She'd finally been able to admit it would be difficult, if not impossible, to commit to a relationship until and unless he could resolve his family issues. Because she desperately wanted a family. Including children of her own. She suspected, however, he wouldn't be ready to consider having another child until he'd made peace with Pete and Libby. If then.

She put a stack of plates into the sink and ran water over them, aware of a heaviness in her heart. What had started as a heaven-sent attraction now involved burdensome baggage. She closed her eyes briefly, inhaling the steam from the hot water. "Please, God, help us find our way," she intoned under her breath, before wiping her hands, arranging her facial features into a pleasant expression and returning to the living room where, just inside the front door, stood a harried-looking Tom, a teenage boy with a shock of dark hair, ruddy cheeks and a sullen look, and a slightly built, auburn-haired girl who seemed to have gathered herself into a taut, expressionless stick figure.

Lynn crossed the room saying, "Welcome to Meacham House. You must be Pete and Libby." Even to herself her greeting sounded falsely cheery.

Tom stepped forward, pressing a palm into his son's back. "Pete, this is Lynn Kendall, the minister I told you about."

The boy gave her a swift appraisal, but mumbled only, "Hi."

"And this is Libby." He sent his daughter a smile of encouragement.

"Nice to meet you," she dutifully replied, her braces causing an unnatural thickness in her words.

Lynn swept her arm expansively toward the others. "Please come join us."

Pete glowered at his father. "I can hardly wait," he muttered.

Rachel saved the day, shoving away from the dining-room table and coming to greet her great-niece and -nephew. She put an arm around each of the children. "Nice to see you both again." She ushered them toward the group of teens. "You might enjoy meeting my friends."

"Friends?" Libby, peering at the group around the table, sounded incredulous. "Those freaks?" she whispered.

Lynn detected Tom's fleeting wince.

Pete said nothing, but over his shoulder sent his father a look of total incredulity.

"Oh, God," Lynn heard Tom groan beside her. "I knew this was a mistake."

Lynn had to admit that the two squeaky-clean Baineses, with their clear skin, designer-label clothes and salon haircuts stuck out here like hothouse orchids in a dandelion patch. She reassured herself that kids are kids and that once they got past appearances, miracles could happen. And looking at Tom's face, they could do with one right now.

But once again she was forcefully reminded that God's timing was not hers, because just then, Sam and Damon emerged from the basement. Damon walked straight to Tom and balanced menacingly on the balls of his feet directly in front of his mentor. "Hey, where ya been? Or was all that talk the other night just so much bull?"

"I don't deal in bull." Tom stared intently at the boy. "What have you been working on tonight?"

"Sam and me was waiting for you."

"It's time to begin counting on yourself."

Damon emitted a lifeless chuckle. "Like whaddaya think I been doin' all my life?"

"With the photography. Trust your instincts. I'll help along the way, but you know enough to go ahead without me."

"Yeah?" There was a catch in Damon's voice.

"Yeah." Understanding seemed to pass between the two. From the dining room Lynn observed Pete scowling at his father.

Sam tugged at Tom's sleeve. "What about me?"

"You follow Damon's instructions. He's in charge."

Something about the words *in charge* caused Damon to straighten imperceptibly. "Okay, kid, c'mon."

"I'll check on you later," Tom said as the pair headed for the basement door.

"It's all your fault," Tom said under his breath to Lynn as he linked his fingers with hers and hid their clasped hands in the folds of her skirt.

"*Genus teenageri?*"

"Getting me into this mess."

"But judging from your intervention with Damon, you're pretty effective."

"Hah!" He nodded over her head to the dining room where Pete had refused to sit, and just stood, his arms crossed, looking down his nose at the group, and where Libby was noticeably cringing from proximity to the ring-nosed Keri.

Lynn attempted to inject a note of levity. "You know what they say. 'A prophet is without honor in his own country.'"

Tom shook his head wearily. "This is a disaster."

Lynn squeezed his fingers. "I'll grant you it looks that way now." She disengaged from his grasp, glancing toward the dining room where Ruth and Rachel were putting on their coats. "Let me see what I can do. Meanwhile, your aunts are about ready to leave. Why don't you walk them home? I can guarantee Pete and Libby aren't going to give you the satisfaction of letting you see them enjoying this place. Your best bet is to keep a low profile."

He looked so hopeless it was all she could do not to give him a hug right there in front of everyone, including his own kids. She nudged him toward the dining room and, taking a deep breath, watched as he offered himself as an escort.

Distaste written all over him, Pete avoided his father, returning to the living room where he flopped into a beanbag chair and picked up the TV remote. He looked up at Lynn. "This thing work?"

"Yes. But we only turn on the television if everyone in the room agrees."

"Yeah, so? It's just you and me."

"The others are saying goodbye to the Steele sisters. They'll be coming in here. Then you can check with them."

His lip curled. "What do we do? Vote?"

"If necessary."

Pete flipped on a baseball game. "If they want to change the channel, they'll have to make me."

"Who is it you're trying to punish here?"

He looked up, his pupils hard as buckeyes. "What's that supposed to mean?"

"What did these kids ever do to you?"

He shrugged. "Nothing. Yet."

"Isn't it your dad you're upset with?"

"Him?" He nodded at his father who was taking the aunts by the arm and assisting them onto the front porch. "He's no big deal."

"That's where you may be wrong, Pete. I think he's a very big deal to you." She crossed her fingers and went on gamely. "And I know you're a big deal to him."

Pete, fiddling with the remote, avoided looking at her. "Right. I'm such a big deal he forced me to come to this stupid place against my will."

Lynn sensed he'd had enough. "Well, since you're here, would you like something to eat?"

"Got any chips?"

"Sure, I'll get them." She knew he wouldn't relinquish his control of the remote to secure the food himself. When the others joined him, maybe he'd relax a bit. Give the Meacham House kids a chance. She was down to small miracles.

On her way to the kitchen, she noticed that Keri Mellon had somehow broken through Libby's reserve, and the two were chatting about the boys at Libby's school. It was a start.

TOM PUT AN AUNT on each side of him and started slowly up the street. Lynn's suggestion had given him a welcome reprieve. Inside, he hadn't known what the hell to do with himself, with his kids, with Damon, with anybody! He had the sick sensation that bringing Pete and Libby there had muddied the waters even more.

"There is no need to escort us," Ruth said. "Nobody's foolhardy enough to attack the Steele sisters at this late date in our lives."

"Or desperate enough." Rachel chuckled.

"I know there's no need, but I'm enjoying your company."

Ruth winked knowingly at Rachel. "Oho, I do believe our nephew wants something."

Tom spread his hands innocently. "Are you accusing me of ulterior motives?"

Rachel nodded emphatically. "Definitely. After all, deviousness runs in the family, doesn't it, Ruthie?"

After a long silence in which he sensed his aunts waiting, Tom explained his dilemma. "I'm glad the kids are here, but—"

"You're scared to death." Ruth matter-of-factly completed his thought.

"Why wouldn't I be? I've never been a candidate for Father of the Year, and they've as much as told me they'd rather be anyplace else."

"Poor babies," Ruth said with an unsympathetic look on her face. "They may have to do something they don't want to do."

"That's the trouble with teenagers today," Rachel added. "They think they control their parents."

"How can I control them if they'll hardly speak to me?"

Ruth laced her hand through his arm. "Why do you think that is?"

"They don't like me."

"Nonsense," Ruth said.

On his other side Rachel linked her arm through his, too. "For starters, show them you care. Don't let them get away with murder."

"Set boundaries," Ruth said.

"Unplug the television," Rachel added.

Tom could hear the strain in his voice when he said, "And then what?"

"Spend time with them," the twins said in unison.

"Doing what?"

Ruth squeezed his arm. "For a grown man, you are incredibly dense."

"What have you done so far?" Rachel asked.

"We went fishing in the river, did some shooting. Believe it or not, Libby liked it better than Pete."

Ruth harrumphed. "That's not so surprising. Libby liked doing something special with you, but Pete is determined not to let you win him over."

"That's encouraging." Tom was more bewildered

than ever. "I compounded my mistakes by bringing them tonight."

"That wasn't a mistake," Rachel said.

"You saw them. They hated it. They have nothing in common with those kids."

"You're judging by appearances," Ruth said.

Tom felt himself getting hot under the collar. He should've known better than to seek their advice. The aunts were too old to have a bead on today's teens. "Hell, yes, I am."

"Then you're a fool." Ruth stopped in front of the bookstore. "Those young people all have more in common than you could guess from the surface. They want to feel good about themselves, to be approved..." She paused, then looked up at him. "To be loved."

Beside him, he heard Rachel sigh. Very quietly she added, "Not so different from you, Tom dear."

Simultaneously, as if they'd communicated their intention by telepathy, they each stood on tiptoe, kissed him on the cheek, then turned toward the house. He watched as they unlocked the door and disappeared inside.

Maybe it was easier to see the big picture when you didn't have any children of your own. Or maybe they didn't have the answers, any more than he did.

But they were right about one thing—he needed to be loved. Why did he find it so damned difficult to admit? And Lynn was standing in the wings, waiting for him to accept her love. He plunged his hands into his pockets, kicked at a pebble and headed back toward Meacham House.

But he was waiting for something more. He was waiting to feel worthy of her.

WHEN HE RETURNED, Tom nearly tripped over Keri, Angie and a boy who looked somehow familiar—all sprawled on the living-room floor, drawing on a huge square of orange cloth. As he studied the kid, a light-bulb went on. "Say," he addressed the teenager, "didn't I see you and Charlie Callahan the other day in Sterling Hardware?"

The boy shrugged. "Prob'ly. I'm Nathan Turner. Charlie's kinda my adopted dad."

Tom had heard how Charlie had taken the young-ster under his wing. "Lucky you. I've known Charlie ever since we were kids. He's one of the best."

The boy smiled shyly. "Yeah, he is."

Tom noticed Libby sitting cross-legged nearby stuff-ing batting into a narrow green cloth sack that looked somewhat like a stem. Pete was nowhere to be seen. Nor Lynn. Apparently she'd already left. Maybe she'd had a call to make. Tom surveyed their work. "What's going on here?"

Keri looked up long enough to say, "We're making Halloween decorations for the retirement center."

"So what's that?" he asked pointing at the cloth.

Libby threw him a long-suffering look. "Dad, it's obvious. It's a pumpkin."

Maybe, but they had a long way to go. Retirement center, huh? That was a picture he could hardly imag-ine—these kids and octogenarians!

Molly, carrying a large piece of white poster board, sailed into the room. "Anybody game to draw a ghost?"

Nathan stood up and relieved her of the poster board. "Casper, here I come."

Tom gestured toward the slowly emerging pump-kin. "Is it that time of year already?"

Molly's eyes twinkled. "Once October comes, it's soon enough for me. Halloween is one of my favorite holidays. How about you?"

Tom's chest felt hollow. "I never had much experience with it. We were almost always overseas."

"We'll fix that, right, kids?" She continued talking as she hunkered down between Keri and Angie and studied their progress. "Meacham House is throwing a party at Golden Fields. Halloween is always such a big deal in Riverbend that this coming Friday was the only weekend night the social director could work us in. I know it's early in the month, but we're having no trouble getting into the spirit. You and your children will be coming, won't you? In fact," she rattled on, "I could use another driver. Can I count on you?"

The three of them—Pete, Libby and him—at a Halloween party for senior citizens? But it was something to do, and at this point he was clutching at straws. "Sure."

"Don't forget to wear a costume."

He stuck his little finger in his ear and jiggled it. "Say what?"

Molly's grin was downright mischievous. "We're all wearing costumes, chaperons included."

Libby looked up with an innocent smile. "Yeah, Dad. You could be the Grinch."

"Gee, thanks." He hopscotched across the room to avoid stepping on the materials. "Seen Pete?"

"I think he went downstairs," Libby said, turning back to her task.

Under the supervision of one of the sponsors, several youngsters with guitars were practicing riffs in the rec room. Pete slouched against the wall, watching them intently. Tom stood quietly in the door observing his son. His dark, short-cropped hair, lean, well-toned build and air of indifference were a far cry from the curly-haired, eager youngster who used to greet him enthusiastically when he returned from overseas assignments. Tom's eyes narrowed. The hell of it was that, sadly, he recognized in his son that same defensive attitude of worldly ennui that had characterized himself as a teen. An unexpected surge of love caught Tom by surprise. Along with an overwhelming feeling of helplessness.

Finally, before Pete spotted him, he turned and knocked on the darkroom door. Damon let him in. Hanging on the wall were several prints of the guitar player, all the same exposure, but each revealing minute variations in the developing or cropping process.

Damon slumped against the wall, his hair obscuring his face. Sam bounced excitedly beside him. "Which one, Tom? Which one's best?"

Tom slowly examined each print. Each had its particular subtleties, and all of them were good. Very good. At the conclusion of his inspection, he stood back and took in the entire display. "It's hard to say."

Sam tugged at his sleeve. "I can't hear you."

Tom turned the boy so he could face both youngsters when he spoke. Sam moved closer to Damon, almost protectively, as if he feared Tom's judgment. "They're all fine in their own way, but I prefer the one where the contrast between the fingers and strings is clearest. It has a lot to say about the way music is made."

Sam hung his head. "I wish—"

Damon punched him lightly and mouthed, "Speak up, kid. Can't hear you."

The next words, high-pitched and uncontrolled,

filled the tiny room. "I wish I knew how music is made. But I can't hear it!"

Damon raked a hand through his long hair, as if he'd never contemplated such a deprivation. "Man—" he exhaled audibly "—I never thought about that. That's tough."

Tom knelt in front of Sam. "Damon's right. That *is* tough. But there are lots of things you can do. Didn't you play basketball this summer?"

"Yes." Sam's eyes filled with tears. "But I couldn't hear the whistle. Coach had to stay right with me."

"Forget it, runt," Damon said. "Sports are for dumb jocks."

"Whoa, fellas." Tom struggled to find the right words. "Sports aren't for everyone any more than music or photography are. The important thing is to find something that you do well and that gives you satisfaction. Your passion." *Like writing.* Out of nowhere the thought burst into his consciousness. A truth he hadn't stopped to examine. Not recently.

"Like what?" Sam challenged.

Tom remembered a comment Mitch had made during their golf round. "Don't you like to draw?"

"Yes."

"And you like photography, right?"

"Yes."

"Have you ever thought about being an artist?"

Sam bit his lip. "Do you think I could?"

"Sure, if you want it badly enough."

As Tom stood up, Damon caught his eye with a look that seemed to say, "I hear you, too."

THIS WAS THE BEST PLACE in this whole crappy teen center, Pete thought as he listened to the CD the guitar dude was playing to demonstrate some musical stuff. He liked the mellow sounds of the music and the way the guy didn't talk down to them the way so many adults did. Some of what the man had said he'd never considered before. He'd just taken the music for granted, never really thought about what went into it. Man, he'd sure been wrong. Maybe he could get his dad to buy him a guitar. He owed him something for making him spend ten days in Riverbend. Yeah, a guitar.

Where was his dad, anyway? He'd just dumped him and Libby the minute they'd come in the door. It couldn't take those old ladies *that* long to walk home. While he'd been waiting, he'd heard some of the kids call his dad Tom, like he was a regular guy, not a pain-in-the-ass parent. Go figure.

Several of the girls had wandered into the rec room and now sat on the floor grooving to the CD. He eyed the one in the tight black T-shirt appreciatively. She had hooters that almost made him forget Polly. Quite a sight as long as you didn't look at her ears—they had enough metal poked through them to activate an airport detector.

He felt weird. He was the one with the stylish threads, the one with the money, the cool one, for cripe's sake, so why did they all look at him like he was the alien? Well, screw 'em. He didn't care. He'd be back home soon where he could forget all about this bizarre—yeah, there was another of those PSAT words—chapter in his life.

The music stopped and the kids stood up, some of them milling around the instructor asking questions and crap like that. Where the hell was his father?

Surely it was time to leave. Maybe he'd gotten too tied up with some loser who called him "Tom."

Finally, at the other end of the basement a door opened and he saw his dad emerging, one arm around the shoulders of a kid of maybe ten or eleven and another arm around a guy who looked kinda like that rocker dude Tommy Lee. A sour taste rose in Pete's throat, a taste like after you heave up your guts.

"Hey," Pete called. The group was heading toward the stairs. Maybe with all the conversation swirling around, his dad hadn't heard him. He shoved some girls aside and got closer. "Where've you been?"

The long-haired dude must've heard him, because he shot him one of those looks that don't need a genius to interpret. *Who the hell are you?* it said.

"Dad?" Finally his father must've heard because all three stopped and turned around. "Where you been?" he repeated.

"In the darkroom."

"With *them?*" Pete couldn't seem to help himself. His famous father, who had never given him the time of day, had holed up with these misfits?

"What's wrong with us?" the long-haired dude said, stepping forward.

"Look at you." Pete pointed to the boy, then back to the long-haired creep. "You're a coupla weirdo retards."

Before he had time to process the shocked expression on his father's face or hear the howl rising from the onlookers, he felt first a blinding pain near his eye, then his nose exploded in blood and snot and he found himself on the floor, looking dizzily at the blurred distorted image of Tommy Lee.

CHAPTER ELEVEN

LILY MAZERIK'S FATHER, Julian Bennett, had been the doctor on call at the hospital when they'd arrived and had recommended keeping Pete in the hospital overnight where the staff could check on him and monitor his pain medication. A concussion and blowout fracture of the orbit, Dr. Bennett had said. After the CT scan and X rays, Tom had been weak-kneed with relief to learn there appeared to be no bleeding into the brain. Pete wouldn't be playing any tennis matches in the next few days, but he was lucky. It could've been much worse.

Looking at his son from the foot of the bed in the light of day, Tom was hard-pressed to recall the handsome face he'd studied in the rec room only hours before. The bruised cheeks, puffy eyes, bandaged nose and pale skin bore testimony to the force of Damon's outrage.

Where did they go from here? All of Pete's pent-up hostility had found a target—Sam and Damon. Hell, who could blame Damon for retaliating? Particularly considering the conversation they'd just had in the darkroom about Sam's impairment. Thank God for Molly. She'd gotten the other kids to go, then driven Sam and Damon home.

Libby had sat in the car, scrunched against the door, not saying a word, while he drove to the hospital.

There had been no way to tell what she was thinking. Nor had she been any more communicative this morning when he'd dropped her off at Ruth and Rachel's. How many more ways could he botch this visit?

A nurse bustled into the room, affixed the blood-pressure cuff and took Pete's vital signs. At her touch, he groaned.

Tom cleared his throat. "How's he doing?"

"Resting comfortably. But he isn't going to feel very well when he wakes up." She smiled reassuringly. "What did the other guy look like?" she asked teasingly.

It hadn't been that sort of fight, Tom thought. Damon had been justified—there'd been no excuse for Pete's insult—and Pete had been in no condition to hit back. Lately he'd been moody as hell and had made no secret of his unwillingness even to try to fit in here. But Tom had never thought his son was bigoted. Pete stirred in his sleep, flinging one arm across his chest. While Tom had had his back turned traipsing all over the globe, had his son turned into a bad kid? Was his hostility that deep-seated?

The nurse paused in the doorway, her ministrations completed. "Can I bring you anything?"

"Thanks, no. I'll get some coffee in the cafeteria later."

Morning sun streamed through the vertical blinds, and Tom stepped to the window to adjust for the glare falling on Pete's face. Leaning against the window ledge, he folded his arms across his chest and continued studying his son. What should he say to him when he woke up? On the one hand he was furious with him, but on a deeper level his heart was in splinters.

He had only himself to blame. He had not been there to help shape his son into a man. Was it too late?

A shadow fell across the entrance to the room. He looked up to see Lynn standing tentatively in the doorway. "May I come in?"

He didn't know when he'd heard more welcome words. When she shut the door behind her, he crossed the room and pulled her into his arms. "I'm glad you're here," he breathed into her hair.

For several seconds neither of them moved, and almost as a physical sensation, he felt himself drawing strength and calm from her embrace. Finally she whispered, "I'm sorry I wasn't there last night."

"You couldn't have prevented what happened." That was the sorry truth. There wasn't anything anybody could have done. Except him. A long time ago.

Gradually she extricated herself from his arms, then walked to Pete's bedside. "How is he?" she asked, laying a hand over the boy's and looking at him with such love and concern that Tom felt his insides turn upside down.

He swallowed the stone in his throat. "His body will heal."

She smoothed Pete's hair off his forehead with her other hand. It struck him that he himself hadn't touched his son even once. "And the rest of him?"

He shrugged. "I don't know."

She paused, one hand on Pete's forehead, one still clasping his fingers, and closed her eyes. The only sound in the room was the gentle exhalation of his son's breathing. In the hall Tom could hear the clatter and conversation that signaled morning hospital rounds. Lynn, however, seemed totally oblivious, deep into whatever she was doing. Praying, he supposed. Well, it couldn't hurt.

When she opened her eyes, it was like the sun rising after a stormy night. She gave Pete's hand a pat, then turned, smiling, to Tom. "Feel like buying a girl a cup of coffee?"

"Don't you have other hospital calls to make?"

She poked him playfully on the arm. "Trying to weasel out?"

"Not at all, but—"

She took hold of his arms. "Yes, I have other calls to make. I'll do them later. Right now, you look like you could use a break. And a friend."

"Both," he agreed. He took one last look at Pete, whose lips twitched in a half smile. A good dream? He certainly hoped so.

Most of the breakfast traffic had cleared out of the cafeteria, so they were able to settle at a table by a window overlooking the cancer survivors' rose garden. Tom cupped his hands around the mug and found himself staring at the cross suspended from a thin silver chain Lynn wore around her neck. The sun had caught it just so, highlighting it against the dark blue of her sweater, making it difficult when he looked up, to forget she was a minister. Even though, to him, she was so much more.

"How did you find out?" he asked.

"About the fight?" She stirred a container of cream into her coffee. "This is Riverbend, remember? Molly called me first thing this morning."

"Did she tell you everything?"

"You mean about Pete's insulting remark?"

He stared into the black depths of his mug. "Yeah."

"Yes. No one thinks Pete's actions were admirable, but they're understandable."

"I wish I thought so." All he could think of was the one time he had mouthed off to Uncle Abe and the very clear lesson he'd learned as a result. Pete came by his mouthiness naturally, but that didn't excuse it.

Lynn sipped her coffee and gave a small sigh of satisfaction before continuing, "He's jealous."

Tom sputtered a mouthful of coffee. *"Jealous?"* He picked up his napkin and wiped his lips. "Of what?"

"Of your work, of your glamorous career, of all the other people in your life. Of anything that takes you away from him. In this instance, Damon and Sam. Can't you see? They're a threat to him."

Tom set down his cup, then leaned forward and rested his elbows on the table. "Let me get this straight. You're suggesting this kid who ignores me, turns away from me any time he can, is jealous?"

"His belligerence has root causes. Can you suggest anything else?"

When she put it that way... "Okay, for the sake of argument, let's suppose you're right. If he's jealous, it must follow he doesn't hate me."

"Far from it. Forgive me for smiling, but is it so hard to believe he loves you very much?"

"Then why does he act like he hates me?"

"Because it's safe."

"Safe?"

"It's a natural protective response. He rejects you before you reject him."

Tom shook his head, confused and frustrated. "But that's just it. I'm *not* rejecting him." He didn't know how much longer he could bear to look into the crystal depths of those understanding gray eyes and find himself mirrored there.

"Not *now*. But how's he supposed to know that?"

"Hell, I've come home, haven't I?"

"Have you?"

He turned and stared out the window at the cold stone statue of St. Francis standing ankle-deep in a carpet of autumn leaves. He heard someone scrape a chair across the tile floor and set down a tray on a nearby table. The sound grated.

Had he? Come home? Or was this just another way station on his life's journey? Was his kid supposed to be a mind reader?

Over the tinny intercom, he heard a female voice page a doctor, but the words didn't seem connected to his brain. At last he turned back to Lynn, patiently awaiting his answer. "Are you always this perceptive?"

Her mouth curved gently. "Not always."

"So you're saying I have something to prove to my kids."

"No, I'm not saying that. *You* are." She pulled both his hands into her warm grasp. "They've said goodbye to you so many times in their young lives. They don't want to have to say it again."

"But their experience suggests this isn't any different from any other time. Is that it?"

"They're very bright children, Tom."

"I know." He paused, his chest tightening. "I love them."

She squeezed his hands. "That's obvious, at least to me. Now you need to make it clear to them."

"How?"

"Think about it. Are they so different from you when you were their age? What did you want? What would have made you feel loved and secure?"

Unbidden, that remembrance of not belonging rose like gorge in his throat. He hadn't wanted to be on his own. Hadn't wanted to grow up before it was time. Hadn't wanted his father's handshake. What he'd wanted was...a hug. A place to call home, where he had people he could count on.

He withdrew his hands and picked up the tab. "I have no idea why you bother with me, but I'm grateful as hell. Thanks, Lynn, for being you." He shoved back his chair and stood up. "Now if you'll excuse me, I want to be there when Pete wakes up."

"Good. You know something? I think the rest of Pete is going to heal, too." She placed her forefinger and middle finger against her lips, then withdrew them and turned them to him in a silent kiss.

As he walked briskly toward the cash register, he wondered what in heaven's name she saw in him. Whatever it was, he never wanted to lose it.

AFTER VISITING two hospitalized parishioners, Lynn decided to stop by Ruth and Rachel's to check on Libby, who had to be wondering what was going on. Rachel greeted her with a worried frown. "I'm glad you've come. Our young guest hasn't said much, and she's tight as a tick. Ruth's taken her over to the bookstore, hoping to interest her in some reading. But I'm not optimistic that'll help. She's an unhappy little girl."

Rachel took Lynn by the arm. "Come through here." She ushered Lynn to the passage connecting the house and bookstore. "Good luck, my dear."

Lynn figured she could use it. Tom, of course, needed to be with Pete, but Libby had to be feeling very alone in a strange place, not to mention worried about her brother. She seemed to be a quiet, introspective girl. It might be difficult to get her to share her feelings, but it was worth a try.

When Lynn entered the bookstore, Kate waved, then advanced toward her, arms extended. Lynn gratefully stepped into her embrace. "You've had an interesting last few hours, I imagine," Kate said as she stood back and studied her friend's face. "How's Tom's son?"

"Not a pretty sight at the moment. But he'll be fine, at least physically. Emotionally, I'm not so sure."

Kate cocked an eyebrow. "Oh?"

"Beyond the damage to his pride, there's the underlying issue of his feelings about his father."

"Heavy stuff."

"Heavy for Tom, too. And Libby, of course, in a different way. I've come to see her."

Kate nodded toward the young adult section of the bookstore. "Ruth's trying to keep her occupied, but I know she'd welcome reinforcements."

Lynn fingered her cross. "That's why I'm here."

Laying a hand on her arm, Kate momentarily delayed her. "I care how *you* are, too. This whole thing must raise some interesting issues for you and Tom. If you need to talk, just give a jingle."

"Thanks, I know I can count on you," Lynn said. She approached the table where Ruth and Libby were bent over a stack of books, examining them one by one. "Mind if I join you?"

"Not at all," Ruth said, sounding relieved. Libby merely shrugged.

Lynn slipped into a vacant chair. "What have we got here?" She picked up *Cold Sassy Tree* and thumbed through it. "This is one of my all-time favorites."

"It is?" Libby appeared mildly curious.

Lynn slid it across the table. "I think you'd like it."

"The main character is a boy. I like female narrators."

"I do, too, usually." Lynn tapped a finger on the cover. "But this one's different. Tell you what, why don't I buy it for you, and if you don't like it, we'll donate it to Meacham House?"

"Better yet, why don't I give it to you?" Ruth interjected. "I'd really like you to have it."

Libby pulled the book closer to her. "Thank you," she mumbled.

"Have you had breakfast, kiddo?" Lynn asked.

"Dad gave me a bowl of cereal."

"But you're still hungry, I'll bet." Lynn waited for the nod of the head. "I'm dying for one of the Sunnyside Café's gooey caramel rolls. Will you let me treat you?"

"I am kinda hungry," Libby admitted.

"You're in for a treat," Ruth said as she stood up, then aligned her chair under the table. "Lucky neither of you has to worry about calories."

Libby threw Ruth a skeptical look. Lynn sighed. Adolescent girls always worried about calories. Too much.

As Lynn and Libby crossed the street to the Sunnyside, Lynn reassured her about Pete. "He isn't going to win any beauty contests, but he'll be fine. In fact, he'll be coming home this afternoon."

"None of this would've happened if Dad hadn't made us go to Meacham House." She studied the courthouse cupola while they waited for the green light. "Or if Mom hadn't made us come to Riverbend."

"But it *has* happened." Before Lynn could go on, the light changed and Libby jumped ahead of her, as if eager to put distance between them. Lynn gave up pursuing the subject until they were in the café and had ordered their rolls. "I don't mean to intrude, Libby, but I'm a good listener. Aside from last night's unfortunate events, what is it about Riverbend you don't like?"

"All my friends are in Chicago. There are things to do there. Dad thinks this is such a wonderful place. For him, maybe. But not for me."

"Have you given it a real chance?"

"I went to Meacham House, didn't I?"

"Yes. And it looked to me as if you were getting along all right."

"Not really." Libby set her menu aside when the waitress delivered the rolls. "Those kids are such freaks."

Lynn, affecting a nonchalance she didn't feel, picked up her fork. "All of them?"

"Well, certainly that Damon guy. What a creep!"

Lynn let that pass. "What about the others? Keri, for instance?"

Libby carefully tore off a corner of the roll and put it into her mouth. "She dresses funny, but she's okay."

"So you might give her a chance?"

"I guess I'll have to if we're going to that dumb Halloween party."

"Is bringing cheer to some senior citizens 'dumb'?" Lynn chewed contemplatively on a morsel of roll, waiting while Libby mulled over the question.

"Not the old people. That part's okay. But if I was at home, I'd be going to the football game."

"You're not home."

Libby looked straight at her, her neck stiff. "You keep saying that. I know I'm not home. So what's your point?"

"My point is that, whether you like it or not, you're here. I want to help you make the best of it."

"Fat chance."

Lynn carefully kept any anger out of her voice. "How do you feel about spending time with your father?"

With daintily crooked fingers, Libby pulled off another piece of the roll. "I dunno," she said tonelessly.

"I think you do know." Lynn prayed she wasn't pushing too hard.

"It's kinda weird being at his house." Lynn said nothing, hoping Libby would go on. "It's like he doesn't know what to do with us. Oh, we've done some stuff—fishing, shooting, hiking. But it's like, I dunno…" She screwed up her face in concentration. "He can't relax around us."

"Maybe he's scared."

"Scared? *Dad?*" Libby gave a brittle little laugh. "He's bailed out of a plane, had people shoot at him and all kinds of scary stuff."

"I'm not talking about that kind of scared. His physical courage is a given. But maybe there are other things he doesn't feel so confident about."

"Like what?"

"Being a father." Lynn deliberately took her time

chewing another bite. Watching Libby, it was as if she could actually see the wheels turning in her brain. "As I understand it, he hasn't had much experience. But I can tell you one thing." Libby looked up hopefully. "He's finally figured out he wants to be a good father."

"You think so?" The girl's voice wavered.

"I *know* so. Maybe you could help him out."

"How?"

"By not fighting him every step of the way."

"I haven't been."

"Haven't you?"

Libby licked her finger and lowered her eyes. Her thin shoulders protruded from the tank top she wore underneath her designer overalls, and Lynn's heart melted. The girl was trying so hard to maintain her stony defenses. "Maybe."

"Love is hard, isn't it?"

When Libby raised her eyes, Lynn was moved to see tears gathering. The girl, in an effort for control, merely nodded.

Giving Libby time to compose herself, Lynn went on, "It's hard for adults, too. The most difficult part is the risk. I mean, what if we show or tell someone we love them and they reject us? It hurts. Worse yet, it makes us afraid to risk exposing our feelings again. Nobody likes to be hurt." Just as she'd told Tom she loved him and... But she couldn't go there, not now. Getting through to Libby was too important. She spoke softly. "Did it hurt, Libby, every time your dad left to go on assignment overseas?"

With her finger Libby made circles in the gooey caramel frosting on her plate. "Yes."

"And when your parents got divorced?"

A nod.

"So you don't like saying goodbye. I don't blame you, especially when it's someone you love."

A noisy group of city street workers sat down in the adjacent booth, masking the awkward silence with guffaws and loud voices.

Lynn had to lean forward to hear Libby say, "What if Dad leaves again?" The vulnerability in her eyes was heartbreaking.

"He won't."

"How do you know?"

"You'll have to take my word for it. He has put his work and his other relationships all aside for one reason. You and Pete." Lynn picked up her paper napkin and dabbed her lips. "So do you think you could cut him some slack? Give him a chance?"

Another pitiful shrug.

"I know it's scary. But your dad is a brave man, and once he makes up his mind to do something, he's very good at it. Can you risk letting him love you?"

Libby picked up *Cold Sassy Tree* and clutched it to her small chest. "I'll try."

Lynn nodded and smiled. "Great. That's all anyone could ask."

The waitress put the check under the saltshaker and inquired if they wanted anything more. Lynn dug out change for a tip, then looked at Libby. "Ready to go back to the bookstore?"

"Yeah." The girl slid across the seat and stood up, the top of her head reaching only to Lynn's shoulder. "You must be a pretty good preacher," Libby said softly.

"Why do you say that?"

Libby's answer brought a huge grin to Lynn's face. "Because you ask such good questions."

Thank you, God. This conversation could have been a disaster. But Libby was quite the young woman. Lynn hoped she'd get an opportunity to know her better.

But that all depended on the results of her one very big risk. The risk of loving Tom Baines.

TOM SAT IN THE CAR outside Mitch and Sam Sterling's house late Wednesday afternoon waiting for his son to come out. When Pete had awoken yesterday morning in the hospital, he had complained groggily. He hurt. He hated Riverbend. And he particularly hated Tommy Lee. At first Tom had been puzzled, but finally Pete had made it clear that he'd identified Damon with the rock star. Despite his inclination to light into Pete, Tom had restrained himself, concluding he needed to let the pain medication wear off before they had a serious discussion of the incident. Besides, he needed more time to think about what Lynn had said.

Finally, on the way home from the hospital, when Pete had seemed more himself, Tom had spoken up. "It's time we talked about the situation. Help me to understand why you lashed out like that."

Pete had given him the usual rationalizations—the Meacham House teens were weird, the little kid had no business being there, it was Tom's fault for making him go. Then he'd said, "Besides, you couldn't care less. You took us there and then disappeared."

Tom admitted that by taking the aunts home and then going into the darkroom, he had seemed to disappear, but he argued the point about his concern for

Pete. "I'm sorry if you think I don't care. Nothing could be further from the truth."

Pete had merely grunted. Just before they'd reached the farmhouse, Pete spoke again. "What's wrong with that little kid?"

"Sam? He's hearing-impaired. But he reads lips. Can you imagine what he must've felt when you called him a weirdo retard?"

Nothing more had been said, but when Tom had gone upstairs last night to check on Pete before turning in himself, he'd found him lying on his back, his hands behind his head, staring through puffy eyes at the ceiling.

"You okay, son?"

"I'm thinkin' I should apologize to that Sam kid."

Tom sat on the edge of the bed and laid a hand on his son's shoulder. For once, Pete didn't wince when he touched him. "That would be the right thing to do."

"I'm not a bad person, you know."

"I know that." Tom listened to distant thunder, wondering how to phrase his next question. He decided the less said the better. "Damon?"

"*Him?*" Pete snorted. "What about him?"

"Don't you owe him an apology, too?"

"For what? He almost knocked my head off. No way."

Tom's shoulders sagged. From Pete's point of view, it was asking a lot. Then again, he needed to take responsibility for his part in the altercation. "I won't say any more tonight, Pete, but I want you to think about why things got out of hand. Then we'll talk about it tomorrow."

"If you think I'm gonna go crawling to that dude—"

Tom stood. "Tomorrow," he said with finality.

And now tomorrow had come. The day had passed, yet neither of them had raised the issue of Damon. Tom hoped fervently that Pete would spare him having to insist. Compelling him to apologize would simply widen the already serious breach between him and his son.

When Tom looked up, he saw both Mitch and Sam accompanying Pete to the car. Mitch held open the door for him and waited until Pete climbed in. Then, with a broad smile at Tom, he clamped the boy firmly on the shoulder. "This is a good kid you have here, Tom." He turned to Sam. "Right?"

"We're friends now," Sam said proudly.

"I'm glad," Tom said. "Thanks, Mitch, for giving Pete the opportunity to tell you how sorry we are."

"It's over," Mitch replied. "Forgotten."

Tom had driven several blocks before Pete said anything. "Sam doesn't have many friends."

"Is that what he told you?"

"Yeah." Pete seemed surprised by the concept. "I guess some of the kids his age make fun of him. He told me about how he'd like to be an athlete or a musician, but how that'll never happen." Pete looked out the window for a while. "I said we could be buddies. At least while I'm here."

"How about *whenever* you're here? I hope you'll be back often."

Tom drove along River Road back to the farm, encouraged that Pete hadn't said, "No way."

After last night's rain the fall foliage was particularly vivid, and the setting sun burnished the copper-orange of the oak leaves to a high luster. Even without Pete's next words, the sight was cause for optimism.

"Dad, I've been thinking."

"Yeah?" Tom held his breath.

"Do you know where Damon lives?"

"Uh-huh."

"Could you take me there?"

Tom executed one of the speediest U-turns in driving history. "You got it, son."

NOW WHERE HAD THAT DUMB IDEA come from? Pete wanted to talk to that Damon guy like he wanted to throw himself over Niagara Falls. Then there was this weird look in his dad's eyes. All soft and glowy. A friggin' Hallmark moment!

Damon was a creep, no denying that, and Pete hadn't the foggiest idea what he'd say to him when they got to his house. And getting there seemed to be taking forever. They went clear through town and into this ratty neighborhood where people had rusty old boats and dented cars parked in their front yards. Some of the houses had paint peeling off them, and this one dump had aluminum foil covering the windows. If he'd known Damon lived someplace like this, he might've changed his mind. But Dad was counting on him. Like this was a big deal.

When his father parked in front of some crummy garage, Pete asked, "Why are we stopping?"

"This is where Damon lives."

Pete looked around. "Where?"

His dad pointed at these ramshackle wooden stairs. "Up there. In the apartment over the garage."

"You're kidding, right?"

Tom stretched an arm across the back of the seat.

"No, Pete. I'm not." It was nearly dark, and only one dim-wattage bulb illuminated the steps. "Do you want me to come with you?"

Oh, sure, that'd be really cool. "No. I'm fine." He climbed out of the car and slammed the door.

An odor of motor oil and stale garbage greeted him at the foot of the stairs. As he climbed, he could hear faint canned laughter from a TV getting louder and louder. Was Damon hard of hearing, too? Pete drew in a thick breath and knocked on the door. Nothing. Just another outburst of audience hysteria. He knocked again. Louder. He figured that was plenty. If nobody was home, he could at least say he'd tried.

The door opened so suddenly Pete nearly fell inside. "What do *you* want?" Damon slouched in the entrance, holding a fork and a can of pork-and-beans and barring Pete from seeing much of anything except the tube and a sagging, mud-brown sofa.

"I was outta line Monday night," Pete mumbled.

"No kidding," Damon responded with a sneer. With the handle of his fork, he nudged Pete's face into the light of the entry lamp. "Gotcha good, didn't I? Serves you right, dork."

Pete pulled himself to his full five foot nine. "I *said* I was sorry."

"Let me give you a clue. Damon Hudson don't need no candy-ass preppie tellin' him which way is up. Got it?" Without losing eye contact, Damon spooned a forkful of beans into his mouth. "Did Daddy make you come?"

Pete was aware his hands were clenched at his sides. But no way was he going to give this jerk the satisfaction of getting his goat. "No. It was my idea."

"Gee, maybe you're not as dumb as I thought."

"Besides, my father and I don't get along. I make my own decisions."

Damon continued chewing. "Your old man seems like an okay guy to me."

"Well, lucky you." Pete had just about had enough. "Maybe you've had better experiences with fathers than I have."

"Ha! Mine?" Damon swallowed just before the beans were in danger of spewing out of his mouth. "The mysterious disappearing man? The one who calls a bar stool his office? That's rich."

For a brief moment Pete felt a weird kinship with this guy. "Look, I've said my piece. I'm going now."

"Don't do me no favors. See ya around."

And the door shut firmly in his face.

Okay, he'd done it, but he sure as hell didn't feel any better. Screw it!

RACHEL STOOD in the doorway of the guest bedroom, her mind going in several directions. "Papa's tuxedo isn't in here. Where could it be, Ruthie?"

Ruth emerged from her bedroom and stared at her twin as if she'd taken leave of her senses. "Good Lord, we haven't had it out in years. Why do you need it?"

"Tom just called. He's in a panic."

"Somehow I can't visualize our intrepid nephew in a panic."

Planting her fists on her hips, Rachel peered over her glasses. "Well, you didn't talk to him. I did. He needs Halloween costumes for Pete and Libby for Friday night's party at Golden Fields. I suggested Pete could be the Phantom of the Opera. That way his poor face won't be such a problem."

"Why didn't you say so in the first place?"

Rachel shook her head in frustration. "Because you didn't let me."

"Be that as it may, I've got another idea. Mama's opera cape."

Rachel relented and clapped her hands. "Great idea, and Papa's white gloves. But..."

"Where are they?" they both chirped at once.

"Let's try the trunk in the attic," Ruth suggested. "Maybe we can unearth one of Mama's old evening gowns for Libby."

They hurried up the attic stairs. "What about us?" Rachel paused at the top, panting.

"Us?"

"We're Meacham House volunteers, right? When was the last time we were at a costume party, Ruthie?"

Ruth hugged her sister impulsively. "Years and years. And you know what I think?"

"Yes, I do," Rachel responded smugly. "We'd better go while we can before we're the ones in the wheelchairs."

"Exactly," Ruth said, crossing to the old steamer trunk under the eaves.

Rachel hugged herself. This was going to be such fun!

LYNN LEANED BACK in the claw-foot tub in her tiny bathroom and laid her head against the rim, closing her eyes and relishing the delicious drowsy feeling induced by the hot water, fragrant with almond-scented bath oil. Had it been only this morning that Molly had called with the news about Damon and Pete? It seemed days since she'd been to the hospital.

And she would need days to process her conversations with Tom and Libby. It was next to impossible to maintain her objectivity where that family was concerned. Had her personal stake been too high? Had she overstepped her boundaries? Said too much?

Was she being foolish to wait for Tom? Once he finally got his situation with his kids straightened out and decided what kind of work he was going to pursue, what was to keep him in Riverbend? She opened her eyes with a start, realizing she'd never contemplated that obstacle. She reached back and fanned her hair over the edge of the tub. So many unknowns. Would he stay here? Could he give her emotional support in her work? Would he want more children?

And, of course, the big one. Did he love her?

Surely kisses don't lie. Or do they? His kisses. Just thinking about them was dangerous. Even though the water was still warm, she trembled. She wanted him as she had wanted no other. *Oh, please—*

The phone rang in the bedroom. She was tempted to stay where she was, but it could be Mae, who was extremely vulnerable now and who found lonely nights the worst. The phone rang a second time. She shoved herself up, grabbed a towel and stepped onto the bath mat, quickly drying herself before dashing to the phone, where she stood clutching the towel sarong-style. "Hello?"

"Reverend Kendall, this is Prentice Jewett." His solemn tone held no hint of amiability. She should've stayed in the sanctuary of the tub. But of course that had been out of the question. Now the other shoe would drop. "I just heard about the brawl Monday evening at Meacham House. What do you have to say for yourself?"

Thud.

CHAPTER TWELVE

LYNN HAD AGREED to take a carload of the Meacham House girls to Golden Fields an hour early Friday so they could decorate the activity center before the residents assembled. They stashed their costumes and several jack-o'-lanterns in her trunk and held the rest of the decorations on their laps, all except for the huge stuffed pumpkin. Tom was bringing it in the pickup.

"Do we have everything?" Lynn asked before they set out. "Masking tape? Staple gun? Candles?"

"I don't know where we'd put anything else," Angie said.

"You've got a point." Lynn turned on the ignition. "Okay, here we go."

Keri, sitting in the front seat, tuned in a radio station, and for several minutes the girls sang along with Shania Twain. In the rearview mirror Lynn observed Libby, who was smiling as she sang, her fingers snapping rhythmically, seemingly at ease with the group.

Angie punched Libby on the shoulder. "You go, girl. That's some voice you got."

"Yeah," Rosita Diaz, perched in the middle of the backseat, seconded. "You oughtta sing with a band."

Lynn risked another glance in the mirror. Libby was blushing. "I'm not that good."

Keri squirmed around to look at Libby. "Don't

gimme that crap. I'd give anything to sing like you do."

"And I'd give anything to have your boobs."

Lynn managed not to laugh and simultaneously keep the car on the road.

"These?" Keri placed her hands under her breasts and hefted them. "They're nothing but a pain. How would you like to look like me and be cursed with the last name of Mellon? It's not funny, I can tell you, but guys seem to think it's hysterical."

"They're still better than nothing," Libby said. "Which is what I've got. Boys never even look at me."

Keri folded her arms, as if attempting to hide her breasts. "Count your blessings, kiddo. They wanna do a lot more than look with me. It's disgusting."

"Damon, too?" Angie asked knowingly.

"He's different," Keri mumbled. "At least when we're alone."

Rosita leaned her elbows on the back of the front seat. "Like how?"

Keri shrugged. "I dunno how to explain exactly. He's not so tough." As if reluctant to say more on the topic, she cranked up the radio, effectively ending the discussion.

Amazing what you can learn when you keep your mouth shut, Lynn mused. Who would have thought that brazen, assertive Keri, who at times seemed to flaunt her sexuality, was so sensitive? And it wasn't too surprising that Libby at her age was concerned about her developing body and about boys. The fact that she had felt comfortable confiding her insecurity to the others gave Lynn a warm feeling. Libby had let her guard down, an encouraging sign.

Lynn ventured a remark. "I looked like a piece of string until the end of my sophomore year in high school."

Keri's jaw dropped. She adjusted the radio volume. "Well, the boob fairy certainly came through for you."

In the backseat, the other girls giggled. The Golden Fields sign was just ahead. Lynn flicked on her turn signal. "I used to wear these huge baggy sweaters, hoping no one would notice I was flat as a pancake. I didn't have a real date until I was a junior."

"I'll bet you don't have that trouble now," Rosita said.

"As a matter of fact, I don't date much."

"Why not? You're a hot-looking woman," Keri said.

Little was to be gained from telling them that a minister has more trouble attracting a man than the average woman. "Thank you for the vote of confidence. I guess I just haven't met the right guy."

"We'll fix that." Angie looked at the others as if soliciting their agreement. "Any of you guys know somebody for Reverend Lynn?"

Keri, Angie and Rosita began suggesting names, then arguing over suitability. Amid the babble, Lynn thought she heard Libby say softly, "I might." But the others didn't hear her, and then they arrived at the parking lot.

The girls piled out of the car, and after loading themselves with costumes, strings of cardboard ghosts and one or two skeletons, made their way to the main entrance of the retirement center. Libby fell into step beside Lynn. "They're not so bad," she said, nodding at the trio ahead of them.

"I know."

After several seconds Libby moved closer to Lynn. "Were you really flat-chested, or were you trying to make me feel better?"

Lynn chuckled. "I really was."

Libby looked up, a tentative smile bringing a sweetness and vulnerability to her expression. "Maybe there's hope for me, then. Thanks."

If her arms hadn't been full, Lynn would have given Libby a hug. Sometimes it was easy to forget that kids had a whole lot on their minds, not all of which was obvious to adults.

PETE STOOD IN A CORNER of the activity room observing, glad as hell that his half-mask covered the worst of his bruised face. Nathan's life-size ghost, propped in the doorway looked good, and the girls had done a pretty decent job of decorating this place. But, jeez, the old people. Some of them never changed expression except that their eyes would shift from side to side like tortoises checking to see if they could cross the road. Lots of the old ladies, though, seemed real excited and were making a big deal of the kids' costumes.

So far he'd been able to avoid Damon. Just as well. Damon wasn't wearing a costume and would probably laugh his ass off when he caught sight of Pete's old-fashioned cape and tux. Guy'd probably never heard of *Phantom of the Opera*. Anyway, old Damon was so busy acting like a hotshot photographer he maybe wouldn't notice.

Libby, who didn't look half-bad, for a sister, in the long dress Aunt Ruth had given her, and several of the other girls were distributing plastic jack-o'-

lanterns full of cough drops and tissues and junk like that to the residents. If that was the "treat," he'd hate to see the "trick."

Just then, those standing near the door began pointing and laughing. Pete stepped forward to see what the ruckus was about. And almost lost it. There, framed in the doorway, stood Aunt Rachel and Aunt Ruth wearing knee-length red-and-white-striped stockings, balloonlike bright blue knee-length pants, red suspenders and matching white shirts with huge red bows around their necks. On their frizzy gray heads they wore funny little hats with propellers on the top. Their cheeks were bright with spots of rouge. Aunt Ruth wore a sign that read Tweedledum, while Aunt Rachel's read Tweedledee. Pete had a vague recollection of his mother reading something like that to him when he was a little kid.

The aunts held their pose so that Damon, the "boy wonder" photographer, could snap away with his camera, then they laughed and started around the room greeting some of the old people. Prob'ly a bunch of their friends lived here. It was a nice enough place, he guessed, but he sure hoped the aunts didn't end up here. He felt a sudden twinge of guilt remembering he was in Riverbend because his mother was putting his grandmother in just such a place.

He noticed that his dad seemed to know a few of the folks here, too. Pete was glad his father hadn't made an idiot of himself dressing up. All he'd done was wear a cowboy hat, western shirt, jeans and boots. Not too embarrassing.

"Hey, Pete. Come join the party." Ms. Linden, looking kinda foxy in her Peter Pan suit, took hold of his arm. "I want you to meet Axel Morrison. He knew your grandmother."

And before he could say anything, she steered him over to a wheelchair-bound man with a carefully trimmed silver beard and piercing black eyes. Pete tried to avoid looking at the empty pant leg neatly pinned above the man's left knee.

"So you're Celia Steele's grandson, eh?" He extended his hand and they shook. "She was quite a gal. If your grandfather hadn't grabbed her, I'd have had a go myself."

Weird to think of this old geezer having the hots for his grandmother. "What was she like?"

After ten minutes Pete had learned more than he'd ever wanted to know. It was a relief, then, when Damon came up to him and said, "Hey, dork, lemme take your picture." He started walking toward the lobby. "Over here. I like the light."

He flipped off the overhead and moved a floor lamp so that it illuminated only one side of Pete's face. "I'm goin' for the sinister look. Stand still."

Damon fiddled with the camera settings, then had Pete tilt his chin. "This is stupid," Pete groused. "Hurry up."

"Hey, you look cool, man. Classy. This could be a great shot." When he clicked the shutter, Pete started back to the party.

"Not so fast." Damon looked up and down the hall. "Want a cigarette?"

His dad would kill him if he saw him smoking. Besides, Pete had tried it. The stuff tasted like crap. "Not particularly."

"Keep me company, then."

Pete hesitated. It was either go with Damon or go back to the golden oldies. "Okay."

Out in front of the retirement center was a row of metal lawn chairs. Pete remembered seeing a bunch of seniors sitting out here one time when he and his dad had driven past. Damon wasted no time lighting up. Then he threw back his head and exhaled three smoke rings. "Have a seat."

They sat side by side, their feet on the porch railing. Damon drew on his cigarette again. Out here in the cool night air, the tobacco didn't smell half-bad compared to that antiseptic smell inside. Pete didn't have a clue what to say. He'd said all he needed to the other day.

"You got guts, man."

Damon's words took him by surprise. His tone was almost admiring. "Me?"

"Yeah, you. See anybody else out here?" He took one last drag and flipped his cigarette expertly, end over end, into the flower bed bordering the porch. "Most guys wouldn't have apologized."

Pete fingered his sore cheek. "And most guys don't connect with such a kick-ass punch."

"Hurts, huh?"

"Not especially."

Strains of "Monster Mash" filtering from inside kept the silence from being awkward.

"You see much of your father?" Damon asked.

"No."

"Me, neither. Mine, I mean. He's either at work, sleeping or drunk."

Pete had a sudden flash of the dump where Damon lived. Of the can of pork-and-beans. He glanced side-wise at Damon, sitting with his shoulders hunched, his hair falling across his face. Pete felt a peculiar sense of allegiance to his dad. "Mine's not so bad, I guess."

Damon raked his fingers through his hair. "Hell, yours is great. Don't you like him?"

Pete considered the question. He didn't know whether he liked him or not. But an ache slowly grew inside him. Even if he didn't like him, he guessed he loved him. That was why it hurt so bad that he couldn't seem to get through to him. Maybe that was what made him so angry. Even old Damon could get his father's attention, spending time in the darkroom and stuff. But it was like the guitar. He'd told his dad yesterday he wanted one. And what had he said? "You've never shown any interest before. It's a big investment." Like his dad was poor or something.

Damon leaned over and cupped his ear in an exaggerated way. "Hey, I didn't hear you."

"That's because I didn't say anything."

"That heavy, huh?"

Pete looked into Damon's eyes, again registering with surprise the growing bond between them. He sighed. "Yeah, that heavy."

Damon was reaching for another cigarette, his hand poised at his pocket, when he cocked his head. The front door opened. "Boys, I've been looking for you." Ms. Linden looked faintly disapproving. "We need some more partners for 'Monster Mash.' We don't want any of our guests to be wallflowers."

Damon shot Pete a commiserating glance and muttered, "Jeez, Louise." Dutifully they followed her inside, where to Pete's amazement, the costumed teens had the old people, even the ones in wheelchairs, out in the middle of the floor gyrating to the thumping beat of the Halloween perennial.

"Yoo-hoo, Phantom!" A little raisin of a woman waggled her fingers at Pete. "May I have this dance?" she said, and then, honest to God, she—wait the word was coming—simpered. He gave himself a mental high five. *Simpered.* His finest pullout yet.

LYNN HAD BEEN so busy at the refreshment table, helping the youngsters fill cups and load plates for the residents, that she only now had time to survey the scene before her. In short, it was wonderful. Something about being in costume had helped the Meacham House kids overcome their initial shyness with the residents. Nathan was holding a woman by the elbows, her walker between them, swaying to one of the classic big-band numbers the kids had selected in deference to the elderly folks; Rosita sat at a table, helping a gentleman with palsied hands direct his cup of punch to his lips; and Pete, bless his heart, had in his arms a tiny little lady who daintily held up a corner of her long skirt as they swayed to the music.

Lily and Aaron Mazerik, their arms entwined, left the dance floor and approached the punch table. "You two still have that honeymoon glow," Lynn teased.

Lily looked adoringly at her husband. "I hope we always will."

Aaron gave his wife a killer smile and pulled her closer. "This is a great party, Lynn. The generation gap has all but disappeared."

"It was nice of you to come. Thank you."

"Wouldn't have missed it," Aaron said. "Besides, a couple of my students would've blacklisted me if I hadn't come to see their costumes."

Lily glanced at the refreshment table. "Do you need any help here?"

"No, I think we've served just about everyone. The kids can handle the rest."

"In that case," Aaron said, "I'm going to get my wife back out on the dance floor."

"You don't fool me. You just want to get your hands on her again."

Aaron pointed a finger at Lynn. "Bingo." With that, he gathered Lily and twirled across the floor.

Until that moment Lynn had done her best to avoid looking at Tom. No tall-drink-of-water Texan could've looked leaner, meaner or sexier than he did. He was lounging against the wall, his hat pulled dangerously low over his eyes, one foot cocked over the other, and it was all she could do not to rush over and drag him out onto the dance floor just to feel his arms around her. Until this moment it hadn't hit her how much she'd missed being alone with him since his children arrived. But then, being alone with him might not be all she hoped. Unfinished business stood between them.

As if reading her mind, he lifted a finger to his hat brim and nodded at her before shoving off from the wall and making his way through the crowd toward her. She hoped no one could overhear the timpani of her heart. Finally he stood before her, his eyes hungry, his voice husky. "I should have known. I like it."

"Like what?"

"Your costume." He touched the tip of her hood. "Little Red Riding Hood never looked *this* good."

She lowered her eyes in studied demureness. "Thank you, sir."

"Red's very becoming on you."

She wondered if that included the flush coloring her cheeks. Out of the corner of her eye she spotted Keri, dressed like a Gypsy fortune-teller, bearing down on them. On her way she motioned to someone. "Hey, Libby, come over here. Get Angie and Rosita."

Tom turned just in time to avoid having Keri run him down. He reached out and took hold of her shoulders. "Whoa, there. What's your rush?"

Keri looked somewhat embarrassed, but recovered when Libby joined her, trailed by Angie the witch and Rosita the ballerina. "I wanted to ask your opinion about an idea I—" she checked with the others, who all nodded "—er, *we* have."

Lynn stifled a grin. No telling what this group of connivers was up to.

In an affected Texas drawl, Tom said, "Well, ma'am, if ah can, ah'll be happy to oblige."

"Good." Keri looked smugly at the others.

"Go for it," Libby said softly.

Keri nodded, then, like an approving duenna, placed one hand at the small of Tom's back and one at Lynn's. "We think you should ask Reverend Lynn to dance."

"Why, ladies, if y'all will excuse me, ah'd be more than happy to step around the floor with this little lady." Then, sweeping his hat from his head, with a flourish, he said, "Miz Kendall, may ah have the honor of this dance?"

Lynn was flabbergasted, first that the girls would try such an obvious maneuver and second that Tom had gone along with the fun so obligingly. She hadn't seen much of his playful side before. She had no time though for further reflections, because Tom grabbed her elbow and escorted her to the center of the floor.

There, amid the witches, monsters and ghouls, he took
her in his arms, just as she had imagined, and holding
her closely, fit his body to hers and began moving to
the music.

Her hood fell back, freeing her hair, and when he
spun around, he pressed his chin to her temple. He
was a breathtakingly good dancer, and she, who seldom had the chance to dance, felt detached and feath-
erlike in his arms. Slowly she became aware that others had stopped dancing and had formed a circle
around them. She caught sight of the aunts beaming,
of Keri and the matchmakers giggling delightedly,
and then, more disturbingly, of an unsmiling Pete
standing with Damon.

Yet she was helpless to break the spell. The beautifully nostalgic strains of "Let the Rest of the World
Go By" moved her even more profoundly than when
she'd first heard it in the film *Out of Africa*. It so fit
Tom. Like the singer, he, too, needed someone, good
and true, with whom to find a place where he could
forget, where he could indeed let the rest of the world
go by. The haunting violin carried them, as lost in
each other's arms, they danced until she barely had
the wit left to pray she could be that someone.

Just as the last chord quivered in the air and before
the onlookers started to applaud, she overheard Damon say, "Hey, dork, it looks like your dad's got the
hots for Reverend Lynn."

"Will you friggin' shut up?" she heard Pete hiss.
Then out of the corner of her eye, she watched as the
boy made a hurried exit, stage left.

Tom dropped her hand. "Now what?" he muttered.

"Go to him, Tom. If he was jealous before, how
do you think he feels now?"

Tom nodded his head, then threaded his way through the crowd toward the door where, to Lynn's horror, stood the last person she'd expected to see here tonight. Prentice Jewett.

"SON, WAIT A MINUTE." Pete was halfway down the walk to the parking lot before Tom finally caught up with him.

When he grabbed his son's elbow, Pete shook him off. "Leave me alone, will you?" The boy continued walking.

Tom maneuvered in front of him, blocking his path. "Not until we get a few things straight."

Pete ripped off his mask, revealing stony eyes. "Great. Now I have to listen to the fatherly lecture."

"I'm not here to lecture. I'm here to find out what's going on with you. With us."

"And what would that be? I'm here visiting because that's what Mom wanted us to do. I'm going home Sunday and you'll be rid of me. So what's to discuss?"

Tom felt exasperation threatening to choke off reason. "Maybe the fact that I love you. You're not a nuisance to me, you know."

"Gee, you coulda fooled me."

"Pete, I know I haven't been the world's best father." The withering look on Pete's face said it all. "I want our relationship to be different. Better."

"How?" Pete regarded him coldly.

"First I need to change some things about my life." Tom took a deep breath. "I need to stay in one place so I can spend more time with you and Libby. Be a part of your lives."

"Why start now?"

"Because now is all I have." He corrected himself. "All *we* have."

"What about Reverend Lynn? What was *that* all about?"

Tom plunged his hands into his pockets, wondering how the hell to explain when he didn't know the answer himself. "First of all, there will always be room in my life for you and Libby, and I intend to do a better job of proving that. Believe it or not, Pete, I'm not too old to learn a thing or two. I used to think I could take on the world single-handed. That I didn't need anyone else." He paused, searching for an explanation. "I was wrong."

At those words, his son turned and looked at him strangely, as if seeing a father he didn't know.

Tom struggled to continue. "I need my family and my friends. And I need that someone special."

Pete looked up. "Reverend Lynn?"

"Maybe." Tom cleared his throat. "I hope so. But she and I have quite a few things to work out first."

"It figures." Pete was giving no quarter. "So Damon was right, huh?"

"About?"

"You having the hots for her."

Tom pulled his hands out of his pockets and dared to drape an arm around his son. "That's one way to put it, I suppose." Tom started strolling back toward the retirement center, Pete at his side. It was good to be able to touch his son with affection. "What do you think about that?"

He felt Pete's shrug. "She's a nice lady, I guess." They walked a few more paces. "Does that mean you might stay in Riverbend?"

Taut muscles somewhere in the vicinity of Tom's

gut suddenly relaxed. A slow grin spread over his features. "Yeah, son, I think it does."

When they reached the porch, Tom spotted a furtive movement to their right. Damon putting out a cigarette. Tom chuckled to himself. Some things never change. How many clandestine smokes had he sneaked in his day?

"Hey, butthead, where ya been?"

Pete looked up to see if Tom was going to object to Damon's language. After a beat, Pete responded, "Talking with my dad."

"Lucky you," Damon replied. Tom looked at the boy. There was nothing in either his tone of voice or his expression that indicated sarcasm.

"I'll leave you here, son. I have a little unfinished business inside."

In Pete's eyes was the faintest glimmer of a smile. "Good luck."

TWEEDLEDUM ELBOWED Tweedledee. "Uh-oh. Here comes trouble." Ruth nodded toward the door.

"Saints preserve us," Rachel said, shaking her head. "What's Prentice doing here?"

"Who knows? But I don't like that look on his face. C'mon." Ruth grabbed her sister's hand and they made a beeline for their nemesis, who was charging directly toward Reverend Lynn, his face reddening with each step.

Rachel had no idea what her sister had in mind. All she knew was that somehow Prentice needed to be headed off.

"Prentice, why, what brings you here this evening?" Ruth trilled in a delighted falsetto. She clutched his arm with her free hand and maneuvered herself and Rachel between him and Lynn. "Isn't this a grand party?"

Prentice gaped. "What in tarnation are you two thinking? You look ridiculous in those outfits." He harrumphed. "Grown women," he muttered.

Rachel pasted on her most welcoming smile. "We're Tweedledum and Tweedledee."

"And I'm the Mad Hatter, emphasis on the *mad*." He craned his neck to look beyond the twins. "Where's Reverend Kendall? She's making a mockery of these senior citizens. Whose idea was this, anyway?"

Out of the corner of her eye, Rachel saw Lynn making her way toward them. "I think the staff of Meacham House is to be commended. We're all having a grand time. Why, even old Mrs. Hankins did the Monster Mash and—"

"The *what?*" Rachel had only thought Prentice was red-faced before. Now he was positively beetlike. "She could've had a heart attack right on the spot."

"Prentice," Ruth said acerbically, "the staff approved the party and they've been on duty. Somehow I think they're more qualified than you to judge the suitability of this affair."

"Besides," Rachel added, "better to have a heart attack having fun than to expire of boredom."

Prentice threw the sisters a scathing look just as Lynn reached them.

"Prentice, how kind of you to drop by." Lynn's smile didn't conceal the worry in her gray eyes. Rachel held her breath.

"Kind, is it? I see that nothing I said to you in our little meeting yesterday made a bit of difference."

Lynn's voice was steady. "I told you then and I'll

tell you now—this program deserves a fair trial. We can already point to positive results."

"Like what?" He gestured helplessly around the room. "Upsetting a bunch of old people?"

"Upset? Who's upset?" Axel Morrison rolled his wheelchair between Prentice and Lynn. "About what?" He looked around. "This? Why, Jewett, it's the best thing that's happened here since they got rid of that sorry excuse for a cook."

Rachel pursed her lips, not daring to smile. The twinkle in Ruth's eyes was unmistakable. *Sometimes God just steps in and takes a hand.* She censored the thought. She didn't mean to be blasphemous. Although with that elegant beard, Axel did look a bit like Moses.

Axel clamped a hand on Prentice's arm. "You've met Reverend Lynn, of course. Great things she's doing with our young people, if you ask me. Why, I've half a mind to help 'em out at Meacham House. The reverend here—" he nodded in Lynn's direction "—was telling me about some needs you have over there."

At the *you,* Rachel noticed Prentice cringe. But he couldn't afford to cross Axel, who was the major investor in Jewett's real-estate holdings.

"I'm thinkin' about donating a van for the kids so they can go on field trips. And your preacher here, she told me they could use a—whaddaya call it?" He looked inquiringly at Lynn.

"A scanner for our computer."

"Right, and you could probably use another computer or two maybe?"

"That would be very welcome." Wonder was written all over Lynn's face.

Axel smiled broadly at Prentice. "So ante up, Jewett. Help the kids out. Tell Reverend Lynn you're good for the computer stuff."

Rachel had to hold a hand over her mouth. This was too delicious. Prentice's eyes bulged and his cheeks went in and out, but finally he choked out his answer. "I'll send a check first thing Monday morning."

Axel winked conspiratorially. "It's only fair, Jewett. After all, think of the trouble you and I used to get into."

At that point, Ruth piped up, a mischievous grin on her face. "Yes." She eyed Prentice pointedly. "Just think."

BY THE TIME Tom returned to the activity room, the party was breaking up. Earlier he had noticed Prentice Jewett and was surprised to see he was still there. Tom hoped the man had been visiting a friend, not causing trouble.

He sidestepped aides who were wheeling some residents back to their rooms while some of the kids assisted those who were ambulatory. Molly, Lily, Aaron and Lynn were packing the decorations into sacks and boxes as the teens handed them over. Libby, Angie and Keri were huddled around Axel Morrison, and at one point, he heard Keri say, "Cool. Now we can have photos in our newsletter."

Ruth and Rachel sat at one of the tables, their heads together, absorbed in conversation. Tom wondered if they ever ran out of topics. When they spotted him, they motioned for him to join them. "Have we got news for you!" Ruth crowed. Then Rachel filled him on Jewett's latest comeuppance.

When she finished, Ruth surveyed the room. "Where's Pete?"

"Outside. With Damon."

"Damon?" they chorused.

Tom chuckled. "An unlikely pair. It's funny, though. I think they'll be good for each other."

"I think so, too." Rachel patted Tom's hand. "Rather like you and your cousin," she added wistfully.

Ruth suddenly straightened and looked over their heads toward the hall. "Hmm, I wonder what that's all about?"

"What?" Tom followed his aunt's line of vision.

"Lynn. She just went racing out, looking very worried. I hope it's not trouble."

Tom jumped to his feet and went after Lynn, who began running once she cleared the front door. "Lynn," he called. But she was already too far away to hear him. He hesitated, heard an engine sputter to life and then watched her car pull out of the parking lot onto the main road.

"Tom?" Aaron laid a hand on his shoulder. "Lynn had an emergency call from the hospital. She seemed unusually rattled. Stayed only long enough to ask me to tell you, so you could take Libby home since she came with Lynn. Lily and I will drive Damon and the other girls."

Tom registered one word. "Rattled?"

"Yeah. Lynn's usually pretty calm, especially in emergencies. But she looked about ready to cry."

Without making a conscious decision, Tom started toward the parking lot, backpedaling to speak to his cousin. "Aaron. Change of plan. Please ask our aunts to keep Libby and Pete until I get back." Something powerful was propelling him toward his car. Something he had no right to question.

"Go," Aaron said. "I think Lynn needs you."

Tom was halfway to the hospital before he realized he'd referred to Ruth and Rachel as *our* aunts. Naturally. Without thinking about it.

CHAPTER THIRTEEN

TOM SPOTTED Lynn's car under a halogen lamp in the hospital parking lot beneath a sign reading Reserved for Clergy. He circled until he found a place near the street. How many times had she been called for this kind of duty? Not knowing whether she would be dealing with the living or the dead? Yes, she, too, was well acquainted with death. How arrogant he'd been to suppose he had a corner on it. Violent or peaceful, it was still death. Still a wrench for loved ones left behind. What had she found tonight?

He hurried through the double automatic doors and found himself in the brightly lit emergency-room waiting area. A burly man with bloodshot eyes and a day's growth of whiskers sat in a corner staring into space. A worried young couple holding an obviously sick youngster across their laps didn't even look up. The irritating hum of vending machines was the only sound, besides the child's whimpering. He stepped up to the reception window and waited impatiently, thrumming his fingers on the laminated surface. Finally a woman dressed in maroon surgical scrubs entered the cubicle. She had a harried air about her, but paused long enough to say, "May I help you?"

"I hope so." His chest felt tight. "I'm looking for Reverend Lynn Kendall."

"She's with a patient right now." She eyed him

quizzically. "Do you want to wait? She may be a while."

Again that weird stomach lurch. He didn't even know what was wrong, but intuitively he knew whatever it was, it was bad. And that somebody needed Lynn far more than he did. He glanced around for a pay phone. Spotting one, he said, "Yes. I'll wait."

He made a quick call to Ruth and Rachel's, explained the situation, told them he might be very late and asked them to keep the kids overnight. That done, he helped himself to a cup of stale coffee, picked up a dog-eared copy of *Golf Digest* and tried, unsuccessfully, to read.

His conversation with Pete pecked away at him. He'd more or less committed to staying in Riverbend. Close to Chicago and close to Lynn. Close to home? All kinds of people—Uncle Abe, his aunts, Mitch Sterling, hell, even Aaron—had made it home. Almost all his childhood associates. Except for Jacob. He looked at the ceiling. A longing, born of memories and nourished by hope, welled up. Could he make Riverbend his home? Even...his and Lynn's?

Across from him, the parents shifted their son, who cried out in his fitful sleep. Just then a nurse appeared in the door. "Mr. and Mrs. Hayes, we'll see Parker now." The mother sagged in relief, while the father lovingly cradled his son in his arms.

"Good luck," Tom said softly.

The father paused. "Have kids of your own?"

With an ache in his heart, Tom nodded. "Two."

"Then you know how it feels. Thanks." The three of them disappeared beyond the partition.

Setting the magazine aside, Tom steepled his fingers and placed them against his lips. Did he? Really?

Know how the worried parents felt? Selena would for sure. What had she handled on her own that he never even knew about?

Pete had every reason to be skeptical of him. Tom knew he'd still make a few mistakes, but maybe that was what parenting was all about. Making mistakes and going on, anyway, because you love your kids.

After fifteen more minutes, the same nurse reappeared. "Mr. Jankowski?"

"Yeah?" The man in the corner stood up.

"We've moved your mother to a room. You can see her now. Please follow me."

The silence closed around Tom. He couldn't imagine what could be taking Lynn so long. Then the image came to him of her leaning over Pete's bed, of the calm and compassion she exuded, of his gratitude to her for touching his son when he had not thought to do so. Someone else needed her now. Just as he had. Just as others would. Who was he to question or begrudge her gift? Especially when, he realized with sudden clarity, that was one of the main reasons he loved her.

The hands of the overhead clock crawled to eleven. A few minutes later the woman in the maroon scrubs poked her head through the window. "Sir, the chapel is open. Perhaps you'd be more comfortable there. It's down the hall on your right."

More comfortable? He doubted it, but the cafeteria was closed and he'd welcome a change of scene. "Thanks. I'll give it a try."

His cowboy boots echoed in the empty corridor. Near the end was a sign reading All Faith Chapel. He pulled open the door and stood in the back of the small sanctuary, just big enough for an altar and six rows of pews on either side of the center aisle. The dim interior lights contributed to the comforting aura of the place. He slipped into the far side of the back pew and sat quietly. Muted spotlights were focused on a Star of David and a cross on the wall behind the altar, above which an illuminated stained-glass window, rich in rainbow crimsons, golds and sapphires, carried the message "Peace to all who enter here."

Tom sighed, then rubbed his hands up and down his denim-clad thighs. Admittedly there was a different kind of silence here. Not the humming quiet of the waiting room, but a hush, both expectant and calming. He fingered the worn velvet of the pew cushion, wondering how many had sat here beseeching their God to heal pain, end suffering.

He stretched out his legs, leaned into the corner and closed his eyes. Lynn. Almost subconsciously he found himself saying over and over again in his mind, *Please be with her, please be with her.*

THE FORMLESS MASS crowded her lungs, pressed against her throat. Somehow Lynn managed brief polite farewells to the night-shift personnel before turning the corner and hurrying toward the chapel. If she could just get there before…before… She grabbed the cool metal handle, opened the door and sank gratefully into her customary place in the second row. It was coming. She wasn't going to be able to control herself any longer. She pulled down the kneeler and sat forward, gripping the pew in front of her and resting her forehead on the smooth wood. "Oh, God. Oh, God."

The mass gave way in a cataclysmic sob, and Lynn yielded at last, releasing the bottled-up anguish of this horrible night, succumbing to the temptation, so long and necessarily held at bay, to cry out her guilt and loss.

Her shoulders shook and the tears came, flowing in runnels down her cheeks. She sucked in breath after gasping breath, helpless to stop. She fumbled in her skirt pocket for a tissue, then wiped at her eyes, which continued to rain tears. Another paroxysm seized her and she bent nearly double with the painful emotions.

Why hadn't she seen it coming? It should never have happened. What could she have said? Done?

Slowly she eased back and contemplated the window and its proclamation. *Peace to all who enter.* She prayed it would be so.

When she calmed her breathing, she had a strong sense she was not alone. Looking around, her eyes widened, and then, when she recognized Tom, began streaming once more. He slid into the pew beside her and gathered her into his arms, cradling her head against his shoulder, smoothing her hair away from her face, murmuring soothing syllables in her ear. She couldn't stop shaking, couldn't stop crying. "There, there," he whispered. "It'll be all right." She nestled closer, seeking his warmth, pulling strength from the storehouse of his arms.

She didn't know how long she stayed protected by his embrace. It could've been seconds or minutes. She only knew that gradually her tears abated and her breathing slowed and became even and calm.

At last she raised her head and found his eyes, molten with concern. "Oh, Tom. Thank you for coming. I've never needed anybody so much in my whole life."

"Anybody?" His voice sounded thick.

"You." She buried her head in his neck, inhaling the special scent that was Tom. Only Tom.

He ran his hand up and down her arm. Finally he tilted up her chin. "Can you talk about it?"

She lowered her lashes, bit her lip, then locked her gaze on his. "Remember the night I had to leave you and respond to an emergency?"

He nodded.

"Mae Farrell's husband had just left her. I've done everything I knew to help her. Referred her to counselors, social workers." Her breath hitched. "But it wasn't enough." She felt his hand on her face, his thumb wiping away fresh tears. "She committed suicide tonight." She clutched his arms. "Tom, I couldn't do anything to save her."

FINALLY HE PERSUADED LYNN to let him take her home. They left his truck and took her car. He figured she shouldn't be alone. Besides, he didn't want to leave her. In the morning he could walk from her house to the aunts' and get one of them to take him back to the hospital.

Lynn permitted him to lead her outside like a child. During the silent ride to her house, she huddled close to him, winding a tissue around and around her fingers.

When they reached her front porch, she was still so shaky she couldn't insert the key in the lock. "Here, let me do it." Tom took the key and opened the door, then stood aside to let her in.

She paused, then said, "Thank you, Tom. I don't know what I'd have done without you."

"I'm coming in." He put his hand at the small of

her back and nudged her over the threshold. "You shouldn't be by yourself tonight. I'm staying."

"But Pete and Libby—"

"They're at Ruth and Rachel's. End of discussion." He removed her red cape, no longer a symbol of playfulness, and led her to the living-room sofa. He sat her down, gathered the afghan around her, then picked up Benedict, who had been meowing fiercely at his feet, and placed him in Lynn's arms. "Tea or coffee?" he asked.

She managed a wan smile. "Tea, I think."

He left her and went to the kitchen, filled the kettle and located the tea bags. While he waited for the water to boil, he leaned on the counter trying desperately to sort out his emotions. She needed *him?* Throughout their relationship, he'd assumed she didn't need anyone. That she had it all together. She always seemed so capable, so...hell, perfect. Tonight had shaken him to the core. He'd felt helpless in the face of her massive need. Yet she'd clung to him, holding on to him in a way that made him, at the same time, feel almost indispensable to her.

The kettle whistled just as the lightbulb went on in his head. He needed her, too. Life without her was unimaginable. He grabbed the kettle from the burner. In the sudden silence he realized he was as scared as he'd ever been. Scared of being that needful of another human being. *Human being.* Yes, that was what she was. All she was. A human being, not a saint. The thought was reassuring. A beautiful, loving, giving human being. And she needed him.

He dropped tea bags into two mugs, then poured the water over them, watching intently as the liquid in the cups grew deeper and richer in color. The comforting aroma calmed him. Finally it was ready. He carried the mugs into the living room and set them on the coffee table. He studied her closed eyes, her ivory complexion dusted with faint freckles. Her lids fluttered, then she smiled gratefully.

"Here," he said. She scooted upright, her back against the arm, snugged the afghan around her and nodded at the space at the other end of the sofa. He settled in the indicated spot, an arm stretched across the back of the couch.

She reached for her mug, then took a sip. "Mmm." She pulled up her knees and balanced the mug on them. "I feel better now, thanks to you."

He studied her thoughtfully before speaking. "Lynn, you can't save everybody."

"I know," she said sadly. "But I try, and it hurts when I can't."

"Yeah. I, of all people, ought to know."

Her eyes found his. "Gordy?"

He nodded. "Maybe that's one reason I've been so disillusioned. Up till then, I'd managed to steel myself, hell-bent on getting a story. Maybe even looked on the wounded and dead as nothing but statistics. That might have made me a more objective journalist, but it didn't make me a better man. Then, like a big wake-up call, came the explosion. Once I permitted myself to relate to events on a personal level, I lost myself."

"And now?"

He considered her question. "I'm feeling my way along. But...I think I'm going to be okay."

She blew on the hot tea. Several moments elapsed. "Maybe we all have our private hells. You, me, Mae, Pete, Libby."

"So how do we face them?"

She looked up, a tiny grin playing on her lips. "Don't do that, Tom. Don't look to the minister for all the answers."

"I'll bet the woman has an opinion, though, right?"

"Okay." She sobered. "How do we face them? Never alone. Always together."

He set down his cup, then slowly and deliberately relieved her of hers and set it aside. His eyes never leaving her face, he took hold of the afghan, pulled her close and reclined into the cushions. She settled against his chest with a contented sigh. He kissed her forehead. "I like the sound of that. Together."

Within a few minutes she was asleep, but he continued holding her, thinking about what he needed to do to assure that never again would she be alone when she had need of him. Or when he had need of her. He moved his hand gently over her back, grateful for the gift she had given him tonight. Her vulnerability.

He, too, had nearly drifted off when he became aware of something soft rubbing against his head. He blinked. To his amazement, Benedict lay curled up beside his head purring with what sounded like feline approval. Tom chuckled softly. Maybe there was indeed hope if he'd succeeded in winning over her cat.

SELENA CALLED TOM at home late the next morning. She said she'd gotten her mother settled and would be returning to Chicago the following afternoon in time for Pete and Libby to come home to attend school on Monday. He realized he'd be disappointed to see them go. After the disastrous start, Tom figured the week hadn't gone too badly. He hadn't made giant steps with them, but he hadn't expected to. He'd happily settle for the tiny cracks developing in their armor.

"Hey, guys," he said, walking out onto the porch where they were carving jack-o'-lanterns for Mitch Sterling's annual Halloween pumpkin-carving event, "your mother called, and I'll be taking you home tomorrow."

"Good," Pete mumbled as he wedged the paring knife into the thick top of the pumpkin.

"How's Grandma?" Libby asked, a worried frown creasing her brow.

"She's comfortably settled, your mom says."

Libby set down the pen she was using to draw a face on her pumpkin. "Do you think her place is as nice as Golden Fields?"

"*Nice?*" Pete scoffed as he worked at hacking out a lid. "Don't be stupid. Nobody wants to go to one of those homes."

Tom eased down onto the top porch step. "For some people, it's the best alternative. Aging is no fun, but you're given good care, and you get to meet a lot of interesting people—like those you met last night." Pete looked skeptical.

"I liked Mr. Morrison," Libby said.

Tom nodded. "Yeah, he's quite a guy. But to answer your question, yes, I'm sure your grandmother's place is nice, too, and that she's getting good care."

He watched Pete dislodge the top of the pumpkin, then dig into the pithy center, coming up with a handful of seeds and stringy pulp. "Look, Libby. Guts!" He threw several strands at his sister.

She shrank back. "Gross. You're disgusting."

"Before you start a pulp fight, there's something I'd like us to talk about." Tom's dry throat closed. It was pretty serious when you couldn't even talk to your own kids without suffering an attack of nerves.

"Yeah, what?" Picking up a large spoon, Pete continued his disembowelment.

"I was wondering how you'd feel about coming here to visit on a regular basis." They both looked up at him. He rattled on. "Of course, I'd come to Chicago, too. Often. I want to see you play tennis, Pete, and come to your swim meets, Libby. And anything else you invite me to."

Libby pulled her pumpkin into her lap and wrapped her arms around it. Her eyes were big and she was biting her lower lip.

Pete simply continued scraping the inside of his pumpkin. Dead leaves, disturbed by the wind, rattled against the base of the porch, and the odor of wet pumpkin filled Tom's nostrils. The sound and smell of disappointment. He'd been foolish to think one week could turn around years of neglect.

Libby spoke first. "How do we know that…" She hesitated.

"I'll follow through?" Tom finished her thought. She hung her head. "Yeah."

"First of all, because I'm not going anywhere."

She looked up wonderingly. "You're not?"

"No." He glanced sideways at Pete, whose lower lip jutted out in concentration as he continued scraping an already hollowed-out pumpkin. "Second, because I want to be here for you in whatever way I can. I told Pete last night that I'd made a lot of mistakes in my life. Not putting family first was one of them. But I hope I'm not too old to learn, to change." He swallowed. "And finally, because I love you guys even more than I realized."

Pete's head jerked up and Libby's eyes filled with tears. "You do?" Her voice quavered.

"I'm sorry I ever gave you occasion to doubt it. So what do you think? Can we start fresh from today?"

Libby played with the stem of her pumpkin, as if considering the matter. Finally she said quietly, "Yes. I think we can."

"Pete?" His heart pounded as he waited for his son's answer.

"How do I know you'll come?"

Tom laid a hand on Pete's shoulder. "Because I am making you a solemn promise."

"And we'd have to come visit you in Riverbend?"

"It's not so bad," Libby piped up. "And Meacham House is cool."

"It'd be better if I had a guitar." Pete, the opportunistic little scoundrel, looked right at Tom.

"I'd like you to be enthusiastic about visiting with or without a guitar."

He pouted. "What about Reverend Lynn? Will she be here, too?"

Libby stared at her brother. "Reverend Lynn? What are you talking about?"

"Didn't you seem 'em last night, dorkess? All mushy-gushy?"

"*See* them? Keri and us girls got them together."

Pete flipped his spoon at his sister. "I don't think so. The way they were lookin' at each other, I'd say they already had something going. Am I right?"

Tom laughed and held up his hands in surrender. "I can see I'm going to have to get up pretty early in the morning to put anything past you."

Libby edged closer to him and rested her head on his shoulder. "It's fine with me, Dad. I like her a lot."

"I do, too," he whispered. "I do, too."

Pete gathered up the newspaper with the pumpkin mess and stood up. "Then do something about it, for crying out loud." Then he walked down the steps past Tom, headed for the garbage can in the garage.

Tom sheltered his daughter in his arms, pondering Pete's challenge. He had a few loose ends to tie up before he could "do something about it," but if he hadn't already had a powerful incentive, his kids had given him one. Their approval.

LYNN BOWED HER HEAD in silent prayer as she always did before entering the church for a service. She gave thanks for the colorful Sabbath morning—the brilliant blue of the October sky, the panoply of fall foliage, the crisp bite of the cool air—for the opportunity to love and serve and for all those who had touched her life in special ways. She opened her eyes and picked up her hymnal and service leaflet. This had been a particularly rich week for having her life touched— Axel Morrison, the girls at Meacham House, the aunts, even Prentice Jewett. But especially Tom. She clutched the hymnal to her chest as the first chords of the opening hymn sounded.

She had never realized before quite how *much* she loved him, not only because of their powerful physical attraction, but because he helped her laugh and play in joyous times, and gave her comfort and support in sad ones. Love, Tom's love and hers for him, was something rare and beautiful. Something to cherish.

At this early service, there was no processional. When the congregation began singing "Morning Has

Broken," she entered from the side and took her place at the top of the chancel steps. At the conclusion of the hymn, she looked out over her flock—and found herself momentarily speechless, unable to utter the words of the opening prayer. There, in the third row, sat Pete, Libby and Tom, gazing expectantly at her. Her eyes filled, and she sent them a smile she hoped conveyed the love in her heart.

With difficulty she drew her concentration back to the worship service, but once engaged, the familiar words took over and she managed to conduct the service with a heaven-sent grace, especially welcome when she led a prayer for the repose of Mae Farrell's soul. When she faced the congregation to give the benediction, she was humbled again, as she was every time, by this role to which God had called her. A moment of silence followed, then Rachel Steele pulled out all the stops for "All Things Bright and Beautiful," the recessional.

As was her custom, Lynn waited outside the front entrance to greet those who'd attended the service. She understood that the "nice sermon" comments were usually perfunctory, but every so often someone would address a specific way her words had lifted their spirits or spoken to a need. She treasured these few moments when she could reach out and touch each person individually.

She noticed Tom and his children loitering in the foyer, letting the stragglers go ahead of them. Finally the threesome approached. Pete was first. "Good morning," she said. "It's a treat to have you here."

"We had to get up awful early," he mumbled as she took his hand.

Libby threw her brother a disgusted look, then elbowed him out of the way. "Don't pay any attention to him. We had to get up early, anyway." Laughing, Lynn put her arm around Libby and gave a gentle squeeze.

Tom stood just beyond his daughter. The way he was staring at Lynn, intently and lovingly, turned her legs to limp noodles. "Their mother is home. I'm taking them back to Chicago today." He hesitated. "They, er, wanted to say goodbye."

She couldn't resist. She smiled mischievously and asked, "Is that the reason you came this morning?"

He locked his eyes on hers and smiled back, as if he was playing along with her, but also as if he had something very important to convey. All he said was, "That, too."

Neither the ringing of the church bells, nor the conversational hubbub on the church lawn distracted them from holding each other's gaze.

Libby broke the spell by throwing her arms around Lynn's neck. "I'm coming back soon."

Over Libby's shoulder, Lynn saw Pete raise a hand. "See ya."

"I'll call you later," Tom said as he turned to leave.

Libby remained beside Lynn, watching her father and brother. "Guys are such dorks," she commented.

Lynn chuckled. "Not all of them."

Libby glanced up at her. "Not Dad?"

"Definitely not your dad."

A huge metallic smile broke across Libby's face. "Good. That means you'll risk letting him love you, right?"

"Oh, honey, that's exactly what it means."

"Good," Libby said before joining Tom and Pete on the sidewalk.

Lynn stood in the doorway of the church, the breeze ruffling her hair and lifting the hem of her robe. Then she looked skyward. "Indeed, Lord, You do make all things wise and wonderful. Thank you."

CHAPTER FOURTEEN

BEFORE IT WAS TIME to begin the organ prelude prior to the later service, Rachel located Ruth in the church fellowship hall where she and Molly Linden were holding the ends of a banner while Lily Mazerik stood back, assessing how high to hang it. "Over that way a little." Lily cocked her head. "Perfect!" She beamed, and Ruth and Molly affixed it to the wall with thumbtacks.

Meacham House
Open House
Sunday, October 22

Rachel hoped Molly and Lynn would have a good turnout for the event, their first attempt to showcase the programs and, more particularly, the talents of the teens. The Halloween party at Golden Fields had been a good start toward helping folks think positively about Meacham House, and if the open house went well, perhaps even the doubters would change their tunes.

As soon as Ruth finished her task, Rachel pulled her off to the side. Ruth, ever the gregarious twin, hissed, "What's so all-fired important? I need to visit with Lily about helping with the open house art exhibit."

"This won't take a minute." Rachel rubbed her palms together in anticipation.

"Well, don't stand there grinning at me like you just gave birth or something. Out with it."

Rachel permitted herself a smug smile. "Guess who was in church this morning?"

Ruth raised an eyebrow. "No. I'm not playing guessing games. I'll be here all morning."

"Hmm, you could be right. Because you'll never guess."

"Then tell me."

Rachel could see that her sister was losing patience. "Aren't you going to beg even a teeny bit?"

"This better be good." Ruth crossed her arms and tapped her foot impatiently. "Okay, I'm begging. Who was in church this morning?"

"The Baines family."

Rachel took gleeful satisfaction from watching her twin's eyes pop and her mouth drop open. *"Tom?"*

"Know any other Baineses?" Rachel took one last look at her sister's stupefied face before heading toward the choir robing room. She'd let Ruth stew for a while before she added the best part. *The way Lynn and Tom had looked at each other.* It was enough to make tone-deaf angels sing.

THE FOLLOWING SATURDAY MORNING Tom sat hunched over his computer desperately trying to get words to flow. Earlier in the week he'd attempted to write a travel piece about Vancouver, one of the places he'd visited before coming home to Riverbend, and had ended up scrapping it. He'd focused, instead, on a profile of a politician he admired. But that wasn't coming together, either. Besides, he wasn't interested in traveling to Washington, D.C., to interview the subject. He had too many things going on here. He leaned back and let his gaze wander to the window and the idyllic Indian-summer day.

He had a sudden, fierce longing for Lynn. It was a day to play in the leaves, eat candied apples and take a long walk in the woods. It would be a night to build a fire, drink hot chocolate and kiss the whipped cream off her nose, before nipping lower and lower... He cursed under his breath. These thoughts were serving little good except to increase the ache in his groin.

Restless, he stood and walked out to the porch, where he inhaled deeply in an attempt to clear his mind of distracting and arousing thoughts. Lynn had left yesterday with a group from the church to participate in the charity bike ride she'd been training for. He supposed this was only one of many times she'd have to go off and leave him. He grinned, then, just thinking about the kinds of little reunions they could have, about the ways he would show her just how glad he was to see her. Ways he hoped would light up her eyes, cause her breathing to quicken, elicit tiny whimpers of pleasure.

He groaned. This was not a helpful train of thought, either. Sexual satisfaction was the least of his worries, but that, too, might soon improve. Just as soon as he figured out what he was going to do. He was a writer, for heaven's sake. Surely he could think of something.

His eyes narrowed. In the distance he saw Shep's ramshackle truck approaching. He walked down the steps and was waiting at the edge of the drive when Shep slowed to a stop.

"Thought I'd bring your mail," Shep said, and proffered the bundle through the open window.

"Thanks," Tom said, taking it. "How's Dorrie?"

"Missing those kids. And I'm suffering for it. I've already gained five pounds eating the leftover cookies."

Tom watched while Shep unwrapped a piece of gum and carefully folded the foil before popping the stick in his mouth. Tom knew the signs. Something was on Shep's mind. He waited.

"So how are you and the reverend gettin' along?" Shep asked. "I been noticin' she's a regular visitor here."

Whether it was his own question or one Dorrie had put him up to didn't matter. They were his friends. "Cross your fingers for me, Shep. I may not be good enough for her, but I'm going to do my damnedest to make her happy."

Shep's cracked lips spread in a grin that exposed a number of stained teeth. "Can't think of anybody better to do it, son."

The vote of confidence meant a lot, because more than anything, Tom wanted to be worthy of Lynn, to be the kind of man who put his wife and family first. "Thanks, Shep."

The older man's lined face wrinkled further with a frown. "She know how you feel?"

"I'm working on it."

Shep nodded his head several times in approval. "Okay, then. See you in church tomorrow." And before putting the truck in gear, he gave Tom a broad man-to-man wink.

Walking back to the house, Tom sifted through the mail, pausing when he came to the envelope bearing Irish postage. *Terence.* The memory blindsided him, as it no doubt always would. He slit the envelope with a knife, then sat back down at his desk and began reading.

> Dear Tom,
> Thank you for your letter. I liked hearing about Riverbend and about the boys and girls at Meacham House. I wish we had a Meacham House. Then I would have more friends. I live far from school. I can't play much as the bus ride is so long. Also, since the explosion, I don't always hear very well. Some of my classmates make fun of me. Terry Whadjasay, they call me. Ma says to ask if you are well. I hope someday you will come visit me again.
>
> Your friend,
Terence

Tom stared at the letter, saddened by the boy's pain and isolation, and maddened by the insensitivity of his peers. If only he could do something to help. Terence did, indeed, need a Meacham House. Just like Damon, Keri, Sam…

Sam. *There* was an idea. He thumbed through the phone directory till he found *M. Sterling*. He dialed and waited anxiously. Mitch picked up on the fourth ring. "Hey, Mitch. It's Tom. Got a question for you. How would Sam like a pen pal?"

When he concluded the conversation, Tom sat back in satisfaction. It was a natural. Communicating by mail made anybody's hearing impairment irrelevant. And friendships, he knew, could span time and distance.

Friendships. His friendship with Gordy. Tom's fingers hovered over the keyboard, then slowly began tapping out his thoughts as memory after memory flooded his brain. The serious, the profane, the comic and the heartbreaking. More and more rapidly the words appeared on the monitor, but Tom didn't look up. He wanted to capture it all—the jokes, the back slaps, the boredom, the adrenaline rushes, the mind-numbing fear.

Finally, around five o'clock, he stopped and began rereading the text. Halfway through, he slumped forward, burying his face in his hands. "Oh, my God," he whispered. "It's the book."

Not the book he'd been asked to write, but the book he was *going* to write. A book dedicated to Gordy and devoted to exploring, not the cold-blooded atrocities of the end of the twentieth century, but the human beings caught up in events beyond their control, and the heroism and friendships forged in such a caldron.

He couldn't wait to tell Lynn. But first he needed to talk to Harry Milstein.

It was the fourth Sunday in October. Although the temperature had dropped into the midforties, the sky was blue and cloudless. Lynn squared her robe over her shoulders and peeked out her office window, gratified to see the parking lot filling up. She turned back to Molly, Nathan and Rosita. "Looks like we'll have a good crowd."

"That's a positive sign," Molly said, smiling at the two youths.

"If I don't screw up," Nathan said, nervously cracking his knuckles.

"Not possible," Lynn assured him. "Whatever you say will come from the heart. That's what counts."

"We have lots of good things we can tell them about, don't we?" Rosita, dark eyes shining, looked to the adults for approval.

"You certainly do," Molly agreed.

Lynn moved to the door. "Ready?" Nathan gulped and Rosita nodded. "Remember, you'll be sitting on either side of me, and I'll introduce you when it's time."

"Break a leg, kids," Molly said.

Lynn escorted them to the foyer and the processional began. She could hardly keep her mind on the hymn, so full was her heart. The church was packed. Dr. and Mrs. Bennett, the Drummers, the Mazeriks, Shep and Dorrie, the Penningtons, Charlie Callahan, Mitch and Sam Sterling, dear Kate and her dynamic duo, Hope and Hannah, and others too numerous to count. Ahead of her, petite Rosita, her bright red skirt flaring around her knees, and Nathan, tall and handsome in his blue suit, did Meacham House proud. As she passed Tom's row—he was on the aisle—he winked and gave her a thumbs-up.

When the time came for the sermon and she stepped to the pulpit, she couldn't avoid noticing Prentice Jewett, sitting expressionless in the front pew, his arms folded defensively across his chest. She paused, taking a moment to center herself before beginning. "Dear friends, this is a day of celebration for Riverbend Community Church and for Meacham House. As God's people, we must always remember that we are part of a larger community and that He has blessed us with resources beyond our imagining. Sharing those resources, easing others' burdens and enabling each of God's children to build upon his or her unique talents and gifts is what we are called to do.

"At this church, part of our response to that call has been the establishment of a community program for young people, Meacham House. Many of you are already involved. Others may be curious about the nature of the program and its benefits. So, in lieu of my sermon—" she held up her hands and smiled "—I have asked Molly Linden, director of Meacham House, and two of the participants, Nathan Turner and Rosita Diaz, to share their thoughts with you. Molly?" She stood aside as her friend mounted the pulpit.

After thanking the church for its financial and volunteer support, Molly outlined the activities taking place and those planned for the future. "But for the real story, no one is better equipped than our young people to share it. Nathan Turner, who moved to Riverbend this summer, will begin."

"Go get 'em, Tiger," Lynn whispered as Nathan got awkwardly to his feet.

Reaching the pulpit, he gripped it like a drowning man clutching a ring buoy. "Molly asked me to tell you what Meacham House has done for me." He cleared his throat twice. "I didn't want to come live here with Charlie, at first. Not because he's such a bad guy, I mean, well, you know." Several in the congregation tittered.

"But I didn't know anybody here. There was nothin' to do. Nobody to hang out with. The only reason I went to Meacham House, besides Charlie making me go, is that I heard they were offering art classes. So I went, and it's made a big difference. Now I have friends. And I'm not the only one. Damon, Sam and the other guys—we all have friends. Some of them are even grown-ups like Molly and Tom." Appreciative laughter from the congregation.

"I'd like to invite all of you over after church to see some things we've done. I hope you'll like my paintings, too." He turned and looked at Molly as if checking to see if he'd said enough.

She nodded and moved to the pulpit. "Thank you, Nathan. Now, we'll hear from Rosita Diaz."

Lynn couldn't wait. Rosita was a born actress and loved nothing better than an audience. Even though she could barely see over the lectern, she was not intimidated. "On behalf of myself and the Meacham House kids, I want to thank all of you for giving the teens in this town a safe place to go. More importantly, for giving us a place to belong. A place where we can laugh and study and just talk about life. And where there are adults who don't think we're so bad. Who listen. Who think we're worth their time and attention and love."

Lynn held her breath. You could have heard a pin drop in the sanctuary. Molly threw Lynn a teary look that clearly said, "Aren't these kids something?"

Rosita went on, her confident voice filling the building. "There's lots of bad stuff going on. You know that. You watch TV. You read the newspapers. But there's good stuff, too. And we want you to come see some of it today. Please, after church, come home with us to Meacham House."

When Rosita returned to her seat, Lynn was nearly too overcome with emotion to go on. But, she realized, there was really nothing further to be said. So instead of more words, Lynn caught Rachel's eye, confident of her organist's musical flexibility. Rachel peered over her glasses, then nodded. Lynn stood, and after she announced a hymn number, the congregation rose and began a heartfelt rendition of "Now Thank We All Our God."

By the time Lynn reached Meacham House after the service, the crowd was spilling out into the backyard, where the teenage musicians were holding forth. Inside, little kids ran up and down the stairs shrieking delightedly, grandmas perched on folding chairs brought in for the occasion, and men stood in groups, balancing cookies and coffee.

A young couple engaged Nathan in an intense discussion of his art, while next to him one of the girls explained to an elderly gentleman the media she'd used for an abstract collage.

After being stopped numerous times by people greeting her or asking questions, Lynn finally made her way to the rec room where Damon and Sam had mounted a collection of photos. The display was entitled "Our Town." In the center was a striking photo of the courthouse at dawn, surrounded by studies of Victorian homes, Riverside Park, the First World War memorial statue and other points of interest. Lynn clapped her hands delightedly. Damon, his hair hiding his face, skulked in a corner, as if daring the world to like anything about him.

Lynn felt an arm snake around her waist and looked up to see Tom smiling with satisfaction. "They're good, aren't they?"

"Very good." She turned and, with Tom at her side, walked over to Damon. "You do us great credit," she said softly. "Those are incredible photographs."

He tossed his head. "You think?"

"Yes, I do."

A tall man with a craggy face and a crooked smile approached them. "Baines, is this the fellow you were telling me about?"

"Yes. Damon, this is Court Reeves, editor-in-chief at the *Riverbend Courier*. He has something to say to you."

Damon eyed the stranger warily. "You have a great future ahead of you," Reeves said to him. "I'd like to do a full-page spread in the Sunday paper of your photos. I can't pay you what they're worth, but something is better than nothing."

Damon stood stock-still. "You're kidding, right?"

Reeves laughed. "No. Not only am I not kidding, I hope you'll come around and see me at the newspaper office. I'd like to put you on the payroll."

Damon looked from Reeves to Tom. "Does he mean a job? Taking pictures?"

Tom put an arm around Damon's shoulders. "That's exactly what he means."

Lynn linked her fingers through Tom's and squeezed just as Damon blew out a breath and uttered a single word. "Awesome."

Leaving Damon and Reeves to work out details, Tom and Lynn wandered hand in hand upstairs. Either everyone knew they were an item, or no one noticed their joined hands. Regardless, it felt so right to have Tom there with her, touching her, claiming her.

"Psst." Putting a finger to her lips, Ruth motioned them to join her. "Over here," she said in a low voice.

Lynn normally disapproved of eavesdropping, but it was too late. Ruth pointed to a group of men standing just inside the downstairs game room. Prentice

Jewett faced away from them, holding court. "Listen," Ruth whispered.

Prentice clasped his hands behind his back and rocked on his heels. "...so I said to them, never mind. I'll take care of it. These Meacham House people are doing fine things, and if I can provide them with state-of-the-art computer equipment, it's the least I can do for such deserving young people."

Ruth signaled a "Watch me" look and sailed into the middle of the group. "I couldn't help overhearing, Prentice. We all know you as a very generous man. I understand Meacham House can use a new oven. May we count on you for that, as well?"

Lynn almost felt sorry for Prentice. Like a fish mouthing the side of an aquarium, his lips moved, but nothing came out. The other men looked at him expectantly. Finally he sputtered, "Why, Ruth, dear, it'd be my pleasure."

Tom led Lynn into the living room. "I don't want to be anywhere near the scene of that crime." He leaned over and whispered in her ear. "Where I want to be is alone. With you. You busy later?"

"What a lovely idea. Will four o'clock suit you?"

"Perfectly."

Lynn smiled up at him. Days didn't get much better than this.

WHEN HE PICKED HER UP, Tom noticed that Lynn had changed into jeans and an avocado turtleneck that brought out greenish highlights in her eyes. He helped her into her gold fleece anorak and whisked her out to the truck. She looked puzzled. "I thought we were planning to be alone."

"We are."

"Then where are we going?"

"It's a surprise," he said.

"I like surprises."

He certainly hoped so. He couldn't believe how nervous he was. He'd been in tight situations before, but never one where the result depended so heavily on saying just the right thing.

A bulky object knocked against the front seat. "What's that?" she said, cranking around to look.

"A guitar."

She giggled. "Are you planning a serenade?"

It was a good idea. Too bad he hadn't thought of it. "No. It's for Pete. I'm going to Chicago tomorrow. Libby asked me to come. She has a swim meet. I'm taking it to him."

"He'll love it."

"I hope so. He's been bugging me about one. I figured it might be a good way to involve him with the kids at Meacham House."

"Like I've said before, you're a good man, Tom Baines."

Good *enough?* That was the question.

"Ah." With one hand she braced herself against the dashboard. "You're taking me to the cemetery."

"Yes, I am." He squinted at the road, studiously avoiding looking at her. "I kind of think of it as our place."

He slowed, then pulled off the road and parked. After helping her out, he took her by the hand and began the ascent.

"It's funny," Lynn mused. "Most people wouldn't pick a place of death as a sentimental landmark."

"I don't think of it as a place of death," he said seriously. "I figured I could make a choice. To let death control my life or to make peace with it. It was here I began to find that peace." He squeezed her fingers. "With you."

When they crested the rise, Lynn sucked in her breath. "Oh, Tom." She turned tear-filled eyes to him. "It's...it's lovely."

He'd loaded the pots of vermilion and yellow chrysanthemums into the pickup after church and had had just enough time to decorate the cemetery with them before picking her up.

She slowly turned her head, taking it all in. "They're everywhere. By each and every marker. On the wall. It must've taken hours."

He shrugged, then grinned. "You're worth it." He sobered and tilted his head toward the graves. "And they're worth it." With a thudding heart, he pulled her toward the wall. "I want to show you something and ask you something."

He put his arms around her waist and lifted her onto the low wall, as nervous as if he were still that scared little kid at a new boarding school. Slowly, standing before her, he extracted a thick envelope from his inside jacket pocket. "Here," he said, handing it to her.

Her eyebrows knit in inquiry. "What is it?"

"Open it."

She pulled out the papers and began to read. He could tell when she came to the important words, because her mouth fell open. Then she looked up, her eyes shining in wonder. "Is this what I think it is? A book contract?"

He took the sheaf of papers from her and refolded them. "Yes. I didn't want to bring you here and ask you what I'm going to ask you until I figured out who I am."

"And now? Have you figured it out?"

He picked up both her hands and drew in a deep breath. "I am a writer. But beyond that, I am a man who has learned a lot and has a lot still to learn. The main thing is, I'm willing to try." He cleared his throat and concentrated on the encouragement he saw in her eyes. "The most important thing I've learned, and what I couldn't say until now, until I felt worthy, is that I love you, Lynn Kendall, and want you to be my wife."

The love he read in her face nearly undid him. "Tom, you've always been worthy."

He was gripping her fingers so hard it was a wonder she didn't cry out. "Is that a yes?"

Her merry laughter warmed his soul from the inside out. "Of course it is." She flung her arms around his neck. "I've been waiting for you all my life."

Before she could kiss him, he held up his fingers and stayed her. "There's one more thing." He thought he knew what her answer would be, but he needed to hear it from her. "Up until recently, I've not been the best father. If you're willing," he stammered, "I...I'd like to try parenthood again—from the beginning. With you."

She pushed herself off the wall into his hug and fastened her lips to his. Her mouth was sweet and warm. He hadn't known such joy, such oneness, was possible. And he had a lifetime of this to look forward to. How long they stood locked together was anybody's guess. The sound of geese calling to one another finally brought him back to his senses. He pulled his mouth away and pointed to the sky. The flock flew closer and closer, almost directly overhead, winging their way south.

"They're leaving home," he said. "But they'll return in the spring."

She leaned against his shoulder. "And what about you? Have you returned? Are you home?"

He thought about her question and realized he'd known the truth for several weeks. He turned her in his arms so they faced the distant river and the setting sun. "Riverbend is a wonderful place, full of fine people and good memories. But it isn't home."

She lifted her head, bewilderment darkening her pupils. "It isn't?"

"No, love." He cupped her face and drank in her serene beauty, knowing he would never forget this moment. "My home is wherever you are."

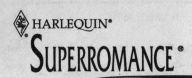

HARLEQUIN®
SUPERROMANCE®

You are now entering

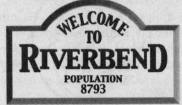

WELCOME
TO
RIVERBEND
POPULATION
8793

Riverbend...the kind of place where everyone knows
your name—and your business. Riverbend...home of
the River Rats—a group of small-town sons and
daughters who've been friends since high school.

The Rats are all grown up now. Living their lives and
learning that some days are good and some days
aren't—and that you can get through anything
as long as you have your friends.

Starting in July 2000, Harlequin Superromance brings
you Riverbend—six books about the River Rats and
the Midwest town they live in.

BIRTHRIGHT by Judith Arnold (July 2000)
THAT SUMMER THING by Pamela Bauer (August 2000)
HOMECOMING by Laura Abbot (September 2000)
LAST-MINUTE MARRIAGE by Marisa Carroll (October 2000)
A CHRISTMAS LEGACY by Kathryn Shay (November 2000)

Available wherever Harlequin books are sold.

HARLEQUIN®
Makes any time special ™

Visit us at www.eHarlequin.com

HSRIVER

**Don't miss
an exciting opportunity
to save on the purchase of
Harlequin and Silhouette books!**

Buy any two Harlequin or
Silhouette books and save
$10.00 off future Harlequin
and Silhouette purchases

OR

buy any three
Harlequin or Silhouette books
and save **$20.00 off** future
Harlequin and Silhouette purchases.

**Watch for details
coming in October 2000!**

PHQ400

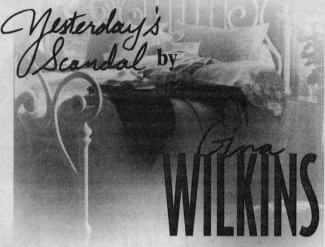

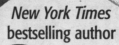